P9-EEI-855

3 1833 04482 1905

VOODOO WAREHOUSE

Repelled by the stink and the sounds, yet drawn by curiosity, Clark peered in to see bars like a jail cell enclosing a roomful of zombies. The tall figure of a dark-skinned man, his face half-eaten away, with bulging eyes that looked glassy and empty, clutched at the bars, as did others in various states of decomposition.

As if sensing him by scent, they looked toward him with unseeing eyes. Arms and legs flopped and shuffled as a host of drooling, jagged-toothed jaws moved with increasing frenzy.

Clark backed away from the zombies and scanned the rest of the rooms with his X-ray vision. Behind one of the doors, he saw a storeroom piled with plastic sacks that had the familiar LuthorCorp logo on them . . .

ACCLAIM FOR *SMALLVILLE*, THE WB SERIES

"What *Smallville* has is soul—that, and an intuitive feel for the zeitgeist."
—*New York Times*

"A fresh reinterpretation of one of America's most beloved and enduring pop icons."
—*TV Guide*

MEDIA TIE-INS

DEC 0 9 2003

OTHER BOOKS IN THE SERIES

ATTENTION: CORPORATIONS AND ORGANIZATIONS:
Most WARNER books are available at quantity discounts
with bulk purchase for educational, business, or sales
promotional use. For information, please call or write:

Special Markets Department, Warner Books, Inc.,
135 W. 50th Street, New York, NY. 10020-1393
Telephone: 1-800-222-6747 Fax: 1-800-477-5925

SMALLVILLE

SILENCE

NANCY HOLDER

**Superman created by
Jerry Siegel and Joe Shuster**

WARNER BOOKS

An AOL Time Warner Company

All titles, characters, their distinctive likeness, and related elements are trademarks of DC Comics. The characters, names, and incidents mentioned in this publication are entirely fictional.

If you purchase this book without a cover you should be aware that this book may have been stolen property and reported as "unsold and destoyed" to the publisher. In such case neither the author nor the publisher has received any payment for this "stripped book."

WARNER BOOKS EDITION

Copyright © 2003 by DC Comics

All rights reserved. No part of this book may be reproduced in any form or by any electronic or mechanical means, including information storage and retrieval systems, without permission in writing from the publisher, except by a reviewer who may quote brief passages in a review.

Cover design by Don Puckey

Warner Books, Inc.
1271 Avenue of the Americas
New York, NY 10020

Visit our Web site at www.twbookmark.com

Visit DC Comics on-line at keyword DCComics on America Online
or at http://www.dccomics.com.

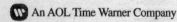 An AOL Time Warner Company

Printed in the United States of America

First Printing: November 2003

10 9 8 7 6 5 4 3 2 1

This book is for the one and only
Rebecca Morhaim. Rock it, girlfriend.

ACKNOWLEDGMENTS

With sincere thanks to the cast and crew of *Smallville,* in particular to THE PRODUCER/CREATORS and to Mr. Tom Welling; to my DC editor Rich Thomas; and to my Warner editor, John Aherne. To my agent Howard Morhaim and his assistant, Ryan Blitstein, thank you so much. Anna Robinson, Lily Gile, Laura Newman, and Michelle Taliaferro, thank you for being Rebecca Morhaim's good friends. Dal Perry and Matt Pallamary, thank you, boys, more than I can say. To Debbie and Scott Viguié, thank you for being my friends. My beautiful daughter, Belle, you are the answer to a mother's prayers. Finally, to Kym Rademacher . . . who walks the walk, and is showing me her moves: Thanks for the choreography lessons. I'm grateful beyond words for your generosity. And for her mother, Suzy, who knows how to treat a kid.

SMALLVILLE

SILENCE

CHAPTER ONE

"'Listen, do wah do, do you want to know a secret?'" Chloe sang out as she sailed through the doors of the Talon with all its Egyptian–Art Deco fashion stylings. She loved the brilliant colors of the columns and the way the shiny mirrors bounced the light all over the busy room. It reminded her of Metropolis.

As she scooted around one of the beefy football players—*I think his name is Ty Something*—her reporter's brain automatically began searching for his last name, but stopped, realizing it didn't matter because at the moment, Ty had done nothing newsworthy. Not today, anyway.

She caught sight of Clark and Pete, and hurried toward them. She was beaming; she was euphoric. In her hot little hands, she held the mock-up of tomorrow's edition of the *Torch*. And in that mock-up, the most amazing scoop of her reporting life. It was like a dream, and the fact that she was wearing the new embroidered corset Lana had talked her into buying, and that she looked, well, *super,* just added to the mix. Heads were turning, male heads, and one never knew: where a few might turn, others—one in particular— could follow.

"'Do you promise not to tell?'" she crowed, ending her cover of the old Lennon-and-McCartney Beatles song.

She gave her short blond hair a shake as she made her way through Lana's noisy, crowded coffeehouse. The shiny copper espresso machine was steaming away, reminding her of a calliope in this circus of life. Accessorized with mugs, books, or cell phones, school kids were chatting in friendly groups, rehashing the day, dishing gossip, or hooking up. Right now she loved each and every one of them.

It's a great day to be ... me!

Of her own friendly group, Clark saw her first. He raised his brows and gave her a pleasantly inquisitive smile as she approached, taking in her state of high elation. *Okay, not an oh-my-God-you're-here-at-last-my-darling* smile, but at least she rated a reaction from tall, dark, and not-hers. Not that it mattered, of course. She'd moved past her crush on Clark.

Right? Right! And so, who cares what I wear in front of him? Well, caring beyond having my personal dignity ... as a girl and as someone he abandoned at the Prom ...

"Hi, Chloe," Pete said for Clark and himself. "What's up?"

"Plenty." With a dramatic flourish, she displayed the mock-up of the *Torch,* stretching it between her hands. A banner headline in seventy-two-point font announced, *SH Teacher of the Year Caught in Drug Bust!*

"What?" Clark said, raising his brows.

"Read it and gasp," she said, holding out the paper.

Warily, Clark took the paper from Chloe and scanned her prize-worthy prose. She was sometimes amazed by how fast he could read. His eyes moving rapidly, he started to flip to page three, where the article continued, then jerked as if he had been caught doing something wrong. *Speed-reading is not a crime,* she wanted to remind him.

He looked up at her, and said, "This is pretty harsh, Chloe."

She was disappointed. *Harsh?*

"The words you use ..." he continued, trailing off and flashing her a patented Clark not-trying-to-hurt-you grimace.

"Clark, I'm breaking a story," she ventured. "A big story. I have to grab the reader's attention."

He shifted, clearly not agreeing with her. Pete looked on, brows knit as he worked to read the paper upside down.

"Drug bust?" Pete echoed, shocked. His eyes widened. "Mr. Hackett? You gotta be kidding me."

"Not a bust exactly," Clark told him, shaking his head. "Not that bad."

"Not that bad?" she said. "Clark, you did start reading it, right?"

He moved his shoulders. "I'm sorry, Chloe, but it seems . . . severe."

She frowned as she took the paper back from him. "It's all true," she said. "Every word."

Clark looked uncomfortable. "Yeah, but . . . 'cover-up'?" He gestured to one of her columns of tightly written journalistic prose. "I mean, you wrote that Mr. Hackett is going to resign from his job. It's not as if he was going to get away with something."

With a look of complete astonishment, Pete extended his hand for the paper. "Resign? He's been here forever. What's he got until retirement, like a couple of years?"

"And now he's leaving? Just like that?" Clark asked, trying to process the enormity of what Chloe had reported. "He's such a great teacher. He deserved to be named Teacher of the Year. Even the kids who get in trouble all the time like him."

I am so right to break this story. Look at their reactions! This is big news.

"Yes," she replied with satisfaction, as Clark handed Pete the paper. "They did. He *was* good at his job. And he had less than two years until retirement. But he sold steroids to Jake Brook!"

"The new tackle?" Clark asked. "He's a big guy. I don't see him needing anything to beef up."

"And yet," Chloe drawled. She nodded at the two guys. " 'An anonymous source' saw the transaction in the parking lot and reported it to Principal Reynolds. Reynolds confronted Hackett, and the rest is . . . on page three."

Pete took that in, or tried to. In his more idealistic world, school officials did not sell drugs to students. Showing him that his own reality was not conforming to the school reality at large was like telling a little boy that Santa Claus wasn't real.

Grinning at him, she clucked her teeth sympathetically and shrugged as if to say, *What can you do?*

"I was shocked, too. You would have never guessed he was such a scumbag. And I used to think he didn't have any school spirit," she added, chuckling ironically. "But here he was, helping the football team pump up the volume. What a guy."

"Chloe," Clark reproved. "It's not funny."

She huffed. "Excuse me, guys, but he's only getting his due. Hey, *I* wasn't the one selling illegal drugs to minors."

"One minor," Pete said as he turned to page three and read her stuff. "Chloe, this is hard-hitting stuff, but . . ."

"Are you suggesting I shouldn't run this story? You guys, it's *huge*."

Pete glanced first at Clark, then at Chloe. He pointed at the first paragraph on page three and began to read aloud. " 'A closed meeting took place, with the aggrieved parties, Mr. Hackett, and members of the administration and the school board in attendance. The meeting was not discussed on any publicly disseminated agenda or memo between the administration and the school board. And yet, it occurred last Monday at 6 P.M." He looked hard at her. "How did you find out about it?"

"The public has a right to know," Chloe said, feeling confused. She did sense that now was not the time to admit she'd accidentally hacked her way into the digitally transcribed minutes of that off-the-record meeting—which had felt to her at the time like finding buried treasure. She had scarcely been able to stop herself from whooping aloud when she'd realized what she had found. Reporters dream of finding dirt like this on public figures. And in a small farming community like Smallville, one of the teachers at the only high school in town *was* a public figure.

"Hey, I didn't commit a crime," she snapped. "I'm reporting one."

"I don't know," Pete ventured, shuffling the mock-up back together. "It says Jake's parents consented to keeping it private." Pete nodded. "And I'm not sure you should drag his family into this."

Chloe was even more confused. "His family?"

"Mr. Hackett's family," Pete continued.

Just then, Lana arrived at their table with a tray in her hand. "Hey, Chloe," Lana greeted her housemate. "How'd the *Torch* turn out?"

Chloe didn't answer, and Lana had already started wiping off their table. Her long hair was pulled up, wisps tickling her jawline. She was obviously busy, but she looked great—which might or might not have explained the adoration on Clark's face. Then Lana smiled at the three friends, and added, "I just took some cinnamon buns out of the oven, and we're frosting them right now. They're fantastic. Any takers?"

"I'm not hungry," Chloe said grumpily.

"No thanks, Lana," Clark added.

Lana frowned as she looked around the table. "Is something wrong?"

"Clark and Pete think I'm a troublemaking muckraker." Chloe snatched the mock-up away from Pete and crisply folded the pages. Opening her cherry-appliquéd shoulder bag, she crammed them inside. Her treasured story seemed like a piece of garbage now. She was embarrassed and angry.

They're not journalists. They don't understand these things.

"Is this about the Hackett article?" Lana asked cautiously as she straightened and put her cleaning towel on the tray. Chloe was hyperaware of the look that passed between Clark and Pete.

Chloe grimaced. "Not you, too." Lana had stopped by the *Torch* office just after school let out for the day, and glanced through the parts Chloe had already edited and pasted together.

Lana hesitated. "Well, it was a little . . . strong."

Stung, Chloe scowled at the trio and said, "*Strong?* I can't believe you guys! We're not talking about coffee, Lana. We're talking about a grown man who sold steroids to a high-school athlete. Hello? If we were in college, this would be on the evening news."

Pete gestured at Chloe's purse. "It says that part of the agreement Hackett has with the school board is that he won't be prosecuted." He looked at the others. "No criminal charges have been brought against him. So I think, technically, he's still presumed innocent."

"Did you read my sidebar interview with my source?" Chloe demanded, her voice rising. Didn't her own friends understand that the public had a right to know what was going on in the world around them? "He saw Hackett selling Jake the steroids. Hackett admitted it. In other words, he's guilty, guilty, guilty."

Pete pondered her words, but still looked quite troubled. "Maybe you're right. It's just . . . Marshall Hackett's in my biology class. If you print this . . . everybody will know that his father did something illegal."

"*Wrong,* Pete," Chloe said for emphasis. Her frustration level was beginning to match the pressure inside the hissing espresso machine. "His dad did do something wrong, whether or not he's prosecuted for it."

She could see from his expression that Pete was moving to her side of the argument, so she decided to push him a little further over the line.

"And come on, guys, Marshall *must* already know. Something like this can't exactly go unnoticed in a family unit. What's his father going to tell him? 'Hey, kid, I decided to stop working all of a sudden. For no good reason'?"

"But what if Marshall *doesn't* know?" Clark asked. "What if nobody in his family knows this secret?"

"That'd be something you're familiar with," Chloe shot at him. "Secrets."

Clark flushed. Lana ticked a warning glance toward Chloe; Chloe knew she should back off. They'd often discussed Clark's own penchant for being secretive. It bothered them both, and they'd both told Clark that it was an issue. And yet, he was still all mystery guy on them.

Chloe ran out of steam and remained silent, considering the effect hearing about this from a third party would have on Marshall Hackett. Mr. Hackett's son was one of the nicest guys she vaguely knew. He had a wicked sense of humor, too. And fact of the well-known matter was, he flat-out worshiped his father. They had the kind of close relationship greeting card companies extolled every Father's Day.

"Mr. Hackett's been an inspiration to a lot of people with disabilities," Clark pointed out, as the uncomfortable seconds stretched into nearly a minute. "If you print this, it's going to tear him down in their eyes."

"Disabilities?" Chloe echoed, surprised. She gestured to the group at large. "Guys, he uses a wheelchair. That's all. No heroics involved. It's not like he . . . like he's some kind of victim who should be coddled and protected because he . . . he can't walk. Justice should be blind." She added, "Don't you think?"

The others said nothing. Chloe huffed. "Fine." She pushed back her bangs as she exhaled, frustrated, and said, "I'm . . . I'm going now. I have a paper to finalize."

As Chloe turned on her heel, Clark said gently, "Chloe, hey. Wait. It's just—"

Chloe waved a hand at them dismissively and moved away. Her face was hot; she was uneasy with the feeling that it was she who was in the wrong, not Hackett. Keeping secrets was not part of her job description. Exposing them was. She had every right to print this story. What if the teacher had sold steroids to other students as well? What if revealing the truth prompted just one other kid to come forward, tell his parents about it, get some help for whatever damage taking the drugs had done? The facts should come out, even if they did hurt a few people. After all, *she* wasn't the one hurting them. Mr. Hackett was.

I'm only doing what a reporter is supposed to do. Aren't I?

Without another backward glance, she shoved open the double doors and stepped outside. The fresh air helped her clear her head as she took a deep breath, then let it out.

The crack about Mr. Hackett and his wheelchair had come out all wrong. She wasn't an insensitive jerk. He *had* done a lot of things in the community for kids with disabilities. He'd spearheaded a drive to get wheelchairs to disadvantaged kids and worked tirelessly to ensure that all the public areas in town provided wheelchair access.

It was just that he'd always seemed so competent and . . . complete . . . that Chloe hadn't ever regarded him as someone with a disability. She'd stopped paying attention to his wheelchair long ago. And to be truthful, she hadn't considered that aspect of her story, either, until Clark had pointed it out.

Maybe I'm completely wrong, she mused, as she walked down the street. *And if I'm not, maybe I should have at least done a little more checking.*

The late-afternoon sun lengthened her shadow, stretching it into a Chloe she didn't know. Birdsong trilled from a lamppost, and, somewhere distant, a dog barked. A trash can beneath the lamppost urged passersby to *Keep Smallville Clean!*

The urgency of the exhortation, with the exclamation point and all, made it somehow endearing. Chloe felt an unusual twinge of tenderness for the town she usually despised. For all its own weirdness, Smallville was a place where real people lived. They had houses and pets and kids.

The story about Mr. Hackett was more than just a story about a crime. It was a story about a man. The school board had promised him he could resign without his wrongdoing—*alleged wrongdoing*—coming to light. But if she printed her story . . . there would be plenty of light shed on his actions. He would not be allowed to leave quietly.

But shouldn't I print the truth?

She pulled the folded pages of the mock-up from her

purse and examined them. The headline was enormous. She had to admit that she had been gloating over her discovery. In her excitement, she'd forgotten about the individuals involved. It had all been about the story.

I'm not a social worker, she thought halfheartedly. *I'm supposed to go after gems like this. I'm supposed to find the stories . . . if reporters don't come back and inform the rest of the tribe about what's going on, how will they be able to protect themselves from the dark beyond the campfire?*

Secrets are bad. They almost always wind up hurting people.

Nevertheless, she walked slowly to the trash can and stuffed the pages into it. A penetrating sadness hit the pit of her stomach, and her eyes welled with tears. She felt defeated. She had worked very, very hard on the mock-up, and now she had to start over from scratch . . . minus her best story ever.

Then she reached forward, thinking to retrieve it. But no, this was the right thing to do. Deep down, she could admit that that was the real reason she'd gotten so defensive around her friends. They'd hit a nerve. She knew that if she'd been sure about the story, she wouldn't have lost her temper with them.

With one more lingering regret for the one that got away, she turned back toward the Talon to tell the guys that she'd decided to bury the revelations about Hackett after all. But just then, the streetlight winked on. Her dad would be coming home, and it was Chloe's turn to make dinner. She'd suggested pot roast, which would take a while to cook, and now she had to write another story to fill the issue on top of it.

I'll write it at home after I get dinner started, she decided, *and e-mail it to my school account. Maybe Lana can help me think up something.*

Damn. I worked for hours on that story!

Feeling virtuous, she took the crosswalk and reached her car, slid in, and started the engine.

At least I got Clark's attention, she thought ironically.

Maybe I won't be such a great reporter after all, she thought, as she signaled and pulled away from the curb. *Maybe I lack that killer instinct truly great reporters need in instances like this.*

Ahead, a pretty tortoiseshell cat dropped from the curb and began to saunter across the blacktop. Chloe slowed. As if in sync, the cat stopped walking. Languidly it stared at her from its territory of the middle of the road, then plopped onto its side and began to lick its left front paw.

"Excuse me, kitty cat, let's move it," Chloe said to the cat, although, of course, it couldn't hear her.

Unflustered and unhurried, it continued to groom itself.

Chloe drummed her fingers on the steering wheel, then turned her tires slightly to the left and put her foot back on the gas. She'd go around the cat, then.

As Chloe approached, the cat rose, stretched, and sashayed into her path once more. Chloe stopped the car and stared at it through her windshield. It stretched back its little head and yawned, flicking its little pink tongue in her direction.

"About that killer instinct that I lack," she said to the cat. "All I have to say is count your blessings, Nine Lives."

As if in reply, it lay back down and flicked its tail into the air with a certain insouciance that Chloe had to admire. She began to laugh to herself, and by the time the cat consented to allow her to get through the intersection, she was actually smiling.

Maybe I'll write about Smallville's escalating traffic problems.

She snorted, because that was a good one—and edged the car to the right before the cat had time to react.

"Well, that's *one* I win," Chloe murmured.

Glancing into the rearview mirror, she watched the cat rise and saunter the rest of the way across the street.

Game over.

After Chloe left the Talon, daily life there overtook the singular moment of high drama as Lana got back to work, and the conversation about Mr. Hackett eventually died out.

Then Clark glanced at Pete's watch. It was getting late, and Clark had chores to do. If he had been any other farm kid, he would have had to go home immediately after school to help with the family business. Because he was an alien from another planet, he actually had time for a social life.

But despite his otherworldly origins, he was part of a family now—a human family—and he had to go home and do his share. Working the land was a backbreaking way to make a living, but he understood why his parents loved it so much. The sense of accomplishment in a job well-done—growing things, springing them from the soil yielding new life as a result of the Kents' efforts—was hard to beat.

I understand what Chloe felt when she wrote that article, Clark thought. *When you do what you do well, it satisfies something in your soul. I'm sorry she's upset.*

I wonder what she'll do—print it or throw it away?

He knew Chloe well enough to know that seeds of doubt had been planted in her mind, and she wouldn't simply ignore them. Chloe had a lot of integrity. He admired her for that.

"I've got to go home," he said to Pete as he got to his feet.

He picked up his books. "I've got chores. You sticking around?"

Pete nodded. "Uncle Howard is visiting. It's easier to study here."

Clark grinned sympathetically. He'd had experience with Uncle Howard. The man was a sales rep for a feed company, and he had a story for every mile he'd driven his shiny teal Lexus along the country roads of the Midwest. All his stories were entertaining, but there were so many of them. Going to dinner at Pete's when Uncle Howard was in town tired even Clark.

Sighing, Pete hoisted his backpack from the floor and unzipped the pouch section. He pulled out a calculator. "Might as well get the math out of the way. Then the rest will be smooth sailing." He grimaced. "Smooth*er* sailing. Don't forget our history gig, Clark."

"Right," Clark assured him. Then he hesitated.

"Your part is looking around the farm for old farming implements," Pete reminded him. "I'm already finished."

"Yeah. History of pesticides," Clark said, trying to reassure Pete that he was hooked in.

Pete rolled his eyes. "It's pretty bad. What I have to say about pesticide use, I mean. Lex is going to love me if he ever gets a chance to read it."

"The LuthorCorp plant makes fertilizer, not pesticides," Clark observed.

Pete shrugged. "Sometimes it's hard to distinguish the two. Which you'll discover once you read my report," he added pointedly.

"Right," Clark said uneasily, not because he had forgotten to search for antique farm equipment at home, but because of Pete's tone of voice when Lex's name had come up. Clark and Lex were good friends, although that friendship had been sorely tested in the past, and probably would be again. Many people in Smallville didn't like Lex simply because he was a Luthor. Clark knew it wasn't that simple.

He also knew that his own father had had a hand in helping Lex's father buy Pete's family's creamed corn factory. Lionel Luthor had assured the Rosses that the factory would remain in operation. Today, the fertilizer factory stood in its place—to Jonathan Kent's everlasting shame.

It's one of those bad family secrets, Clark thought. On the other hand, Pete was the only one who knew his own secret, besides his mother and father. Lex didn't even know, although he had tried more than once to figure out what Clark was obviously hiding from him. *Pete knows. Lex doesn't. Does that make Pete my closest friend?*

"Hey, Clark, don't freak out or anything," Pete said, as he fished in his backpack. "I'm not going to start a fight with Lex or hold an anti-LuthorCorp rally or anything." He pulled out some pieces of paper from his pack. They were paper-clipped together, and there were some notes scrawled in the margins of page one.

Pete said, "This is the first draft of the report. Take a look, see what you think. There's nothing in here that can really hurt Lex. Not like Chloe's article on Hackett." He exhaled. "Man."

They were back to it. Clark took the pages from Pete, and said, "She was pretty upset."

"Yeah. But not half as upset as Hackett is, I'll bet."

Saying nothing more, Clark rose from his chair. Lana gave him a wave from behind the counter, and he waved back. Her forehead was furrowed; he guessed she was still thinking about Chloe, and he was glad the two girls had become such good friends. It was good to have someone to talk to, a sounding board for issues one couldn't discuss with other people. Pete had learned about Clark's secret by accident, but after the Kents' initial scare, it had proved to be a good thing. More than once, Pete had come to Clark's rescue specifically because he knew his secret.

Lana and Chloe both knew what it was like to lose a mom, and they had a few other things in common. *I like Lana, Chloe knows it; Chloe . . . well, she's over liking me that way. It's awkward now and then. Friendships bring their own complications with them.*

He told Pete he would read the report.

"Cool." Pete settled in to do his math.

With another nod at his friend, Clark turned to go. Pete settled in for math torture.

Then, through the din of the coffeehouse, Clark heard shouting outside. Another voice rose in what could have been anger, might have been fear. He was tempted to use his X-ray vision, but it was just as simple to push open the Talon doors.

Then he was outside. About ten feet away, beneath a lamppost, Marshall Hackett was yelling at another guy from the football team. His face was fire-engine red; spittle flew from his mouth as he screamed, "Give that to me!"

"Marsh, chill!" the other guy protested. It was Ty West-fall, dark-haired, and about the same height and build as Marshall. Both were wearing their letter jackets, jeans, and running shoes. Jocks to the end.

Ty held a wad of paper in his left hand. Marshall flailed for it; Ty took a step backward and held them out of Marshall's reach. Marshall rushed him, and Ty easily side-stepped him, saying, "I just want to see what it says, man!"

"Give it to me!" Marshall shouted, flailing at him. Clark thought about how coordinated he was on the field. But right now, Marshall was so upset he couldn't control his movements.

Ty dodged Marshall again. "Is it true?"

"No!"

"But it says he's resigning," Ty persisted.

Uh-oh.

This time Clark did use his special vision; he zeroed in on Ty's hand; among the bones, the words *Drug Bust!* appeared in a negative image—the way Clark saw things when he used his X-ray vision—and Clark realized Ty had a copy of Chloe's mock-up of the *Torch.*

How'd he get hold of it? Chloe usually makes only one, and then she puts it in Reynolds's in box when she's finished. She never wants any spare mock-up copies floating around until the finished copies are distributed.

"Give that to me!" Marshall bellowed. Then he doubled up his right fist and slammed it into Ty's solar plexus. The force of the impact made Clark wince.

Grunting, Ty contracted around the punch. The tatters of the *Torch* mock-up flew around his head like a circlet of tweeting birdies in a cartoon.

With brutal force, Marshall slammed Ty against the trash can, so hard that Clark heard a crack. Clark took a step toward them, aware that guys did not bust up other guys' fights, but it sounded as if Ty had broken a rib. As he scanned Ty's torso, his X-ray vision caught sight of the remainder of the pages of the mock-up inside the trash can.

Chloe threw it out. And Ty and Marshall must have found it.

Marshall pulled his fist back to his ear and prepared to lay into Ty again when Clark said, "Hey."

The two looked up at him. Despite the fact that he was getting hurt and could use a hand, Ty was no more happy to see him than Marshall—Clark got that; it was an embarrassing situation—but Clark was glad to see Marshall unball his fist and take a step away from his teammate. Without another word, Marshall dropped to his knees and began grabbing up the shreds of the mock-up.

Ty remained where he was, his hand pressed against his rib cage. He muttered something about Marshall being a psycho, but eventually he said, "Marsh, it's cool, dude."

Marshall glared at Ty as he snatched up the pieces and cradled them against his chest. "Get the hell away from me."

An unwilling witness to his pain, Clark steadfastly looked away. Ty did the same.

The two stood in acute discomfort until Ty sneered at Clark, and said, "What you lookin' at, Kent?"

Clark knew he couldn't do anything to help, and the knowledge frustrated him. He wasn't friends with Marshall Hackett, and any attempts to step in would be highly resented at a time like this.

The papers in his arms, Marshall began to get to his feet without using his hands. He fell back. Ty reached to help, and Marshall shouted, "I told you to leave me alone!"

Retreating as if Marshall had socked him again, Ty shook his head. Then, as he watched Marshall dropping the same pieces and then picking them up again, he muttered, "No. No, I won't leave you alone."

"My dad . . ." Marshall breathed. "My dad, he couldn't have sold drugs to some kid. He wouldn't do that. He's a good man!"

"Marsh, it's cool," Ty said again. "She probably just made it up. It's in the trash because Reynolds told her it was bogus."

Then he narrowed his eyes at Clark and took a threatening step toward him. "Get the hell out of here!" Ty shouted.

Clark remained stoic and walked on by.

I've got to tell Chloe about this, he thought. *Talk about bad news.*

"My . . . father . . . didn't . . . do . . . anything!" Marshall Hackett screamed. "He wouldn't do this! I know my father! I know him! He's my *father*!"

His voice echoed down Main Street.

His agony came tumbling after.

CHAPTER TWO

Cap du Roi, a small village in Haiti

Maria del Carmen Maldonaldo Lopez had never run faster in her life.

Her short, spiky hair was slicked back with blood and sweat. Dressed in an olive tank top and khaki shorts, she was smeared with mango, mud, and sweat. Her arms and legs were slashed by the stalks of sugar cane as she raced through the field, the reedy stalks breaking off and acting as a medieval abatis—the pointed ends of the broken cane at the ready to run through anyone unlucky enough to fall on them.

Her field boots were caked with mud; her right boot was stretched tight over her swollen ankle as she staggered past the cane field and shuffled through a pitiful vegetable patch. She could smell the crops as she helplessly destroyed them—bean plants, overripe pumpkin, the overturned earth hot and thirsty. She slid over some fallen plantains, grinding them into mush. She knew how hard the villagers worked on their subsistence-level gardens, and that she had just wiped out a good portion of the village's food supply.

She couldn't help that now. She kept running. She ran as if her life depended on it.

It did.

She could hear her own breath as she flew through the thick night, the steamy air practically boiling on her skin. Salt mixed with the blood that dripped after her, leaving a delectable trail of odors for the nightmare that wanted nothing more than to rip her body open like a plantain and devour her.

She couldn't take a second to gauge the monster's progress. She didn't need to. The thing that was hunting her was a nightmare—tall, gaunt figure of a dark-skinned man, his face half-eaten away, his eyes bulged glassy and empty. His mouth hung open, as the mouths of the dead often do, but the jaw clacked shut at a frighteningly steady pace— *click clack click clack.*

Starving for her flesh, the creature was hunting her down. She had been running for what seemed like hours, and its pace had never slowed. It was like being stalked by the Terminator.

No, it's worse. This thing is real. It's a zombie, and it's real!

She burst into tears as she ran, though consciously she was unable to register any emotion to go with those tears. She was drowning in a numbing, free-floating terror, and yet some part of her brain demanded that she keep moving, past the intense pain in her ankle, past her exhaustion. It was a miracle to her that she had enough energy in her body to cry. That there was any moisture left in her body for tears. She kept seeing an image in her mind of herself half–eaten away but still alive. And that was her goal now—to get away from him before he ripped the flesh completely off of her bones. It was as if she didn't believe she could hope to get away unscathed, and that only if she kept running, kept praying, kept dodging it, could she manage to survive at all.

Beneath the moonlight, she saw at last the pathetic string of yellow lights that signified the perimeter of the AYUDO compound. *Home!*

Gasping, she reached for the lights; they were her lifeline.

Inside the gate she would be safe from this monster . . . if she could only get to the gate before *it* reached *her*.

"*Ayudame*," she tried to scream. *Help me.* But nothing came. Any sound was strangled by her shallow panting. She was light-headed with fear and the desperate need to take deep breaths to fill her lungs; how on earth could she ever hope to scream?

"*Ayu . . .*" she tried again.

And then, in view of the watery lights, it grabbed her around the waist and flung her to the ground. She went face-down into the mud. And even though her nose and mouth were immediately plugged with mud, she could smell the foulness of the zombie as it straddled her. This was Haiti, and people died here; she had seen death and smelled it.

But this was worse.

This was the stench of hell itself.

Finger bones gripped her shoulders and dug deep, slicing through her flesh. Something hard pressed against the back of her neck; a sharp pain pierced her skin.

The zombie was beginning his feast.

She went rigid. Somewhere deep inside herself, she realized that if she didn't act now, she was going to die. Horribly.

I can't die. I'm a good person! I was doing good here!

The shock of actual words in her mind galvanized her. Though the zombie had a big frame, he wasn't as heavy as a normal person. Portions of his flesh had either fallen off or been devoured by the packs of wild dogs that plagued the village. Before arriving in Haiti three months before, Maria del Carmen had taken six months of self-defense classes. Three months of classes were required before joining the AYUDO Project; her parents had insisted that she double that amount of time.

Don't panic, Marica, she told herself, using the diminutive of her own name, as her family, friends, and coworkers did. *You're dead if you panic.*

But oh my God, I'm in a foreign country and a zombie is devouring me . . . piadosa Virgen Maria de Guadalupe, dale clemencia, amor y compasion a aquellos que te queieren y vuelan a tu proteccion . . .

She prayed to the Virgin of Guadalupe with all her heart and all her soul. She kept her mind on the words of the prayer, forcing down her terror as she willed herself to focus.

You can save yourself, she heard her interior voice whispering. *It's within your ability. Think of your self-defense classes. You can do it.*

It was as if the Virgin herself was speaking to her.

Marica listened.

And she remembered what to do.

She hadn't taken enough lessons for the movements to be automatic. But if she could manage not to completely lose control, and take a few seconds to work through her offensive postures, she might be able to survive.

The zombie bit into her again, and she grunted in horror. Blinded by the mud, she was pinioned tightly as the monster's jagged, broken teeth sank into her. Then she went strangely cold.

Am I going into shock? Is it injecting me with something?

Her panic level shot up; for a moment she could do nothing. Groggy from lack of oxygen, she sensed that if she didn't do something soon, she really, truly was going to die.

Marica . . . remember your training . . . execute putar kepala . . . putar kepala . . .

Sí!

She sprang into action.

In its eagerness to grab hold of her neck, the zombie had loosened its grip on her wrists. This was her only chance, heaven-sent. As she yanked her arms free, a fiery pain shot from her wrists to her shoulders, and she wondered if she had broken something. The monster didn't appear to notice that it had lost hold of her, so lost it was in its feast.

Miraculously, through the haze of white-hot agony, she managed to draw her hands toward the center of her chest. She balled her fists as best she could, although her strength was fading, and she was in danger of passing out.

In the semblance of a double fist, she anchored her hands together, then pushed up and to the right. The zombie stayed on easily, like a cowboy on a very sluggish longhorn.

Her arm muscles shook, but she propped herself up into a tripod by rolling her fists so that she was resting her weight on her palms. Then she rolled herself onto her hip, pushed again with her hands, and flipped onto her back, on top of the zombie.

It grunted, writhing and grabbing at her; Marica summoned reserves she didn't know she had and rolled off the zombie, scrambling to the right. Its flopping hand batted against her right ankle and she jerked out of reach, sobbing for breath. Throwing herself forward, she tried to crawl, and she scrabbled like a baby in the slippery mud.

The zombie sat up, teeth clacking, and dived for her.

She kicked her legs frantically, but it was no use. The zombie grabbed her, and this time, held her tight. She closed her eyes as despair washed over her.

Then she heard another shuffling sound and opened her eyes.

A pair of feet stepped into her field of vision, filthy, blistered, and caked with mud. She glanced up and saw rags covering strong, muscular legs and a well-defined torso and firm arms. It was a man in excellent physical condition. He had a little goatee, and he wore an earring . . .

. . . and his eyes were as sightless and unseeing as the zombie who, even now, was clacking its teeth at Marica's booted feet.

This new zombie before her opened its mouth.

The one behind her flung itself at her. The stench from its mouth was unbelievable. Its blank eyes stared right through her; it was like a machine as its teeth clacked, as if scenting her not from its nose but from its bloody maw . . .

It came closer, leering sightlessly at her, as the first zombie grabbed her around the neck. Instinctively, she grabbed at the bony fingers, pulling as hard as she could, trying to dig her heels into the mud for traction.

The second zombie gripped her forearms.

She screamed again.

Its mouth clacked at her; blood dripped onto her arm . . .

The world began to grow dark. She thought of her mother and father, who had begged her not to come to Haiti, calling it hell on earth. They had known what they were talking about. But the images and memories swam as the world sank away, sank away . . .

Don't let them eat me. Don't let my mother see that . . . merciful Mother of God, intercede for me . . .

A shot rang out.

A sharp pain erupted in her shoulder, and Maria del Carmen Maldonaldo Lopez prayed no more prayers, and made no more wishes.

Field Operative T. T. Van De Ven and two other soldiers marched their zombie captives across the fields of cane, their heavy boots crushing ripe shoots rising beneath the earth-crunching noises. The two zombies staggered along barefoot, their feet covered with blisters. Van De Ven had no idea if the zombies were in pain. He didn't particularly care, either. His mind was on other things.

They got to the artificial boulder that housed the alarm system and the elevator. Van De Ven took off his skullcap and showed the retinal scan his left eye. Three clicks signaled that his scan had been accepted.

They went down in the elevator to where the real action was.

The two soldiers were new, and he could tell they were scared. He smiled grimly to himself.

They ain't seen nothin' yet.

The zombies stood silent, their mouths slack, their eyes vacant. To all outward appearances, they were the mindless hulks the Project had transformed them into. But that was now, after he had captured them and pumped them full of Thorazine. These zombies had gone AWOL, and they had wreaked havoc in a total frenzy that had impressed the war-hardened combat veteran. Gone completely wacko.

Ferocity was good. Aggression was even better. But it had shown up unexpectedly . . . and it was happening more often. There was something wrong with the doctored fertilizer the Project was receiving from LuthorCorp. The formula was incorrect.

The elevator doors opened, and Van De Ven turned his attention from the zombies to the soldiers. As he had anticipated, the stench hit them full force. The one on the left covered his mouth. The other blinked as his eyes began to water.

"Man," Watery Eyes gasped.

Zombies stank. No two ways around it.

"C'mon, boys," he said to the two zombies, who staggered out of the elevator. They began to walk down the tunnel.

A shriek pierced the air, and Watery Eyes swore under his breath. The other soldier made a comment about joining the military and seeing the *under*world.

"Thought I'd end up in Germany or something," he muttered.

Van De Ven was patient with them. Not everybody had the stuff, like him.

There was a second shriek. One of the zombies froze. The other one ran into him. Then the first one turned around very slowly. His vacant eyes stared at Van De Ven, moving just a little bit, as if he were trying to focus, perhaps even to communicate with him.

Interesting, Van De Ven thought.

Down the second corridor they went, deeper into the earth and into a complex of rooms. Van De Ven gestured to Germany, and he fished in his pocket for some keys.

He showed them to Van De Ven, and the quintet moved into the first of a dozen blocks of cells in which zombies were housed.

Some were in good shape—they had been the soldier volunteers, not quite clear on exactly what they had volunteered to do. They were the best results of the Project so far, the ones that made the failures worthwhile.

"In you go," Van De Ven said to the two zombies as Water Eyes opened the door to an empty cell.

That matter dispatched, Van De Ven went to report to his superior, Colonel Adams, a craggy-faced older man, who looked up expectantly from behind his metal field desk and returned Van De Ven's sharp salute.

"At ease," he said.

Van De Ven assumed parade rest and debriefed as quickly as possible.

"They were wild, sir," he told the colonel. "Went completely crazy up there, nearly ate a girl."

The colonel took that in. "Local girl?"

"No, sir. One of the relief workers."

The colonel set his jaw. "Damn."

"I recommend we take them all out, sir. The AYUDO personnel, I mean, sir. Security has been breached. They're sure to get on those laptops of theirs and tell the world what's going on out here."

The other man shook his head. "Killing them will call even more attention to the Project." He smiled wryly at Van De Ven. "Let them look like idiots, trying to make people believe in zombies. They might as well add that they all got in their spaceships and took off."

"But, sir—" Van De Ven protested.

The colonel waved a hand. "I'll take it under advisement, son." He leaned on his elbows, and added confidentially, "Not everyone appreciates a military solution. You know we're working with a civilian."

"Yes, sir."

"And he likes to stay under the radar. So . . ." Col. Adams smiled. "For now, we watch. And wait. If the AYUDO workers get to be too much of a nuisance, you'll be the first one I send to take 'em out."

"Sir, thank you, sir." Van De Ven stood tall, proud, and eager.

"Meanwhile," the colonel said, sighing, "we have to figure out why this batch went so wrong. Thank God no civilians have any of this stuff. Can you imagine what would happen if they actually used it for fertilizer?"

Van De Ven could not . . . but it was an interesting question.

CHAPTER THREE

The phone rang while Chloe was checking her pot roast in the oven. Figuring it was Lana or her father, she left the oven door open as she picked up the cordless and said, "Hello?"

"It's Clark." Chloe nodded, warmth coming to her cheeks. The room behind Clark was very noisy; she figured he was still at the Talon.

She shut the oven door and turned her attention to the phone call, raking her fingers through her hair before she realized what she was doing—primping for a boy who couldn't see her—even when he was standing right in front of her, much less when he was talking to her on the phone.

"Before you start in on me again. I decided not to print the story, okay?" she informed him. "Because you guys had a point, and I—"

"Chloe, Marshall Hackett saw your article," Clark cut in.

Chloe was speechless. As his words sank in, she shut her eyes and felt a wave of guilt wash over her. An image of Marshall's reaction followed after.

Not good.

"Chloe?" Clark pressed.

Then she opened her eyes, and said, "I . . . I threw it away. I threw the whole mock-up out, and I'm going to start over."

"Yes. It was in the trash. By the Talon. I don't know how they found it, but they fished it out and read it."

"They?" she asked sharply. "They who?"

"Marshall and Ty Westfall."

"Oh, my God." She took a breath. "Did . . . Clark, did he

know about his dad? He didn't learn about it from my story, did he?"

There was a beat, and then Clark said, "No, Chloe. He didn't know."

There was a sharp rap on her front door. She walked toward it.

"Chloe, listen," Clark went on. "Marshall's very upset. He was making threats. I'm coming over there."

"Threats . . ." she said slowly as she opened the door.

"Against you."

Marshall Hackett stood on the other side of the screen door. He looked terrible; his eyes were swollen, and he was very pale, like a vampire—and in his fist he clenched her mock-up, the pages torn and filthy.

"Hi, *Marshall*," she said anxiously into the phone. "Marshall who is at my door *right now*."

"On my way," Clark told her.

"That would be good. Are you using a cell phone?" she queried shrilly. Her heart slammed against her rib cage. "Are you coming now?"

"Pete, I'm taking this," he said away from the receiver. "Chloe, I have Pete's cell phone. I'll stay on the line."

"You . . . *bitch!*" Marshall shouted at her. He yanked open the screen door; it smacked against the side of the house, making a noise like a rifle shot.

"Chloe, tell him to leave," Clark told her firmly.

"Go away, Marshall." Chloe's voice shook. *"Now."*

In a bizarre way, the guy was ignoring her at the same time that he was totally focused on her, his face contorted with rage. It was as if he wasn't seeing her. The phrase *blind with rage* snapped into her mind.

Looming over her like a giant, he stepped across the

threshold and stomped into her house. Chloe backed away, clutching the phone and saying into it, "Clark, I need help!"

"What's going on?" Clark demanded. "Chloe, what's happening?"

Marshall loomed over her. Chloe gasped, and said, "Marshall, listen . . ."

"No, *you* listen!" he shrieked at her.

He smacked the phone out of her hand. It arced across the room and hit the wall, narrowly missing a framed picture of Chloe holding a copy of a newsletter called "Chloe's Room" she used to edit in middle school. Then it ricocheted off the wall and smacked the coffee table, hard.

Chloe held up her hands like an unarmed cowboy, backing away from him as she mentally counted how many minutes had elapsed between when Clark had called her and now. She came up with thirty seconds—far too early for Clark to come to her rescue. She was going to have to handle this on her own—and without any way to call for more backup. Nine-one-one might have been a good idea, but the next available phone was in her father's bedroom, and there was a hallway and a closed door to get through. She was afraid to turn her back on Marshall.

God, I'm scared, she thought. *I'm terrified.*

"Marshall," she began. All she had to defend herself was her wits. She knew she was well armed in that department, and she was grateful for her intelligence. But panic was beginning to overtake her. "I'm not printing the story. I buried it."

"Doesn't matter," he gritted at her, still moving toward her. "Now everyone knows."

"No. Nobody . . . very few people know. And they won't tell a soul. I promise."

"Ty's already told half the football team." He glared at her. "My dad's out of a job."

Westfall, her helpful reporter brain informed her. *Ty Westfall is his full name.*

Don't go there, she ordered herself. *Last names are unnecessary details. That is so not the point right now.*

"I'm so sorry, Marshall," she said, and she meant it.

"Not half as sorry as you're going to be."

He rushed her. Maybe his fury made him clumsy; maybe her adrenaline rush made her unusually agile. Whatever the reason, Chloe dodged him, and he stumbled forward, colliding with the coffee table with a grunt. He managed to stop short of flying over it and whirled around, his face contorted with even more fury than when he'd appeared at her front door.

Chloe went numb from head to foot, unable to believe that this was actually happening.

Hold on, Sullivan, you are talking about Smallville, right? Guys have tried to freeze you to death, burn you to death, and throw you off a cliff. Having a guy break into your house and threaten to beat you up . . . hey, rolling off a log here . . .

"Marshall, please, calm down." She tried to smile, but her mouth said *no way.* She tried to swallow. Also not possible.

She tried to run. That she managed, but it didn't matter. Marshall was a football player, and this time, he tackled her hard and flung her to the floor. The contact was rough, and it was hard to stay conscious, but Chloe's self-preservation instincts went into overdrive as she screamed and started kicking her feet into his chest as hard as she possibly could. She might as well have been kicking a bale of hay for all the effect it had on the burly ballplayer.

Grunting, she scanned the area ahead of her for something

to hit him with. There were chair legs attached to chairs, and sofa legs attached to sofas, and that was about it.

If this were a movie or a TV show, she thought, *or even a badly written novel, I'd have conveniently played baseball with the gang sometime before Marshall showed up, and left my Louisville Slugger on the floor, within reach. Then I could whack him with it.*

It's really too bad that reality doesn't provide for contingencies that way.

"Marshall, this is stupid," she said in a rush. "Really stupid."

He said nothing in reply, only got to his feet and yanked her up as easily as if she were a feather. Dangling in his grasp, she looked up at him; his eyes were red and swollen. He'd been crying, and she detected behind the blaze of anger a very frightened, very wounded guy.

"I don't mean stupid," she said. "I mean, tragic."

For a second, she thought she was going to get through to him. Emotions warred across his features. Then he sneered at her and made a fist.

Oh, my God, Chloe thought. *He's going to hit me.*

"Marshall," she said desperately. "Marshall, please . . ."

His fist flew at her.

Behind her, a loud, wrenching sound covered her scream. Then before she knew what was happening, Marshall flew backward, arcing into the air before he slammed onto her sofa. The force of his trajectory was so strong that the sofa tipped backward and Marshall rolled over the back and onto the floor.

Then Clark's arms were around Chloe, and his face was inches from hers.

He stared at her hard. "Are you okay?" he demanded.

She nodded, and Clark released her, running to stand over Marshall in case he got back up.

How did he get here so quickly? Chloe wondered. She pressed a hand over her chest, trying to catch her breath.

As she turned around, Clark was helping her attacker. Marshall was red-faced; he didn't look at Chloe or Clark, only focused his attention on the floor.

"Marshall," Chloe tried again. "I'm sorry. I wasn't going to print the story. Honest."

"You . . ." He began, then sagged, utterly defeated. Still avoiding her and Clark's gazes, he lifted the sofa back off the floor and righted the piece of furniture. He appeared dazed, as if he was wondering what he was doing in the Sullivan living room.

"Would you like a glass of water?" Chloe asked gently.

He nodded. Clark took a couple of steps backward, giving Marshall some space. Marshall sat down on the sofa and buried his face in his hands.

Exchanging looks with Clark, Chloe hurried to the kitchen to get some water. She poured herself a glass, too, and chugged it down at the sink.

"Clark?" she asked.

"I'm good," he replied.

By the time she handed the glass to Marshall, he had calmed down. He took it and said in a rush, "You got it wrong, Sullivan. Wrong . . . and a little bit right.

"My dad wasn't selling steroids to Jake Brook because of football. Jake . . ." He shook his head and clamped his mouth shut. A muscle jumped in his cheek. His hands were shaking.

After a sip of water, Marshall stared up at Chloe. The look of despair on his face was far worse than the anger he'd shown her.

Chloe sat on the arm of the sofa and waited. She was a good listener, and she knew that the silence before someone's words was usually part of the message.

"My dad has MS," he said, and his voice was saturated with equal parts of sorrow, anger, and relief. Chloe's lips parted in shock, and she ticked her gaze to Clark. He looked back, equally surprised, and raised a brow.

The room was pin-drop silent while Marshall struggled to speak.

Chloe guessed that no one else knew what he was about to tell them. She wasn't sure Marshall even remembered that Clark was in the room. This connection was between her and him.

"Multiple sclerosis," Marshall clarified. "My father has multiple sclerosis."

Chloe's heart caught, but she stayed quiet. This wasn't about her reactions or her sympathy. This was his chance to talk it out.

"He's been on an experimental medication, but it didn't seem to help. You can't get it with a prescription. You can only get it as part of an approved medical trial."

She nodded to show that she was hearing him. She didn't know very much about the disease, but she vaguely recalled that there was no cure . . . and that over time, it usually got worse.

"Does Jake have MS, too?" Clark asked, his tone respectful.

"That's none of your business," Marshall said harshly. His moment of connection was over, and now he was pulling back. As he scowled at Chloe, she sensed that in that instant he had stopped seeing her as someone he could talk to; she was the enemy again.

"My dad's disease was none of your business, either." He

balled his fist and brought it down on his thigh, hard. "Reynolds and the school board were to let him resign so he could get another job in the district. Jake's parents were going to cooperate.

"But now that you've blown it open, that is not gonna happen."

He took a hefty swallow of water and rubbed his forehead wearily. "And without a job, he doesn't have health insurance."

Chloe closed her eyes.

"And he has a preexisting condition, so it'll be next to impossible to get private insurance," she filled in. She felt sick. No wonder Marshall had gone ballistic.

"Maybe it *was* a cover-up," Marshall went on, his voice dull and sad. "Maybe what he was doing was wrong. I don't know. But he was trying to help somebody."

His voice lowered. He spoke so softly Chloe had to crane toward him to hear him. "All I know is that my father is a great teacher, and he had a lot to offer another school. No one's going to hire him now. He's finished. My family's finished."

"Marshall, no," Chloe said earnestly. "There . . . there are always options. There's a solution."

"Is there?" He stared at her. "Do you have a way to change that headline you wrote to 'Happily Ever After'?"

"If he explains to . . . to the education board or whatever it is, " Chloe ventured.

"We live in an age of lawsuits, Chloe. By the time this is resolved . . ." He shook his head in disbelief. "We can't afford a lawyer. All our money has gone for medical bills, even though we do have medical insurance. At the moment."

"I'll—I'll print a story about that," she offered. "I'll get a campaign started to reinstate him. We'll have a fund-raiser."

"Don't. You've done enough already." Marshall handed her the glass. "I'm going to go now," he told them both, "unless you want to call the police and press charges against me for assault."

Chloe's brows shot up. "Marshall, I would never do that."

He stuffed his hands into the pockets of his letterman's jacket. "It's hard to say what you're capable of, Chloe." He said to Clark, "No hard feelings?"

Clark shook his head. "No, man. Do you need a ride?" He was carless, but Chloe would let him use hers.

Marshall moved past them. Then he turned around and stared at both of them.

"When he was diagnosed, my dad told us kids to walk as much as we could, whenever we could. He told us that health is a gift, and we needed to do everything we could to take care of our health. Because in the good old USA, it's a really expensive gift.

"I don't need a ride, Clark. I need a time machine."

There was nothing Chloe could say, no way to make things better. But in her mind, she was already surfing the net, searching for some way to help the Hackett family.

Chloe and Clark turned to watch Marshall leave. When he got to the threshold of Chloe's house, he gestured to the screen door, which Clark had ripped off its hinges and thrown onto the porch.

"Wow, dude. You really should try out for the team," he said, impressed.

"Been there," Clark replied.

Marshall nodded, stuffed his hands back in his pockets, and trudged away. His receding figure was hunched and lost.

Clark shut the front door.

"Oh, my God." Chloe began to shake all over. "Clark, what did I do?"

"You didn't know." He was at a loss to comfort her. "You thought it was a good story, and when you felt otherwise you tried to dump it."

"I ruined their lives." She burst into heavy, racking sobs.

Then Clark moved to her and put his arms around her. She closed her eyes and leaned her head on his chest, the pain of loving him magnifying her misery. She was lost in guilt and sorrow and hurt. And Clark was there for her, holding her close.

They stood that way for a couple of minutes.

Then Lana's voice penetrated the sound of Chloe's weeping, as she said, "My God, what's going on?"

Standing in the doorway, Lana was holding a Talon to-go box. The scent of cinnamon mingled with Lana's perfume as she tentatively walked toward them.

"What happened to the screen?"

Awkwardly, Chloe pulled herself out of Clark's arms. She realized that she was still holding Marshall's water glass, and that she had accidentally spilled water down the back of Clark's sweatshirt. Clark hadn't said a thing about it.

"Ty Westfall fished Chloe's mock-up out of the trash," Clark explained to Lana. "Marshall was there. I guess Ty's telling people all over town what happened."

"So, no quiet resignation." Chloe hugged herself, exhaling heavily. "Mr. Hackett's got multiple sclerosis, and Marshall figures he won't be able to get another teaching job. He'll lose his health insurance benefits."

"But . . ." Lana frowned. "They'll be okay, right?"

"They're not okay now," Chloe observed, her voice

cracking. "They haven't been okay for a long time. Only none of us knew it."

Chloe fought back tears. "Mr. Hackett is sick, Lana. He's got a chronic, progressive disease."

"That's not your fault," Lana said firmly. "You didn't make him sick."

"It's okay, Lana. I have to accept responsibility for my part in this fiasco. I'm past the rationalizing," Chloe said, flashing her a faint, wry smile.

"But it's not rationalizing," Lana protested, reaching a hand toward her friend. "You threw it out, Chloe. It's not your fault that those two guys went rooting through the trash."

Chloe let that sail right past her. She pursed her lips together and shrugged, then said pleasantly, "I have a pot roast to check on." She gestured toward the box in Lana's hands. "Cinnamon buns?" As Lana nodded and held it out to her again, Chloe carried it into the kitchen.

Clark stood with Lana. There was a beat of silence between them, then he said, "Marshall was going to beat Chloe up."

"Oh, my God." Lana covered her mouth. "Did he hurt her?"

"No. I called her to warn her, just as he reached the house."

"And you miraculously got here in time to stop him," she said archly. "How do you manage it, Clark? All the great timing, I mean?" She turned her beautiful brown eyes on him. "And the rescuing?"

He raised his brows, realizing that the innocent look he cultivated had long ago stopped working on both Lana and Chloe. He didn't insult her intelligence by saying, "Just lucky, I guess," which he would have said—used to say—back when they were younger.

I wish my having a secret didn't bother her so much. I wish she could just let it go.

Finally, he said, "I ran into Marshall and Ty Westfall outside the Talon. I wanted to let Chloe know that Marshall had read her story, so I called her on Pete's cell phone." As if offering her proof, he pulled Pete's phone from his back pocket.

"It all happened really fast, but I was in on what was happening as soon as it started," he finished.

Flushing, Lana ticked a glance at the cell phone. She shifted her weight, and said, "I guess that sounded a little bit accusatory. I'm sorry. I didn't mean it to be." She hesitated. "I should go help Chloe. She's pretty upset."

"Yes. She is." He tucked the cell phone back into his pocket and headed for the screen door. "I'll fix this," he assured her. "Tell Mr. Sullivan that the hinge was broken. That's why it came off so easily."

"Sure. Thanks for helping her, Clark. We're both lucky to have you around."

She gave him a smile—his chest tightened in response—and Clark took off.

CHAPTER FOUR

It was a beautiful new day, and all was really, really good in the world.

Pausing at the sink with her dad's new LuthorCorp coffee cup in her hand, Rebecca Morhaim looked out at the brilliant wildflowers decorating her front yard. There were sunflowers and bluebonnets, and small magenta-colored blossoms whose name she didn't know, laid out like a magical road leading right up to their new ground-floor apartment. The sun glowed a warm, welcoming yellow. Sunbeams sparkled and capered over the breathtaking beauty. In the distance, a rooster crowed, and Rebecca giggled with delight at the reminder that she was living in the country now.

We made it.

She and her dad, the notorious jewel thief Thomas Morhaim, had finally escaped Metropolis, the mean, gray city she had come to despise. For them, there would be no more skyscrapers, no traffic, no pollution . . . and no one who knew that her father was a convicted felon.

He paid for what he did, but nobody in Metropolis would let him get past it. Daddy was a marked man, and there was no way anyone was going to give him a break, ever. We were outcasts, and we always would have been.

I'm not going to let a single person in Smallville know about our past. They don't need to know. And Mr. Luthor promised Daddy he wouldn't tell a soul.

Of course her father had had to check "yes" on the

LuthorCorp job application that asked, *Have you ever been convicted of a crime?*

So many times, checking that box had ended her father's job search right then and there. But Lex Luthor had given him a chance.

"I've had some scrapes of my own," was all the young, bald-headed billionaire had said, and that was the last time he brought up Tom Morhaim's descent into crime.

She would be grateful until the day she died for Lex Luthor's faith in her father. Given the terrible economy, no one in Metropolis would hire a criminal when there were so many other, more deserving folks going without.

Now, down the hall, her father hit a high note as he showered and got ready for his first day on the job. He had always loved to sing in the shower. Even though she had been a preschooler when he had been sent away to prison, she remembered his Top 40 Shower Hits concerts. Sometimes, when she'd felt all alone in the world, she had closed her eyes and listened to his voice inside her head.

Sometimes, the memory of those songs was all that kept her going.

But when he'd gotten out fourteen months ago, the singing had not resumed. Trips to the welfare office, the unemployment office, and handing over food stamps at the market had kept her father very silent, very worried, and very ashamed.

That had all changed six weeks ago, when Lex Luthor hired him. Tom had sung "Bye Bye Love" the morning he had given their Metropolis landlord—*more like slumlord*—their thirty days' notice.

Now Tom tried another high note. It was more a raspy shriek, but she loved him for straining to reach it. As far as she could tell, this morning's selection was "I'm as Corny as Kansas in August."

She grinned broadly.

We're safe from all the gossip. We're going to start over. And we're going to have a life.

Everyone in their Metropolis neighborhood had known she was the daughter of the man who had gone to prison for shooting a security guard during the robbery of a Metropolis jeweler's. A hush would fall over the kids at school when he came to pick her up. And some girls' moms told them to stop hanging with Rebecca once they realized who her father was.

Over winter break, Rebecca had met a guy named Ryan Gile at the skating rink. He was sweet, a boy a year older than she, and he went to a different school. They went out a couple times, going to the movies, then making out like crazy afterward. She was thrilled; she'd never had a boyfriend before.

Then Ryan abruptly stopped calling her. When she called him to see what was up, he said in a strange voice, "I've just been busy. That's all."

But a few days later, Lily Newman told her that Ryan had heard about Rebecca's father, and he had decided that dating her was "just too freaky." His very words.

But here, in Smallville, I'll have a chance to be judged on my own merits . . . and my own drawbacks. No one will think I'm "just too freaky" because of my dad's mistake.

"Good morning, baby doll," her dad said, sailing into the kitchen. He was wearing khaki pants and a shirt with an embroidered patch with his name on it.

She tried not to think about how much it looked like a prison uniform. He was making slightly more than minimum wage—better than in prison, where he got a few cents a day for cleaning the laundry—but still not really enough to live on. But she knew that and had been trying to focus on the good. Things were going to have to get better.

The only reason they could afford their apartment in Smallville on top of their moving expenses was because Grandma Morhaim had died a year ago and left them some inheritance money. Rather than saving it—for college, as Rebecca had hoped—Tom had used it to finance the move, calling it "an investment in our future."

It had been tough going all her life, and he had reminded her over and over that there was no money to cushion a fall and no health insurance if something should happen to him. Then the grandmother Rebecca had never known left them some money, and things had eased up a little.

The foster families she had lived with hadn't stayed in touch with her, so it was just she and her dad. But being together made it a lot easier to face the future.

Things were going to get better. They already were, in fact.

I hope it lasts . . .

She smiled for her father, and told the ghosts in her head to shut up.

"Hey, Daddy. I made coffee and scrambled eggs," she told him. "A nice, healthy breakfast to start the day."

It was a momentous occasion, the first breakfast on his first day of work and her first day at a new school. It was also noteworthy because in Smallville, the Morhaims had not applied for food stamps. They had paid for this breakfast with their own money.

"We're not going to be the 'poor lowlife Morhaims' here," Tom had told her. "We're going to be a nice, normal family."

And we are, she thought proudly.

Back home, the local church had helped the Morhaims a lot—with a subsidized apartment, food donations, and access to good medical care from St. Theresa's mobile medical unit, a van that traveled to the homes of different parishioners.

It had embarrassed Rebecca to be one of the parish's charity cases, but as her father had once reasonably pointed out, doing good works was the church's job. While that might be true, she had flushed with mortification when one of the other girls in catechism class had sung out, "Oh, my God! Becca, you have on my little sister's sweater! I thought she threw it out!"

Rebecca tried not to become fashion-obsessed the way girls who were not poor could afford to be. Although she was tall for her age, she was very slender, and sometimes she could still buy clothes in the kids' section. That was one trick—kids' clothes usually cost less than juniors, even if the styles were the same.

Her thick, dark hair curled down to her shoulders, and she knew how to French braid it, bead it, and twist it into an elegant chignon, holding it in place with a chopstick or a lacquered decorative stick. Her father had once commented that she'd inherited her mother's artistic flair.

Rebecca wouldn't know about that. Her mother had died seven years ago.

"You look handsome in your uniform, Daddy," she teased him as he took his cup from her. She always put cinnamon in with the grounds. He liked it that way. She couldn't resist adding, "For an old guy."

"Hey, hey, easy on the 'old guy's' ego," he chided her, leaning against the counter as he sipped his coffee. His profile was to her; he was a good-looking man in a dad sort of way—silvery blond hair and silver in his beard. He had sharp features and a firm jaw. Despite having been in prison for so long, he looked young for his age, and well-groomed.

He moaned softly, closing his eyes with pleasure as he swallowed the coffee. "Good job on the java, Becs."

She beamed with pleasure. "Sit down. Have some scrambled eggs." She fussed over him, taking his cup from his hand and setting it on the table, indicating the simple plates heaped with fluffy yellow eggs, two slices for each of them of cinnamon toast, and orange juice. In the center of the table stood a plain clear-glass vase brimming with flowers that she had picked at sunrise.

"Well, this is beautiful," he told her appreciatively.

She pointed at the cinnamon toast. "I got it all on sale. I even snagged some day-old bread at the outlet next to the grocery store."

"Even better." He grinned at her. "A great cook and a frugal housekeeper. You're going to make some boy a great wife."

She snorted. "Yeah, if I go back in my time machine to the fifties and turn into Beaver Cleaver's mother. Then I'll spend all day vacuuming the house in high heels and pearls."

"Trade you. You go be the warehouse clerk at the fertilizer plant, and I'll vacuum the apartment." He waggled his sandy blond eyebrows. "Cuz, honey, I look *good* in those high heels."

"Dad, you are such a dork."

He shrugged with mock innocence and picked up his fork as she sat down in her own chair and surveyed the table with pride.

We're gonna be good here, she thought.

She added, "By the way, we're going to have to eat a lot

of eggs, because they're a lot cheaper when you buy them in flats."

He grinned. "Don't mind a bit."

It's all good, she told herself happily.

About an hour later, Rebecca was not so certain of that.

Smallville High was a busier, larger school than she had anticipated. That was because a lot of kids were bused in from distant, rural farms—and there were a lot of those in the county. Agribusiness had not come to Smallville, and most of the farms were still small, family-run affairs. That made for more families. More families, more kids.

She could have taken Smallville High's busyness. She was used to going to a large urban school, so the number of students wasn't a problem. But she could see she was going to have trouble penetrating the cliquish, small-town attitude of the kids she was meeting—or rather not meeting. They weren't letting her in. These kids had grown up together, and they weren't used to having a stranger in their midst. It wasn't that they were particularly rude; they just weren't very welcoming or friendly. For Rebecca, who had dreamed of having a lot of friends once the onus of her father's past was safely buried, it was a little disappointing.

But that was until lunchtime.

She had stood quietly with her tray, anxiously surveying the throngs of talkative students, and wondering if she could just sneak away and find a quiet place to eat alone. She wondered if they could tell that her lime green mohair sweater was secondhand, and if her jeans were too worn for this school. She'd gone for green in a big way: her eye shadow was green, and she had on her green beads from Grandma.

Nervously twisting her thumb ring beneath the edge of her tray, she swallowed down tears—she had pictured this day so differently . . . and started scanning for the loser table. There always was one. She should know: With a dad in prison—and then recently released from one—she had been relegated to that table, along with the gamers and the geeky kids who had seen *The Lord of the Rings* way too many times.

Then a short, slender blonde with a killer haircut got up from her table and trotted over to her. She smiled, and said, "Hi, I'm Chloe Sullivan. You're new."

"Yes," Rebecca said, feeling shy. "We just moved here."

Chloe smiled. "Poor thing."

"No. It's all good." Rebecca ducked her head. "My dad got this job at LuthorCorp and—"

"No kidding," Chloe cut in, smiling even more brightly. "My dad works there, too." She laughed. "Well, lots of kids' dads work for the Luthor empire around here. And moms, too. Clark's mom, for instance."

She glanced back over at her table, and Rebecca's mouth literally dropped open.

The most handsome guy she had ever seen was sitting there, idly munching an apple. He had dark hair and incredibly blue eyes beneath dark brows, and the way the sunlight hit him, it was like he was from another planet, he was so compelling. His jaw was strong, and he had great shoulders. He was wearing a blue T-shirt that set off those amazing eyes.

Seated next to him was a girl as striking as he was. She was so pretty that she, too, was almost unreal.

Figures, she thought wistfully. *Best-looking guy, best-looking girl.* Chloe was no slouch, either.

"That's Clark," Chloe said archly. "The one you're staring at. His mom works for Lex's dad."

"Lex?" Rebecca blinked at Chloe. "You call Mr. Luthor 'Lex'?"

"We all do." Chloe shrugged and gestured with her hand at the guy—Clark. "Clark is Lex's best friend. And Lex and Lana and her aunt own the Talon together. That's our local coffeehouse."

With a mischievous grin, she jerked her great haircut in the direction of the table. "Come sit down. You're about to drop your tray."

"Wouldn't want that to happen," Rebecca murmured, following as Chloe led her toward Clark and the girl. *Lana? Is that her name? She owns a coffeehouse?*

"We have another castaway on the island that is Smallville," Chloe announced to the others as she presented Rebecca. "A moment of silence for my new friend . . . um"—she chuckled—"shall we call you Poison Ivy?"

Because of all the green, Rebecca thought, wondering if it was too *much* green. Maybe she looked like a leprechaun. Maybe she looked like she was trying too hard.

But how can one try too hard in high school?

"I'm Rebecca," she told them. "Rebecca Morhaim."

"Hi, I'm Lana," the other girl announced. She gestured to the empty chair beside her, and for one small second, Rebecca considered taking the empty chair on Clark's left instead.

"Thanks," she said, and meekly sat beside Lana.

"I'm Clark," the adorably cute guy said, quickly swallowing down his bite of apple. "Kent."

"Hello." *Wow.* His gaze was so intense she could almost feel heat coming off it. He had a square, chiseled jaw and full lips. His hair was shiny and dark . . . but it was his eyes that kept drawing her in. She felt almost dizzy, he was so handsome.

"Hey." Chloe waved at someone. "Here comes Pete."

Rebecca was grateful for the chance to look elsewhere.

Another handsome guy strode toward them. His light blue shirt set off his dark skin; Rebecca found herself wondering if he had a girlfriend, too. Then she caught the look he slid Chloe's way, and figured that he did.

Which is okay, she's awfully nice.

"Guys," he said, ignoring her. His face was drawn, his eyes bleary. "Very bad news."

"How bad?" Lana asked.

"Is it about . . . the Hacketts?" Chloe asked, biting her lower lip. "Do I want to know this?" Lana leaned around and put her hand on Chloe's forearm in a gesture of solidarity, while Rebecca looked on curiously.

The guy named Pete sank into the chair beside Clark and leaned his hands on the table. He looked as if someone had dealt him a harsh body blow, and he was still reeling from it. He scratched the top of his head and sat silently, as if trying to figure out what to say.

"Pete," Chloe begged. *"What?"*

"Maybe I should . . . should I leave?" Rebecca whispered to Lana, assuming that he was hesitating because there was a stranger in their midst.

"No. It's okay. It's just . . ." She trailed off, her gaze on Pete. "Pete, please, you are pretty much killing us with the dramatic pause here."

Pete wiped his mouth, then lowered both his hands to the table.

"Ah, strange choice of words there, Lana. Mr. Hackett killed himself this morning," he announced in a rush, as if he were glad to be rid of the words. He drooped like a deflating balloon, hunching over his hands, shaking his head. "In his garage."

There was silence. Rebecca looked from one face to the other as the three friends tried to absorb the news.

Then Chloe bolted from the table.

"Chloe!" Lana called after her. She got up and ran after her. "Chloe, wait!"

That left Rebecca alone with Clark and Pete.

She had no idea what to say. She didn't know who they were talking about. But someone was dead.

The three sat for a moment. Then Pete looked over at her, and said, "Hey. Are you a friend of Lana and Chloe's?"

"I'm new," she told him, distressed. "We just moved here from Metropolis. My dad and me."

"We had a . . . a tragedy," he said awkwardly. He looked at Clark, as if for guidance on how to proceed. "One of the teachers got caught selling drugs to a student and . . ."

"That's not what really happened," Clark cut in, glancing sharply at his friend.

Pete nodded. "Yeah." He exhaled, looking frustrated and confused. "It's actually a lot more complicated than that. It was being kept silent. But Chloe found out about it, and she accidentally left a story around—

"In the trash," Clark pointed out.

"In the trash," Pete confirmed. "But the teacher's kid's friend found the article, and now it's all over the school."

"Chloe's the editor of the school paper," Clark told Rebecca.

"We got on her back about running the story," Pete added, sounding distant, a bit cool. "Told her not to do it, and she decided not to run it. But it got out anyway."

Rebecca felt as though she were watching a tennis match, the ball bouncing back and forth over the net. They were telling her far more than she had the ability to process. She didn't know anybody in the story besides Chloe, and she didn't really know Chloe yet at all.

"This doesn't happen a lot here," Clark said to her. "People dying."

"Sure it does." Pete frowned at Clark and shook his head. "This is Smallville, man."

"Wh-*what*?" Rebecca was thrown. "What are you talking about, 'people dying'?"

But just then, the bell rang, signaling the end of lunch. Chairs scooted back. Students reached for their heavy backpacks and polished off bits of french fries and the famed Smallville High cafeteria mystery meat surprise.

Above the noise, Pete said to her, "Ask Chloe to show you the Wall of Weird. That'll help explain what we're talking about."

"The Wall of . . . ?" She hoisted her backpack, feeling small and scared.

"Don't worry," Clark said gently. "I'm here and . . . I mean, we watch out for each other around here. Small town." He smiled reassuringly at her.

Watch out for each other . . . from what? she wondered. *What's a Wall of Weird?*

"Seriously, don't worry," Clark said, as they fell into the crowd leaving the cafeteria.

Pete's response was to roll his eyes. "Yeah, right," Pete grumbled.

Rebecca swallowed hard.

What have Dad and I gotten ourselves into?

Lionel Luthor had claimed some extended business in Metropolis, leaving Martha Kent back in Smallville. "In my absence, try to straighten out Lex, all right?" he'd asked her briskly but pleasantly. "See if you can transfer your business acumen into his skull."

She was sorry for the harshness of his words, but she'd grown to understand Lionel well enough to know that he didn't mean them precisely as he said them. He was very proud of Lex. He just didn't want Lex to know it.

It was a very complex and rather sad relationship.

In Lex's office in his palatial mansion, Martha hung up the phone and stared at Lex in shock. He was sitting at right angles from her, he behind his desk and she at the corner beside him, with a PDA flipped open and plugged in to a truly amazing laptop. In anticipation of Lionel's return, they were scheduling some meetings between father and son. They had been snacking on a fruit plate piled high with blueberries, one of Martha's favorites. They weren't as good as the ones she grew in her organic garden, though. In fact, they were somewhat bitter, and she had been dusting them with sugar when the phone rang.

She could scarcely believe what she heard.

"You look as though you've seen the proverbial ghost, Martha," Lex observed. "What's wrong?"

Reflexively moving her hair away from her temples, she said, "That was Jonathan. With very bad news. Do you know Samuel Hackett at Smallville High?"

Lex looked acutely uncomfortable as he shifted in the chair behind his desk. "Distantly."

She gave her head a little shake. "Lex, he's dead."

As Lex stared at her in silence, his lips parted.

"He ran his car in the garage," she added. "He was asphyxiated by the carbon monoxide."

Lex blinked, taking that in as well. Steadily, he said, "Does anyone know why? Why he did it?"

"Why?" She repeated the question as though he were insane. "Lex, does it matter why?"

"Of course it does." He regarded her steadily, but there was a flush on his cheekbones.

She moved her hands. "He was selling drugs to a student. Jonathan told me he was discovered, and . . ." She hesitated. "That's really all I know."

Lex pursed his lips and folded his hands on his desk. He was quiet for a few seconds, then he said, "Jake. Jake Brook. That's the student he was selling drugs to."

"You know him?" Martha asked. "This Jake?"

"In a manner of speaking. I know his disease." Lex sighed. "And it's a bad one, Martha."

"Jake's a drug addict?" Martha asked, trying to process all the information he was giving her. "Mr. Hackett was a drug dealer? Oh, my God."

"No. Jake has a different kind of illness." He looked acutely uncomfortable. "As did Mr. Hackett. And Luthor-Corp is trying to help find the cure."

"What disease . . . ?" she began, then trailed off, shaking her head. "I guess it's none of my business . . ." But actually, she did feel that it was her business. Her son went to that school. If someone had an illness, perhaps potentially infectious, she deserved to know every single detail about it, privacy or no.

"The family appreciates my discretion," he said simply.

She was monumentally put off by his evasiveness, and decided to let him know it.

"If that's the case," she said in a mildly accusatory voice, "why did Mr. Hackett have your experimental drug to sell?"

"That's a point of discretion as well." When she looked at him blankly, he said, "Hackett was also afflicted with the identical diagnosis, and he and Jake were taking part in a clinical trial. Jake was convinced he himself was getting the placebo, and he asked Mr. Hackett to sell him some of his dose. Jake's symptoms were worsening."

He added gently, "Jake's only sixteen. He's scared."

"Oh," Martha said. "Mr. Hackett . . . he was in a wheelchair. That's all I know. I always assumed he'd been in an accident."

"No," Lex said. "Not an accident."

She was trying to understand the situation. "But if they were both in the drug trials . . . why would Mr. Hackett give someone else his share of the medication if he was fairly sure he had the actual drug, and not the placebo?"

Lex sighed. "He was that kind of man, and his family is paying for his generosity. Some people feel too much, try to do too much."

He lowered his gaze to the polished wood of his desk, and added, "Rest in peace, Samuel Hackett." Then he added, "I hope this doesn't invalidate the medical trial. It would be a terrible shame at this late date. My investors will be screaming. We're at the fourth down with ten yards to go on this protocol. Millions will go down the drain."

She flared. "Oh, my God, Lex. How can you sit there so calmly and talk about this as if it were a football game?"

"Not much for football," he said calmly. "I'm more of a polo man myself."

"Lex."

"Martha, I'm not without feelings," he replied, glancing back up at her. "But I am the head of a multimillion-dollar operation, and, as such, I have to think with my head first. Stockholders expect a return on their money. They want results."

He looked philosophical as he leaned back in his chair and crossed his ankle over his knee. "Clinical trials are very expensive. It's disappointing when they show that a promising drug isn't useful after all. But when a trial is halted due to possible side effects of the drug, we have to think about other factors as well. Such as lawsuits. It's a tough game, Martha. For the thick-skinned and the hard-hearted."

Martha decided to press. "What disease is it? What did he have?" She thought a moment, trying to picture any of Clark's classmates who used a wheelchair. "I don't think I know Jake Brook."

"Football team. For now." His eyes grew sad. "He's not doing very well. If he's lucky, he may last the season."

She glanced up sharply at him. He pushed away from his desk and stood, wandering idly to his bookcase, where he picked up a Roman coin from the days of Alexander the Great and scrutinized it.

"There are some very ugly diseases in the world," he said, running the tip of this thumb over the bas-relief of Alexander's profile. "Many of them are thought to be the diseases of aging. Arthritis, Parkinson's. MS. But they strike the young, too."

Lex looked sideways at her. "They're the modern plagues of our time, robbing victims of their memory, their mobility. No one wants these illnesses to exist. So they try to find out how people contract them. Scientists go through fashionable theories the way some women go through shoes, always chasing after that funding. Grants are hard to come by unless people think you're going to make some progress.

"Right now, it's businesses like LuthorCorp that are the scapegoats." He put the coin back down on the shelf and turned his back on it. "Everyone's blaming chemicals in our food. They're saying these plagues are caused by hormones injected into our poultry and the pesticides on our lawns. That we're coating our playgrounds with lethal antiemergents and killing ourselves in the process. That's what they say."

"There's merit to that argument," she cut in. "And a lot of data to back it up."

"Depending upon which side of the argument you're standing on," he said.

Martha reddened slightly. "I'm not naive, Lex. And I don't mean to be disrespectful to you."

"I make fertilizer, not pesticides." He shrugged. "To a lot of people, chemicals are chemicals. But I know what you're getting at. You're an organic gardener, and I applaud your efforts to keep your food as free of man-made additives as possible. I wish everyone could eat organic produce."

"But they can't. The food you grow is also expensive because of all the handwork you have to put in to raise your crops. Agribusiness can't afford to do it the way you do. They need some good fertilizers and some good pesticides. I make very good fertilizer. The best." He smiled wryly. "It's my claim to fame. And fortune, I might add."

Martha began to connect the dots. "And you were funding the drug because . . ."

He smiled. "In part, because I'm a businessman in a controversial field. You know what my father likes to say: 'Plan for the best, expect the worst, and always have a backup plan.' "

"And your backup plan . . ." She considered. "In case a connection is ever proven . . ."

He made air quotes, as if around a magazine headline. " 'LuthorCorp scientists work night and day to find cures for terrible diseases, and they certainly would not want to make products that harmed people. They're in the business of helping the American farmer.' "

"I see," she said slowly.

"But we're off topic." He dipped his head. "And you're upset."

"Yes. I am. And so is Jonathan. Clark's coming home from school because Smallville High has been dismissed early due to the tragedy. That's why Jonathan called." She flicked her PDA closed and picked up her purse. "Lex, I need to be with my family this afternoon."

"Of course. I'll call Clark later myself, see how he is."

"A man he knew killed himself today," she said sorrowfully.

"Clark's had a lot of losses," he observed. "I'm sorry he has to go through another one."

"That's nice of you, Lex," she said. "Seeing as you lost your mother, too."

"Still got Dad," he said.

Martha pushed back her chair and rose. "I'll be in tomorrow."

"I'll look forward to that."

She excused herself and left the room. Lex watched her go, very concerned.

I wonder if Hackett's despondency was a side effect . . . he mused. *Or if it was a natural by-product of life. Which would not surprise me in the least.*

CHAPTER FIVE

Half a world away, in Cap du Roi, Marica groaned in pain as she shifted on her cot in AYUDO's makeshift infirmary. The night was hot, and her arm was on fire. Jean Claudine was her hero, but he insisted that what had attacked her was a couple of wild dogs, not zombies. And he refused to see her when she was by herself. She didn't understand it at all.

The hut was crude, but it was shelter nonetheless. There were a dozen such structures in the compound, used both for housing as well as an on-site lab and place for storing fertilizer, seed, equipment, medical supplies, and the bare necessities such as batteries and some gasoline for an emergency generator.

Miguel Ribero, the team's doctor and chief scientist, informed her that the bullet had missed bone, but not muscle. He was planning to have her transported to a "real" hospital in a few days, once he had made arrangements. She did not protest. She was in pain, but she was alive.

Her other coworkers checked on her all the time, teasing her that some people would do anything to get out of their rotation of helping the villagers with weeding the vegetable gardens.

"Not that there are many vegetables to harvest," Marica moaned. "I ruined most of the gardens when I was attacked by the zombies."

Anna Cruces leaned forward and put her hand over Marica's forehead. "Zombies. *Ay, chica, tienes fiebre.* You've got a fever. You're delusional."

Marica wrinkled her forehead beneath Anna's damp

palm. "I saw what I saw. And don't I have bite marks on my neck?"

"Dogs, as Jean told us," Anna told her. "Marica, think about it. You were scared. Come on; zombies aren't real. They're for scary movies, *chavela*." She giggled at the absurdity of it, and added, "And they certainly can't run after people and chase them. They drag along like mummies. The only way they can get you is if you fall down helplessly and twist your ankle."

She demonstrated, lurching across the dirt floor of the tiny hut. Marica wanted to laugh, but she couldn't. "Her" zombies had been nothing like that. They had been wild and crazy, and they moved as fast as ferrets.

"But I did twist my ankle," Marica insisted, pointing to her swollen leg. "And I did scream helplessly."

"You're right, Anna, about her fever. I was there," Jean announced, striding into the hut. "It was dogs and nothing more. *Grâce à Dieu*," he added, crossing himself. Then he walked away.

Marica sighed. "He's in total denial, Anna. He had to have seen them. Because . . . because they were there."

"Well, if you say so," Anna finally said. But it was clear she remained unconvinced.

Looking ill at ease, she sat beside Marica's bed, not speaking, and Marica began to doze, feeling comforted by her company, despite the fact that Anna didn't believe her.

After a little while, Anna announced that she, too, had to go. "I have to do your share of the weeding," she said in mock accusation. "Crazy lazybones."

She lightly kissed Marica's forehead. "Rest, Marica. You've had a terrible experience."

Marica accepted the kiss, nodding with resignation as she said, "Say hello to Mama Loa for me." Mama Loa was the matriarch of the village. It was she who had permitted the AYUDO workers to help her people, she who decreed after each week of service that the AYUDO team could stay for a little while longer.

Her name was bizarre. *Loa* were the Haitian equivalent of gods. It was rather like being called Mother Spirit. Equally unusual was her son's name: though sixteen, he was called Baby Loa. A bright, fun kid with a future, the team was arranging for him to attend a private school in Mexico City.

"She said she's going to bring you a healing tea," Anna added, making a face. "I just hope it doesn't have any boiled lizards in it, like the one she made for Jean."

"Why did she make him a tea?" Marica asked.

"He hasn't been feeling good," she said. "Lots of headaches. Nightmares."

"Because he's lying about what happened," Marica said hotly. "His conscience is bothering him."

"*Ah, sí.* The Devil has his pitchfork in his brain," Anna said merrily, demonstrating. Then she waved at Marica and left the hut.

After a time, Mama Loa arrived. She was dressed in her signature colorful dress and skirt, a kerchief around her head. She wasn't very old, and Marcia liked her very much. Sometimes it seemed she kept her poverty-stricken village alive through sheer force of will. Baby Loa adored her, and was always at her side, doing for her, making sure she had a sun umbrella, a cool drink—whatever might make his wonderful mother's life easier.

Marica had been dozing. Now she opened her eyes and smiled at the amazing, charismatic woman. Mama Loa smiled back, flashing brilliant white teeth in a face the color of freshly turned earth. She carried a small china teacup in her hand, and said, "*Pour toi,* Marie-Claire."

"Merci, Maman." She took the cup and stared down at it. "Ah . . ." She was afraid to drink it. She spoke enough French to ask her what was in it, but not enough to be able to understand what Mama Loa would tell her.

The woman snorted and put the cup to Marica's lips. Then she poured it down.

To Marica's instant relief, it tasted delicious. Like berries. She swallowed it down, and smiled.

As she handed the cup back to Mama Loa, the woman grew serious. She narrowed her eyes at Marica and nodded very slowly. Then she whispered to her, "Zombie. *Oui.*" She laid her finger across her lips and jerked her head toward the open window of the hut. *"Oui,* Marie-Claire."

"I knew it. I knew I wasn't crazy," Marica said. She held out her hand to the woman. Mama Loa squeezed hers hard, then patted her.

At that moment, Baby Loa stuck his head through the doorway. He was very dark and very cute, with a special sparkle that made people grin around him.

He waved at Marica, and said in English, "Whas 'appeneen, sweetart?" Then he spoke to his mother in rapid-fire Haitian French, gesturing with his hands.

Mama Loa rolled her eyes and answered him, sighing with exasperation. She said something to Marica, but whatever she had put in the tea was already beginning to affect her. Marica's lids were closing, and everything was sliding away, becoming a blur of echoing sound and hazy images.

Mama Loa made the sign of the cross over her and rose. As she moved toward the doorway, the colors of her clothing jittered in Day-Glo hues. Then she left with her son.

Marica slept heavily, dreaming. She felt herself floating, then she was running through the cane field; the pain in her neck was excruciating . . . the crack of the bullet, the pain . . .

. . . and the zombie, gliding silently through the cane. He was different from the two she had encountered—tall, and dressed in a ragged T-shirt and torn jeans. He was a man, his eyes glassy and unseeing. Looking neither left nor right, he shuffled along—not the monster that had attacked her, but something far more docile, almost helpless.

"Vite," a harsh voice ordered it. Hurry. Then something came down against its back, and the zombie groaned.

As if she were a movie camera, Marica's gaze abruptly shifted to the figure behind the zombie. He was a man in soldier's gear, wearing a short-sleeved olive green T-shirt and baggy cammo pants. She couldn't see his face.

The thing that had come down on the zombie's back was a semiautomatic weapon. Though it looked like a compact toy in the soldier's muscular grip, she knew appearances could be deceiving. The damage to her arm was testament to that . . .

As she watched, the soldier pulled out a walkie-talkie and spoke into it. In English, not French. She couldn't quite make out the words except for the single phrase, "Number 320."

Number 320 . . .

. . . and then she was drifting away, drifting away . . .

In the morning, she wondered if she had dreamed it all. But she didn't say anything about it to anyone. She took Mama Loa's message to heart; no one wanted her to be talking about zombies . . . so she wouldn't talk about them.

After that, things started going very wrong for the team members of the AYUDO Project, and for those they were trying to help. Anna Cruces and Jean Claudine both left abruptly, their reasons—family problems, being needed at home—vague and unconvincing. Neither one contacted those still in the village to let them know that they had gotten home safely.

Was it because we talked about the zombies? Marica wondered, terribly frightened. *Did they leave of their own free will?*

Then Baby Loa went missing. Mama Loa went insane with worry.

Dr. Ribero took the matter up with the local authorities, greasing palms, as was the custom in Haiti. In return, the police assured him that they were searching everywhere for the sixteen-year-old. But Baby Loa did not return to the village.

Everything took on a different tenor after that; with guards stopping the AYUDO team members every time they left the village, demanding to see papers. They were rude and threatening, demanding bribes, which they described as "security service fees," and generally making the relief workers feel unwelcome. Most of the others took the hint and abandoned the project. After two weeks, there were only five workers left, including Marica and Dr. Ribero.

Although she continued to write home, at first she didn't tell her family what was really going on; they would insist that she leave, and she didn't want to leave Mama Loa until Baby Loa was found.

But two more weeks passed, making it a total of a month with no sign of Baby Loa and six weeks since Marica had been attacked by the zombies. Mama Loa sank into a deep depression, insisting that her boy had been turned into a zombie and that she would never see him again.

Taking a deep breath, aware that she might be putting herself in danger, Marica sent out queries about what was going on, but she received no replies. She wondered if someone was intercepting her mail.

She became increasingly afraid, listening in the night to strange shuffling sounds that crept throughout their little compound.

It is the zombies, she thought, terrified. *Are they coming for me?*

I came here to do good, Blessed Virgin, she prayed. *Did you call me here to help these people grow food or to save them from zombies?*

AYUDO had come to Haiti to help the impoverished villagers learn new agricultural methods so that they could increase their production and better feed themselves. Dr. Ribero, a Paraguayan professor of agriculture who had once taught at the Sorbonne in Paris, had joined them. He had been instrumental in equipping AYUDO with sturdy strains of rice and vegetables, and prevailing upon several large corporations to provide farming implements, microscopes, and lab equipment for finding ways to increase production.

Aside from his influence in the world community, Dr. Ribero knew how to negotiate the underground economy of the poor, oppressed country. From some gunrunners in Port-au-Prince, he had purchased some used Smith & Wessons, ostensibly for warding off the packs of wild dogs that terrorized rural Haiti.

He had also "lifted" several hundred pounds of the fertilizer destined for the vast cane plantations of some rich landowners. He left sufficient behind in the docking warehouse at Port-au-Prince so that no one would notice the theft. Besides, in Haiti, it was commonplace for anyone who had the means to steal something of value, to go ahead and skim a little off the top.

The fertilizer did miraculous things to the nutrient-hungry soil. Yams and greens grew in abundance. Cane began to grow where it had refused to grow before. The vegetable gardens doubled in capacity, bursting with lovely, sturdy shoots of beans and other vegetables.

But after Marica got attacked, everything fell apart.

With Mama Loa so despondent worrying about her child, the other villagers had stopped working in their gardens, rice paddies, and cane fields. The soil needed nurturing, but they skimped on feeding the plants, and the crops began to show the effects of nutrient starvation.

Her mood affected them all, and the villagers collectively gave up hope that they could do anything to improve their lives. They went back to the mind-set they'd first had when Marica had arrived in Haiti over a year earlier: that anything they did was doomed to fail.

As they grew hungrier, they grew more lethargic. All anyone had to do to believe in zombies was look at the villagers, who trudged through the long, hot days like the pathetic person Marica had seen in her dream.

She was devastated.

During her days at the University of Mexico, Marica had specialized in what she termed "crisis agriculture," and it had been her dream to help people help themselves in just the way AYUDO did. She had known there would be obstacles and difficulties, but she'd been willing to give the mission her all.

It had never occurred to her that despite being given tools, knowledge, and other forms of assistance, people who were starving would refuse her help. But that was what was happening in Cap du Roi.

At first, things had gone so well. In the year that she had been with the project, children had lost the distended, bloated appearance of starvation. Their eyes had begun to sparkle, and they had begun to laugh. Mothers who used to wake up every morning wondering how to feed their babies had worked diligently in their individual gardens and in the communal plots as well. Bonds of sisterhood had formed among the women.

But these days, they hardly acknowledged each other's presence. It was as if walls had risen up around their hearts at the same time that their spirits had been trampled.

Children were crying in the night for food, and Dr. Ribero predicted that even worse starvation than before would hit the village before the year was over—as a result of a better diet, more village women became pregnant. Also thanks to better nutrition, more babies were being born, and the elderly were living longer. These all added up to more mouths to feed. The villagers had worked hard on their gardens, and they had cane to sell to the AYUDO project, who in turn processed it at a local factory and sold it to churches and international benevolent groups.

Now there was very little cane to process. Perhaps even more frightening for Marica, the remaining AYUDO team members absorbed the prevailing mood of lethargic apathy as well. They began to neglect their huts in their compound, and didn't take the time to wash themselves or their clothing. Marshaling the wherewithal to help the villagers with their problems was something the team could no longer manage.

Marica and Dr. Ribero discussed the situation at length. They seemed to be the only ones who wanted to discuss it. Something was terribly wrong, and they had secretly agreed to find out what it was. They had taken the problem and analyzed it piece by piece.

For the last week, they had zeroed in on the fertilizer Dr. Ribero had taken, wondering if something so wonderful for crop production could actually turn out to be harming the people instead of helping them. It had come from a factory in the United States owned by LuthorCorp.

Marica had heard of the Luthor family; they were very wealthy. They had lots of business interests in Mexico, and her own well-to-do family traveled in the same circles. Interesting that Lex Luthor, close to her in age, had chosen agriculture as his way to make a mark on the world, just as she had done.

"Look at this, Maria del Carmen," Dr. Ribero said now as they sat in the lab hut together. All their scientific equipment had been housed in the ramshackle tin shed, and AYUDO paid two local teenagers less than pennies a day to guard it for them.

Marica moved swiftly to his side. He was seated behind their microscope, and he moved his chair in order to give her a better view. She glanced at him, puzzled, then gazed through the viewfinder.

Her heart literally skipped a beat.

"Dios mio," she murmured, crossing herself.

At first she was confused by the tiny particles of a strangely glowing substance. It was green; she wondered if it was some kind of chlorophyll.

But she ignored them as she realized that also present in the compound were molecules arranged in the same composition as several forms of datura, the compound assumed to be the active ingredient in the "magical powders" that Voodoo priests and priestesses—*houngans*—administered to their victims in order to turn them into zombies.

There was absolutely no reason for it to be present in fertilizer that had been processed in a plant in the United States.

She frowned at the doctor, who frowned back and

gestured for her to take another look. His face was drawn and pale. He looked exhausted . . . and worried.

She peered through the microscope again.

It had to be datura. The green material . . . maybe there was a little Voodoo magic involved; some chemical that bonded with the datura in such a way that it took on interesting properties such as illumination.

She took a step away, realizing that her life had just changed forever. Voodoo, in some form, was real. She had proof. And the North Americans were providing it to the Haitian upper class in order to exploit the poor and oppressed.

If that isn't proof that Satan is real, then I don't know what is.

Her heart thudded in her chest, and she became aware of how hot and muggy it was in the lab. Outside, tropical breezes were threatening to burst into winds. Palm leaves rubbed against each other like big pieces of sandpaper. Tree trunks swayed and moaned like ship masts. Snakes slithered in the underbrush. The villagers' chickens shifted uneasily in their coop. A hillock away, a local pack of wild dogs yipped at the moon like Sonoran Desert coyotes.

Datura. The implication boggled her. Could it really, honestly be true that LuthorCorp, the American fertilizer giant, was providing the rich landowners of Haiti with the means to turn their plantation laborers into mindless zombies?

Sweat poured off her forehead, and she felt dizzy and sick. Dr. Ribero placed his hand on her left arm, indicating that she should sit down.

She did so, very clumsily. She was so shocked that she couldn't really even think. She kept her right hand grasped around the base of the microscope, as if anchoring herself to the scientific reality of what she had just seen.

It occurred to her that neither one of them was talking. As if he read her mind, Dr. Ribero pointed upward toward the bare lightbulb and tapped his ear.

We're being bugged? she thought, stunned.

His eyes were sad, his mouth pressed tightly in a frown. He moved to her and whispered in her ear, "Now that we know this . . ." He didn't finish his sentence. He didn't need to.

She swallowed hard. *Now that we know this, we're in terrible danger.*

Are we going to disappear as well?

"Now that we know this, it is the beginning of the end," she whispered back to Dr. Ribero.

Only God can save us now.

Marica was correct. Things got even tenser in Cap du Roi—if that were possible. She tried to find a computer to e-mail her parents but was told there were none. Their electricity was cut off. Then the police took the team's scientific equipment away from them.

Mama Loa went missing, too.

Two more AYUDO team members left. That left her, Dr. Ribero, and a young man from Italy named Marco Taliaferro. Dr. Ribero tried to get a message to the Mexican embassy to request an escort out, but it was no use. No one wanted to get involved with the plight of the foreigners. The locals had enough problems surviving; they had no resources to take on anyone else's burdens.

About a week after their discovery of the datura in the fertilizer, Dr. Ribero slipped into Marica's hut; he had a canteen around his neck and one of the Smith & Wessons slung across his chest.

"Marco saw something," he said. "We have to go. *Now.*"

He pointed to her bed. "If you have anything you need, grab it."

"What?" She was speechless.

"They're coming. He heard someone talking on a walkie-talkie." His face was ashen. "Marica, we're 'targets.' That's what they said of us. In French. Marco translated it. They're coming for us."

Then the drums began.

She raised her head, listening. Low, insistent, the complex rhythms plucked the nerve endings beneath her skin. They stared at each other. Tears of fear welled in her eyes.

"In case," he began, and hoisted a fanny pack around his waist. Unzipping it, he showed her a couple of baggies of LuthorCorp fertilizer.

She nodded.

The drums sounded longer, stronger. He took her hand and began to lead her outside. Then he raised a hand as static and distorted electronic voices overlaid the drumming, very close by.

Too close.

"Wait," he told her. He unhooked the plastic tabs on the fanny pack, leaving it in her hand. Then he crept outside.

"No!" she whispered fiercely.

His boots crunched in the loamy soil; she watched him trot, hunched over, toward the next hut, about six feet away.

"Come back," she whispered to the retreating figure. Then he went inside the hut . . . and didn't come back out.

The wind picked up; she smelled smoke. She moved to the doorway and glanced out anxiously.

The zombies of Cap du Roi were walking.

The slack faces of perhaps eight people were illuminated by flashlight and torchlight as they shuffled toward the scattered huts. They were surrounded by a dozen or more men in military garb.

The zombies moved forward; as she stared at them, she cried out and crossed herself.

She was relieved to see that Mama Loa was not among them. But Baby Loa, Jean Claudine, and Anna were. They stared straight ahead, no light in their eyes. They looked completely dead. They looked like people who'd had lobotomies.

Moving, and yet dead.

The drums beat a thundering syncopation with the footfalls of the zombies. Smoke stung Marica's eyes.

They were torching the compound.

I'm going to die. They want to kill me. I know more than they want me to know.

Dr. Ribero . . . Marco . . .

He still didn't emerge from the other hut.

It was time to go, before the zombies and their guards figured out which huts were occupied.

I have the fertilizer. I have to leave now, with or without the men.

Her mind raced as she tried to formulate a plan. The police had all the team's passports locked in a safe inside police headquarters in Port-au-Prince. Her French wasn't very good, and even if it were, it wouldn't be much help. Everyone in Haiti was used to their comings and goings being monitored, and one didn't just leave at one's own whim. One received permission to leave.

She stood in her hut, her attention momentarily snagged by a large lizard skittering across the wall. She watched it disappear into a hole behind her bed. She had never noticed the small opening before. She never had a reason to notice it.

But it didn't matter now. What mattered was getting out of the compound, away from the oncoming zombies, and finding an official who would listen to her story, investigate what was going on out here, and help her get back home.

Or else, simply running on her own.

That seemed the safer course. There was no one in Haiti whom she could trust now.

I'll try to get to Miami. Or Cuba.

And then she realized that she had waited too long to leave her hut.

For she smelled them, smelled the rank, fetid odor of decomposing human flesh. Heard the scratching shuffle of their feet, which were too heavy for their thin leg bones to pick up and set back down. As the wind whipped the trees, she heard the crack of crushed branches, the odd noise as something was knocked over—garbage cans, a basket of silverware, a wooden bowl loaded with plantains.

The drums provided counterpoint; they were speaking to her in some macabre and incomprehensible language. Then they picked up speed. Their tempo shot from slow and sedate to anxious and threatening, and she felt her body responding with the fight or flight syndrome. She began to hyperventilate. Her mind raced.

The drums beat faster.

She grabbed the fanny pack.

Then firelight threw a sudden silhouette against the cracked, peeling wall: It was of a man walking toward the entrance to her hut. It was not Marco. There was nothing sinister about his shape, except that it was there. She had no idea if he was zombie or living human being, friend or foe, and she knew she couldn't find out.

She yanked the bed back to further reveal the hole in her wall of about two feet in diameter.

As she dived under her bed and scrabbled toward the hole in the wall, whoever stood on the threshold came into the room. Marica prayed that the noise from the drums would cover her escape.

She beat at the sides of the hole with the fist of her good arm. The damp, rotted wood easily gave way, and she kept crawling, feeling like a butterfly bursting from its cocoon. Her other arm was on fire.

Tears streaming down her face, she emerged from her hut and into a copse of trees. The undergrowth was thick and thorny, pulling at her clothes and hair, scratching her.

Her hut burst into flames.

The figure she had seen thrown against the wall emerged, carrying a torch. He was wearing fatigues and a black hood over his head. He was a soldier.

She put her hand to her mouth. She was sobbing, completely at a loss about what to do.

A flare hit Dr. Ribero's hut, and it, too, burst into flame.

Marica flattened herself against the ground, biting her lip so hard to keep from screaming that she drew blood. Throwing her forearm forward, then pulling herself up to meet it, she managed to put a bit of distance between herself and the two blazing huts.

She dived into the forest underbrush.

Footsteps came up behind her; foliage was pushed out of someone's path.

She froze, closing her eyes in an effort to boost her hearing ability. A voice called out, *"Mademoiselle Lopez? Est-ce-que vous êtes ici?"*

Miss Lopez? Are you here?

She clamped her mouth shut, lest she scream with terror.

Her hands were covered with cuts. *I have work to do here. Very important work. Something very, very wrong is going*

*on around here. I have to let someone know about the
datura, and the zombies. I have to stop them.*

She stayed hunkered in the darkness, her heartbeats
counting off the seconds like a time bomb. She heard the
click of a weapon, and she shut her eyes as tightly as she
could. She began to list her sins, preparing herself for the
moment of her death. She hoped that if she died, she would
be given Last Rites in time by a priest. She had been a good
Catholic all her life, and she fervently wished to die a good
Catholic as well.

The searcher evidently gave up. Marica exhaled with a
sob as his presence receded, then disappeared.

As the only home she had known for the last year was
ransacked, Marica hid for hours, shivering like a rabbit.
Moonlight washed over her, and she listened to the roar of a
flash fire and the crackling of burning wood. Smoke burned
her eyes; she struggled hard not to hack as the smoke filled
her lungs and made her feel sick and dizzy.

She heard every building in the AYUDO compound burn
to the ground.

At the end of it, the air was empty of sound. There were
no drumbeats, no shuffle of zombie feet, nothing. It was as
if the world had been frozen . . . the action halted for an un-
specified amount of time.

Those who believe that silence is golden have never listened to the silence of the dead.

Marica let the tears flow, grieving for her friends. She had
no idea where Marco or Dr. Ribero were. But she didn't let
herself completely give way; she sensed that this reprieve
was only the calm before the storm, and she had to get out
of there before she was found.

She was exhausted and terrified, but she knew what she

had to do. She had to keep going, and she had to put an end to the zombie business.

With the rising of the new day, Maria del Carmen Maldonaldo Lopez slipped into the jungle and put as much distance as she could, as fast as she could, between herself and the murderers.

In the pack, she carried evidence . . . and secrets. She made a vow to the sweet and merciful Virgin of Guadalupe then and there that she would find out what the datura-like compound was in the LuthorCorp fertilizer . . . and make sure no one was ever harmed by it again.

She might not be able to now, but she would eventually expose this evil to the light of day . . . before she was silenced herself.

CHAPTER SIX

Mr. Hackett's funeral was scheduled to be held two days after he died, on Friday. That Thursday Principal Reynolds held an assembly in the gym, announcing that there would be no school the following day.

Nobody was tacky enough to cheer.

"I hope to see many of you at the service," he told the student body as he concluded his announcement. He looked shaken. As he gathered up his notes, Clark saw how badly the principal's hands were trembling.

"Man, this is so weird," Pete murmured. "This is unbelievable."

"I know," Lana whispered back. "I can't believe it's happening. It's like it's not real."

Clark, Pete, and Lana had sat together in the bleachers. Chloe was absent. Ever since the news of Hackett's suicide, she had stayed home from school, and Clark figured that made sense. Lana told the guys that Chloe needed some space, so he and Pete gave it to her.

That didn't stop Clark, however, from checking on her house every couple of hours or so. He'd occasionally put on a burst of superspeed and race away from the Kent family farm, run to her house, and make sure she was safe.

Because Marshall Hackett was staying out of school as well.

Clark had checked on the Hackett home, too. It was not a good place. The family was in shock; they were all moving silently from room to room in a daze, not speaking, not eating. Lights glowed in bedrooms at all hours of the night.

TVs were left on in several different rooms, but no one was watching any of them. The mail was piling up. In the kitchen, a carafe of coffee had been sitting in the coffeemaker for days, and a sheen of mold coated the surface. Everyone trudged past it, and Clark figured Mr. Hackett must have been the family coffee drinker.

It was as if everyone had died, not just him.

Marshall was a mess. He mostly sat in his room and stared into the darkness.

When Clark told Pete about it, he shook his head. "That guy's going to need some serious therapy," he said.

They were now sitting in Clark's loft, supposedly working on the farm implement section of their history project while they waited for Clark's parents to drive them to the funeral. Pete's mom and dad would meet them at the church.

On the table sat some old rusty scythes and the remains of a wooden yoke worn by farmers while walking behind a mule when plowing. Pete's report on pesticides and fertilizers was there, too. Truth was, they hadn't touched any of it. School seemed amazingly inconsequential at the moment.

Martha was baking bread; the warm, homey smell permeated the loft, mingling with the fragrance of hay and flowers. She usually baked when she was upset.

Jonathan came up the steps and gave the boys a nod. Like Clark and Pete, he was wearing a suit. None of them looked comfortable.

"Okay," Jonathan said. "We're ready to go."

Clark and Pete nodded. They followed Clark's dad back down the stairs and out to the truck. As Clark and Pete climbed into the truck bed, Martha crossed the yard from the house. She was wearing a black dress and low black heels.

Jonathan helped her into the truck, and they took off for the center of town, to the small Methodist church the Hack-

etts had attended. They had been active in the church, and
Principal Reynolds had cautioned the students that it would
probably be standing room only unless they got there early.

As they jostled along in the truck, Pete and Clark watched
the fence posts blur by. Portable sprinklers chittered in the
fields, spraying the wheat and corn with water, fertilizers, or
pesticides.

After a while, Pete said to Clark, "Do you wonder about
it, Clark? Dying?"

Clark shifted uncomfortably. "Yes. I wonder if I can die,"
he said frankly. "Or how long I'll live. Maybe I'll burn out
quicker than most people."

Pete grimaced. "Man, Clark, that's intense." He gazed at
him. "I mean, I hadn't thought of that. What if you're im-
mortal?"

Clark shrugged. "I'm pretty sure the meteor-rocks can kill
me." He grimaced, thinking about the devastating effect
their poisonous green glow had on him whenever he came
near them. "So I can die. I guess."

"Yes," Pete said. "But sometimes in Smallville, not even
the dead can die." They were quiet for a moment, both
thinking about the ghosts they had tried to exorcise in the
Welles farmhouse and cornfield last year. The bones had
been infused with radiation from the meteor-rocks, which
seemed to have kept the spirits of the dead people bound to
the earth. And their pursuit of Clark had nearly killed him.

Pete grew lost in thought as well. They sat silently, as the
truck bounced down the road.

About ten minutes later, they reached the center of Smallville. At the far end of a U-shaped road, the Smallville
United Methodist Church gleamed like a beacon. It was
made of wood, and had been freshly painted. Clark recalled
a picture in the *Smallville Gazette* of Mr. Hackett in his

wheelchair, holding a paintbrush in his hand as the church pastor pretended to pour a bucket of paint over his head. Like Chloe, it hadn't really dawned on him that the man was confined to a wheelchair—that that may have been the reason the picture got printed. He had simply chuckled at the good-humored teacher being "threatened" by the minister.

All that is gone now, he thought.

"I wonder if that new girl Rebecca will show," Pete said. He shook himself. "Not that I'm hoping, to, like date her at the funeral or anything."

Clark gave him a faint smile. "I guess it's true what they say. 'Life is for the living.'"

Clark's dad pulled over to the curb across the street from the church. Clark took a breath and climbed out of the truck bed, careful not to get dirt on his suit. Pete followed after, and they joined Clark's parents on the sidewalk.

A small crowd congregated around the front of the small, white-steepled building. Outfits were somber. No one was smiling. Pete nudged Clark, and said, "There's Principal Reynolds."

"And there's Lana," Clark said, gazing at her.

She was wearing a black dress with jet beads at her neck. She had on small dangling earrings that grazed her jawline and her hair was pulled back into a topknot. She looked pale and tired.

When she saw Clark and the others, she lifted a hand. Martha waved back as Clark started across the street, glancing both ways for traffic. Although a car couldn't hurt him, it would certainly raise a lot of questions if Jonathan Kent's boy dented the front end of a car when it collided with him.

"Lana," Clark said when he reached her. He glanced over his shoulder and realized that Pete had hung back to give him a chance to talk to Lana privately.

"Hey." Her eyes glistened with tears. She pressed her lips together, and said, "I hate this."

There had been a few times when the two of them had held each other; and others—fewer still—when their lips had touched. But when Lana slid her arms beneath his and sank her head onto his chest, he felt as if she were coming home after having been gone a long, lonely time. As her soft cheek pressed against him, he was overcome with tenderness. Something loosened inside him, and a rush of emotion caught him off guard. He had to hold back tears of his own.

"It's so awful at the Sullivan house," she whispered. "Chloe's going crazy with guilt. She hasn't slept in days. Her father's upset, too."

"She has nothing to feel guilty about," Clark asserted, but Lana shook her head.

"You'll never convince her of that." She lifted her head. "I've never seen her so upset. She's shut down." Then Lana looked past Clark's shoulder, and said, "Hey, Rebecca."

With that, Lana gently broke from Clark's embrace. He was sorry . . . sorrier still that holding her was awkward for them both. But he had no idea how he could ever hope to be close to Lana if he didn't share his secret with her. And he wasn't ready to take that risk—nor saddle her with that responsibility.

"I hope it's okay that I showed," Rebecca Morhaim said. Her peasant-style dress was navy blue, and the embroidery on it looked frayed. And her shoes were scuffed. For the first time, it dawned on Clark that she and her father might be poor. "I mean, I'm new here, and . . ."

"You're a member of the student body," Lana said warmly. "The same as us. You belong here."

Rebecca exhaled, vastly relieved. "Thanks, Lana." She smiled weakly at Lana, then Clark. "This might sound weird, but I've never actually been to a funeral before. Mom . . . my mom died, but we didn't have a service. I'm pretty freaked."

"I have." Lana's voice was filled with pain. "For my parents. When I was three."

"Oh, my God," Rebecca breathed. "*Three?* How awful." She looked questioningly at Lana.

"It was the meteor shower," Lana answered, unwillingly pulling memories and images from the past. Clark knew the story well. Lana had been sitting in her Aunt Nell's flower shop; her parents had gone to the Crows homecoming game.

And the meteor-rocks had screamed from nowhere into the bright Kansas sky, the enormous, fiery boulders slamming into buildings . . . and the Langs' car, just as her parents had gotten out of it in front of the flower shop.

The meteor shower that accompanied my ship to earth, Clark thought, cringing inside. *The same one that turned Lex bald.* His father had told him to let that one go. There was nothing he could have done, nothing he could do now. But it made the burden of his secret even heavier to bear.

Rebecca looked too shocked to speak. Then she managed to say, "You saw it happen?"

"I only remember bits and pieces," Lana answered truthfully. "And it grows a little grayer every year." The thought clearly distressed her; Clark knew that Lana held on to her pain in order to hold on to her parents. She had said as much to him on several occasions.

His own parents, his genetic parents, had no hold on him, nor he on them. Why hadn't they put a message in his ship, tried to explain who he was and where he came from, and told him that they loved him? There was nothing for him to hang on to—no names, no faces. They could have at least left him a photograph of themselves—if they had such things as cameras on their home planet. They had to have had some kind of imaging equipment—Clark's ship was evidence of a vastly advanced technological society.

Why didn't they give me a past? I have no idea who I was . . . who I am . . .

"How's Chloe?" Rebecca asked, startling him out of his reverie. He felt ashamed that he was focusing on his own pain when Chloe was in such distress.

"Bad," Lana admitted. "It's like she's checked out. I mean, she's there—her body's there,—but Chloe's not home. She's just going through the motions. She wanders around the house like a ghost."

Clark was so sorry. He knew how hard Chloe would take something like this. She had a tremendous sense of integrity.

"Guilt's a tough gig," Rebecca murmured. Then she shook herself as if she were remembering where she was, and said, "I would never commit suicide if I had kids. That's so cowardly."

Lana sighed heavily. "I guess the shame was more than he could stand."

"No, it wasn't that." Pete said, approaching the group. As he drew near, he looked as if he were going to be sick to his stomach. "Apparently his symptoms had worsened with the stress. He could hardly move. He couldn't even make his wheelchair go. He got afraid that he was going to drag his family down."

Lana was horrified. "So he . . ."

Pete looked down at his hands, then up at his friends. "He took his own life to spare them. He didn't want to be a burden." He added sourly, "He had a lot of life insurance."

The three stared at him. "How do you know all that?" Lana asked him gently.

"Ty Westfall's blabbing it all over the place. They found

a note," Pete informed them, shaking his head in disbelief. "In Marshall's sports bag. Mr. Hackett put it there because he figured Marshall would eventually find it. Turns out there were more secrets in the Hackett family than the drug sale." He paused. "Marshall was adopted. Mr. Hackett was his stepfather, not his biological father."

"Whoa," Clark said.

"Yeah." Pete shook his head. "Nice parting words. 'By the way, I've kept something from you your whole life.'"

"Marshall didn't know?" Rebecca asked.

"How did that happen?" Lana asked. "I mean, why did they adopt him?"

Pete stuffed his hands in his pockets. "When Mr. Hackett was diagnosed with MS, he and his wife decided not to have any more kids. They stopped with one, Marshall's brother, Jeremiah. But I guess they wanted a bigger family. So they adopted Marshall. That's kind of nice, actually. Tells me they had hope for a future together, as a family."

"Isn't it a bad time to be telling your kid he's adopted, I mean, when you've decided to kill yourself?" Lana asked. "That's a huge revelation. I still have to deal with it, and I've known for years."

"He didn't want Marshall to worry about getting MS," Pete replied. "He wanted to let him know he wasn't genetically related to a man with such a terrible disease. Jeremiah's not so lucky."

"How's Marshall taking it?" Lana pressed.

"Not well. If it was supposed to make Marshall feel better, it did just the opposite. He's all messed up."

Rebecca thought to herself, *These are nice people. Something bad happened, and they're not judging everybody. They're trying hard to understand how it happened. If they ever find out my secret, I hope they're as kind to me.*

"Did Ty mention if Mr. Hackett told Marshall who his biological parents are?"

"I don't think so," Pete replied. "I think it was a—what do you call it—a closed adoption. I suppose he can try to find them. Seems easy enough in this day and age, with the Net and all."

Lana looked troubled, and Clark remembered when Chloe had researched the identity of Lana's natural father—against Lana's express wishes. It had created quite a rift between them, and it had taken some time for Lana to learn to trust Chloe again.

I know how she feels, Clark thought. *If Chloe ever suspected I . . . that I'm more than what I appear to be, she'd probably start investigating me. If she hasn't already. And I don't know how I would stay friends with her after that. I don't know how Lana managed it. I'm glad she did, but that was one place Chloe should not have gone.*

"This must be so unsettling for you," Lana said to Rebecca. "Coming to a new school and having all this to deal with."

Rebecca looked mildly uncomfortable. "It's kind of nice, in a weird way. It takes the spotlight off us. I mean, me." She shifted her weight and put her arms around herself in a defensive posture.

Clark turned. A black limo rolled to a stop in front of the church. On the dashboard was slapped a white sign with black letters that read, "Funeral." The windows were tinted, but he used his X-ray vision to look inside. There were three figures in the stretch—a woman and two young men. Marshall was leaning against the door, gazing blankly at the church. His heartbeat was slow and dull.

They've given him something, he realized. *Something to help him through.*

A tall, thin man in a dark suit had been standing off to the left. He turned and gave a nod, and two more men joined him. They went down the brick steps of the church in a little clump, the guests parting for them. There was an air of professional sadness about them that put off even Clark.

"Funeral director," Pete filled in. "And his two sons." He made a face. "Not the kind of family business I would want to be in."

"How do you know who they are?" Rebecca asked him.

"Believe it or not, that man—" he gestured to the oldest-looking of the three men—"buys feed from my Uncle Howard. They raise beef cattle. Just a few head."

As they watched, the man reached Marshall's limo and opened the door.

A hush fell over the crowd as Mrs. Hackett emerged. She was wearing sunglasses, and her face was slack. She leaned heavily on the funeral director's arm, losing her balance as he guided her away from the limo door.

"She's on something to get her through this," Pete said. "I would be, too. Man, this is awful."

Rebecca turned away. Her face was ashen. She said, "I think I'll go inside. My dad's already here."

"Okay," Lana said. "We'll catch up with you."

Clark glanced curiously at Rebecca as she walked away and started up the stairs. "She's really upset by all this."

"Aren't you?" Lana asked him. But it was clear from her tone that the question was rhetorical. She knew he was.

"Clark," his mother said, as she and Jonathan joined him, "You okay?"

"Hey, Mom." He gestured helplessly. "Um, not really."

There was a stir in the crowd, and Clark and Martha turned to see what had happened.

"Marshall!" someone yelled. It was Marshall's brother, Jeremiah.

After climbing out of the limo, Mr. Hackett's adopted son had fallen to his knees. Now the funeral director and one of his sons were attempting to help him up. But he was a burly football player—sagging and uncooperative because of the tranquilizer he was on—and they were having trouble.

Clark edged his way through the clump of onlookers and hurried to Marshall's side. He said, "Excuse me," to the funeral director, who relinquished his hold on Marshall and gave his place to Clark.

Clark wrapped his hand around Marshall's forearm and gently, carefully raised him to his feet. Using his strength, he held him up, keeping him balanced, although to the casual observer, he was simply giving him a steadying hand.

Marshall murmured, "Get 'way from me, Kent."

"It's okay, Marshall," Clark soothed. He looked over his shoulder at the church. "Can you go in?"

"Dad . . ." Marshall moaned. His eyes opened and closed. He was heavily dosed, and Clark was a little concerned. He listened to his heartbeat, which was slow but steady.

Then Marshall saw Lana. He slurred, "Did Sullivan show? Come to gloat?"

"No," Lana assured him. "No, Marshall."

"Good. I'm gonna get her." He shook his arm, trying to break contact with Clark. But Clark could tell that if he let go of Marshall, the guy would fall again. Clark wasn't going to let that happen to him.

So without saying a word, Clark began to walk him up the steps to the church. Marshall became as docile as a lamb.

Jeremiah came out of the limo next. He was trembling, and his eyes were so swollen from crying that they appeared to be closed. His demeanor was the exact opposite of Marshall's—where Marshall's emotions had been subdued with drugs, Jeremiah's were raw and unharnessed, and as he gazed up at the church, he burst into heavy sobs. His wails rolled up and into the church like physical things. He was so loud and so distraught that people began to murmur.

The pastor of the church came out. A young man with a goatee, he was dressed in a long black robe with a whiter, shorter robe over it. Gently requesting that people move out of his way, he hurried down to the Hacketts, straight past Marshall and his mother, and gathered Jeremiah in his arms.

The older son of the family sobbed openly. He clung to the pastor and practically screamed with grief. Meanwhile, the two other Hacketts made no reaction. It was eerie; as if they had no emotions left.

"Let's go in," Clark said to Marshall. He glanced at the son of the funeral director who was escorting Mrs. Hackett. The man nodded back at him and they each guided their respective mourner into the church.

The scent of chilled, dying flowers hit Clark as he entered the church. The pews were overflowing, and heads were turning in his direction. It was an awkward moment.

His mother and father had gone on ahead. Martha half waved, indicating that they had saved him a place. Pete had joined his own family. Lana was with Clark's parents, and Rebecca was sitting with an older man with blond hair. Clark figured him for her father.

Taking his cue from the man escorting Mrs. Hackett, Clark walked Marshall up the center aisle.

A closed coffin stood before the altar. It was made of brilliantly polished wood, with brass fittings along the side of the lid.

Marshall stopped and took a deep breath.

"You okay?" Clark asked him.

"Don't feel a thing," Marshall slurred. "Gave me something."

"Okay." Clark licked his lips as they walked past row upon row of curious faces. He was hyperaware of his surroundings: the scent of women's perfumes mingled with the odor of the dying flowers.

Organ music began, playing the hymn, "Amazing Grace."

They reached the front pew, and the bearded man said to Clark, "Go on in."

Clark hesitated. He hadn't planned on sitting with Marshall during the funeral. He really wanted to be back with his own family, and with Lana. But Marshall was like a rag doll, unable to move under his own power. So Clark eased him into the pew, making room for Mrs. Hackett and Jeremiah, and reluctantly sat with them. He helped Marshall into a sitting position, rather like a ventriloquist with his dummy.

"Thanks," Marshall managed.

Mrs. Hackett was also eased in. She gazed dully at the coffin, as if she couldn't quite understand what it was. Clark was uncomfortable with how disoriented she seemed to be.

From the back of the church, Jeremiah's shrieks of pain shot loud and harsh, so out of control that he, not Clark, might as well have been from another planet.

Clark half rose to help the pastor with Jeremiah, when he saw his father leave his pew and walk toward the two men. Jonathan touched the minister on the back, talking to him for a few seconds, then put his arm around Jeremiah and walked him to the pew where Clark, Marshall, and Mrs. Hackett sat.

"My boys . . ." Mrs. Hackett's voice was breathy.

"It's okay, Mrs. Hackett," Clark told her.

"No. It's not." Without tearing her gaze from the coffin, she patted Clark. "You're a good boy." She didn't seem to notice that she was patting a stranger, and not her own son.

"Thank you, ma'am," Clark said.

"So polite."

The pastor walked toward the casket, moving to a podium beside it and looking down at what must have been an order of worship. He bent down, retrieved a glass of water, and took a sip.

"Dearly beloved, let us listen to the word of the Lord," he said.

Heads bowed.

Tears flowed.

And Jeremiah Hackett wailed with loss.

CHAPTER SEVEN

At the Scottish castle he called home, Lex, who had skipped the funeral, was seated behind his desk and watching the beautiful, disheveled woman as she paced the floor and yelled at him. She was small but wiry and beautifully proportioned; and her short, black hair and blazing eyes lent her an air of danger—an alluring combination of kickboxer and runway model.

"I fully believe that something sent me here to stop you," she said.

She was limping. Her left arm was bandaged; it had been in very bad condition, and Lex had had one of his own doctors clean and rebandage it. She was now also on an antibiotic protocol.

"Like an angel?" he asked her.

"You are not listening to me!" she shouted at him. "There is something in your fertilizer. In this!" She held a clump of what appeared to be dirt in her hand. "This killed people, Mr. Luthor! Friends of mine!"

"I am listening, Ms. Lopez," he said firmly. "Very carefully." He hadn't yet figured out her angle—blackmail money? A lawsuit? Lex was a Luthor, and therefore, quite accustomed to dealing with both.

And to think I was talking to Martha Kent the other day about this very thing.

Lex steepled his fingers, watching her. She was beyond exhausted, and she had told him an amazing story of hitching a boat ride filled with refugees from Haiti to Cuba. And then an old university friend wired her some money from

Mexico City, so that her parents wouldn't find out and make her come home before she had completed her mission. And then . . . coming to Kansas to talk to him about poisoned fertilizer?

The timing after his conversation about fertilizers, pesticides, and diseases with Martha Kent was . . . curious. But the fact that LuthorCorp might have sold a foreign country some contaminated fertilizer didn't surprise him as much.

If what she's telling me is true, I'll bet my Porshe my dad's mixed up in it. In fact, I wonder if his leaving for Metropolis has anything to do with this.

Her next tirade was cut short by the arrival of Lex's assistant, Drew, who had brought them something to eat. He wheeled in a table. It was covered with a starched white linen tablecloth and a number of elegant silver-covered dishes. Also, an iced champagne bucket and two flutes. It was too late for lunch and too early for dinner, but Lex was not about to let his guest go hungry. From the story she had told, she had been on the run for at least a week, with rarely a chance for a decent meal, much less a good one. By her elegant carriage, she appeared to be the kind of woman who had been raised on the finer things of life.

He hoped she approved of his menu selections.

With a flourish, Drew uncovered the largest dish. A beautiful sliced London broil lay on the silver tray. The next dish revealed new potatoes, the third, fresh asparagus. A simple meal, beautifully prepared.

Lex got up from his desk while Ms. Lopez sank into a leather chair. She glanced around, got back up, and dumped her handful of LuthorCorp fertilizer—if that was what it really was—into one of the champagne flutes. Lex smiled to himself—*feisty, isn't she?*—and began unwrapping the champagne cork. He popped it expertly—practically the only useful thing he'd learned at a string of prep schools, and poured it into the empty glass. He carried it to her and stretched out his hand.

"*Salud,*" he said in Spanish. Health.

That seemed to defuse her. Shaking her spiky-haired head, she sighed, took the champagne, and sipped it. She closed her eyes and leaned back against the luxurious leather chair.

"Better," she said.

His smile grew. He hadn't expected her to apologize, and he was glad that she hadn't let him down.

"Thank you, Drew," he said to his employee, who silently withdrew. Then he picked up one of the plates and began to serve her, watching her as she quietly drank his finest champagne and began to relax.

"There's datura in it," she informed him. "The herbal poison that *houngan* in Haiti use to create zombies."

He said nothing, only finished arranging her meal, and carried it over to her. Before she took it, he fetched her a white napkin and held it out for her to wipe her hand off.

She did so, then handed him the champagne without a single word of thanks.

He liked that, too.

She cut the meat and took a healthy bite, chewing appreciatively. Her eyes flickered with satisfaction, and she cut another piece.

"Did you see any? Zombies?" he asked conversationally.

"Yes." Her look at him was fierce and angry. "I saw friends and colleagues changed into zombies. Their will drained, herded along like pigs . . . and crazy, like demons. And they . . ." She touched the back of her neck, where there was a thick bandage.

She shuddered and lifted her plate. "I've lost my appetite."

"If the *houngan* in Haiti use datura to create zombies, they don't need to buy my fertilizer to get it," Lex pointed out. "Otherwise, zombies would be a new thing in the world. And they aren't. At least the stories about them aren't."

"I am not making up stories!" she thundered. "Don't you patronize me. I risked my life to get this sample to you."

"I don't mean to patronize you," he persisted. "I'm simply thinking aloud, Señorita Lopez. Maybe my father's figured out a way to artificially create datura. With economies of scale, LuthorCorp may be saving the Haitian growers a lot of money."

She looked stunned. "You are admitting it?"

"No." A strange smile played over his mouth. "May I be frank, with the proviso that you will be discreet, at least for now? It wouldn't surprise me if my father was processing custom batches of fertilizer here in my own plant without my knowledge. He's done things like that before."

"And . . . you are your father's son," she said slowly. She sounded nervous, and Lex fell a little bit in love with her right then and there.

"Yes. But our relationship isn't what you might expect. It's . . . complicated." He cocked his head. "He didn't send you here, did he?" *Is this some kind of test concocted by my father to see how I'll handle it? Or less euphemistically put, one of his traps?*

"So you are trying to blame this all on him?" she asked. "Come now, don't play the innocent with me. I'm not some little peasant from the mountains. My family has dealt with people like you before."

"Really?" He was intrigued. He leaned forward, smiling, and said, "Where? If we've met before—"

"—'you would remember it,'" she mocked. She picked up her champagne again and drank. Her hands were shaking and there were circles under her beautiful brown eyes. "All I'm saying, Mr. Luthor, is that I'm here to find out why everyone except me died in Cap du Roi."

"Died . . ."

"Men in uniforms," she said. "Bloodthirsty butchers! They slaughtered everyone. I hid."

"The *tonton macouts*?" Lex asked. "I thought they had been disbanded."

"You know an awful lot about the country," she observed, draining her glass.

He took it from her and began to refill it. "What's to know? It's a poverty-stricken nation with a penchant for ghoulish legends. I've never been there, but I've been known to watch a good zombie movie now and then."

"It's no joke!" she thundered at him. "You arrogant industrialist!"

He lifted a brow, stifling a chuckle. "I don't think I've ever been called that before."

"Don't think that because you're handsome and rich, you can be glib with me," she shot back at him. "I have been through hell. I'm not in the mood for banter."

She rose and set her plate down. "They were not *tonton macouts*, the bogeymen of the old regime, which I suspect you already know. I may have walked into the belly of the beast when I came to you, but I warn you, my family knows I'm here. If anything happens to me—"

"Nothing is going to happen to you. At least not that I have anything to do with," he assured her.

That gave her pause. She looked at him, and said, "Mr. Luthor, I watched people die. *De veras, hombre.* I saw zombies." She crossed herself.

"All right." He inclined his head.

She gave her head a shake, seeming to shiver all over as

she raked her fingers through her hair, and said, "I need a shower, and I need to sleep." They were not requests. "Then I need to talk. If not to you, then to the authorities."

And which authorities would those be? he wondered, fascinated by her air of command. Women usually tried to get his attention through the gentle art of seduction, not by accusing him of turning people into zombies, then insisting that he give her a place to crash for the night. But Maria del Carmen Maldonaldo Lopez most certainly had his attention.

"Here's what I suggest," he said. "I will personally help you investigate the fertilizer. For all we know, there are more bags of it stamped with LuthorCorp labels sitting on pallets in my warehouses, already waiting to be shipped to Haiti. We can at least try to halt any scheduled shipments. And we'll figure out who's behind it, and stop him."

She blinked. "We may be speaking of your father. Your own father."

"I'm aware of that," he replied calmly. He gestured to her food. "Why don't you finish your meal, and I'll see to it?" he suggested, rising. "A bath. A nice bed."

"Bueno," she said. That seemed to appease her. She sat back down and cut herself another piece of meat, her appetite restored. She had obviously dismissed him.

Yes, I definitely think I'm in love, Lex thought, amused.

Without another word, he left the room.

At precisely the same time, just inside the Luthor compound, a tall man dressed in black adjusted his earpiece, having listened carefully to every word that was spoken in Lex Luthor's office. The man had successfully planted some state-of-the-art surveillance equipment in the Luthors' mansion the previous night, and it had been a lot easier to accomplish than he had expected.

First he disarmed the "A" bank of security lasers with a

superadvanced high-tech device he'd first heard about back in prison. It not only detected the beams, but it distorted them so that they were rendered harmless against anyone who brushed up against them, or walked through them. After he'd been let out, he'd gone straight to a man he'd met in the joint who had worked in surveillance for years. The man had sold him some fantastic state-of-the-art equipment that he had boosted from a fancy new high-rise in Metropolis.

Once they'd been satisfied that it was in perfect operating order, the burglar had trotted it down to Smallville. *Time for payback for all those years I made nickels pressing license plates while bastards like the Luthors stole vast fortunes "legally."*

Eavesdropping on the conversation between Lex's visitor—one Ms. Lopez—and the rich boy himself, the thief had decided that he'd better steer clear of Lex Luthor's bedroom that night. He had planned to start there, robbing the rich boy blind, but it was beginning to sound as if someone else might be visiting there.

The rich get richer, even in babes, he thought enviously. *And this one sounds hot. 'Course, when you've been in the joint for a lotta years, any lady sounds hot. And when you're filthy rich, it's not hard to charm the ladies. What have I got? "So, what's your favorite meal at San Quentin?" ain't high on the list of successful pickup lines.*

I'm going to change all that. Smallville's the answer to all my prayers . . . and I've been praying steadily for ten long years.

He kept listening in for about another minute. This was too good to be true . . . there was some weird fertilizer in the mansion that he could snatch along with every single piece of gold or silver he could carry.

A subtle little ding on his handheld readout informed him

that someone was using a LuthorCorp computer to access the Net. And that someone was trying to hack into Luthor-Corp protected files.

Then she—for he figured it was the woman who had identified herself as Señorita Lopez—dialed in an e-mail account—he immediately cloned her password—and wrote a message in Spanish which he was able to intercept. It read:

PAPA, MAMITA. I'M SAFE. I DECIDED TO TAKE A DETOUR HOME TO LOS ESTADOS UNIDOS (EL ESTADO DE KANSAS!) TO VISIT LEX LUTHOR! MORE LATER. TE QUIERO, MARICA.

Marica, the man thought, smiling. *Cute name.*

Then his remote device showed that she had abruptly disconnected.

"Your room's being prepared. There's an adjoining bathroom," Lex Luthor was saying to her. "I can have Drew escort you there." Then he said, more softly, "You're trembling."

"I'm very tired," she replied frankly. "I've been through a lot."

"Do you need something to help you sleep?" he asked.

"No."

"You could always ingest some of my fertilizer."

"I'm quite certain that I have." Her voice was frosty.

"And yet, you seem to have a will of your own," Lex pointed out. "No ill effects."

"You weren't there." Her voice dropped to a whisper. "Some of them did have wills of their own. They were . . . crazy."

There was a moment when neither spoke.

"I'm going to help," he said. "I told you that."

"And why should I trust you?" she demanded.

"I've given you no reason to. I understand that," he replied.

"God will punish you if you've been lying to me."

"Well, I would hate to anger God any more than I already have," he said dryly.

As the thief listened, he detected receding footsteps, two pairs of them. After fifteen minutes of silence, he thought about modifying his plans for the evening. He was still going to break into the Luthor mansion, but he was going after different loot . . . at least this time around.

Looks like I've got better things to steal than tiaras and old coins.

Payback is going to be a lot sweeter than I expected.

CHAPTER EIGHT

No one at the Kent home slept well the night of the funeral. Jonathan tossed and turned in his sleep. Martha eventually got up and made herself some tea.

Clark stared up at the layered indigo night sky through his telescope, wondering if his birth parents were dead; if anyone who had known him when he was a baby was still alive. And if so, how could he contact them? Did they know where he was? Were they looking for him even now?

Breezes rustled through the crops, waving tall stalks of corn and wheat like impatiently snapping fingers. Clark could practically hear the world demanding that life move on, that things happen. He knew that growth was like that. Nonfarmers saw either dormant furrows or cultivated fields brimming with crops. They didn't know about what went on between the sowing and the harvest, the molecules merging and separating, spores germinating, the earth giving up nutrients to millions of tiny units of life as they struggled to sprout and blossom. There was an awful lot of "during" between "before" and "after."

Mr. Hackett is part of that cycle now, Clark found himself thinking, and he hied himself away from the image, which more than bordered on morbid.

When I die, what will happen to me? To my body? To my soul?

Can I die?

Upset, he moved away from the telescope and took the stairs down to the ground. Wandering through the barn, he saw the light on in the kitchen and heard the kettle's insistent whistle, announcing that the water inside was boiling.

Clark watched, expecting his mom to appear to retrieve the kettle. But she didn't come.

The kettle kept whistling, the valve sputtering like the espresso machine at the Talon.

Clark made his way toward the kitchen, pushing the door open.

"Mom?" he called. "Mom?"

There was no answer.

Puzzled, he took the kettle off the stove with his bare hand and placed it on a back burner. Then he walked toward the living room, wondering if she'd forgotten about her tea and gone back to bed.

"Mom?"

There was a shape in the darkened living room. Clark's heart jumped as he ran toward it.

Martha Kent lay crumpled on the floor, unconscious.

"Mom! *Dad!*" he bellowed, as he dropped to his knees beside her. He picked up her wrist and found a pulse. Her skin was warm and she was breathing.

"Mom, Mom, what's wrong?" he whispered, leaning over her. Then he yelled again for his father.

"Clark?"

Jonathan's hair was tousled and his eyes laden with sleep; he wore a T-shirt over pajama bottoms, and his feet were bare.

Then he saw his wife and raced to her. Clark moved out of his way as his father crouched over her, opening her lids and examining her eyes.

"Clark, call 911!" he shouted.

"Dad, I can carry her to the hospital faster—"

Jonathan vigorously shook his head. "We shouldn't move her. Call them. *Now.*"

Clark responded to the demand for action in his father's voice. He moved in a blur to the portable phone in its wall cradle, then forced himself to slow down as he jabbed in the numbers. Now was not the time to break the phone by employing too much strength.

"Emergency services," a male operator answered.

"Hello? It's Clark Kent, at our farm. My mom . . ." He took a breath and tried to calm down. "Our address . . ."

"Your address is on my screen," the man assured him. "It came up as soon as you dialed. Tell me what's going on, Clark."

"My mother . . . my mother is unconscious." *This isn't happening. It's happening too slowly. It's happening too quickly. I can't keep track of what's happening.* His mind was racing. He took another, deeper breath.

"I just found her. She has a pulse. Her skin is warm."

"Her pupils are normal," Jonathan called to him. "She's breathing on her own."

Dazed, Clark repeated the information.

Clark heard the clack of the computer keyboard on the other end of the line. Then the man said, "I'm sending an EMT right now, Clark. Don't move her. Keep her warm. If she regains consciousness, don't let her get up. Do you understand what I'm telling you?"

"Yes." Clark glanced anxiously over his shoulder. "They're coming, Dad. EMT."

Jonathan nodded.

The man on the phone said, "Clark, I want you to stay on the line with me until they get there, all right? Keep talking to me. Let me know what's happening."

"Yes." Clark gripped the phone as waves of fear washed

over him with a roller-coaster sensation. He was trembling. "Please hurry."

"Hang in there with me, Clark. They'll be there soon, son."

Clark closed his eyes, nodding, though of course the man couldn't see him.

"How's your history report coming?" the man asked.

Flustered, Clark opened his eyes and frowned quizzically. *My history report?*

"My son Dennis is in your history class. He said you and Pete are doing something about pesticides."

"Fertilizer," Clark murmured, his mind not at all on history papers and guys named Dennis. "It's . . . it's fine."

"Dennis still isn't done with his."

Clark vaguely understood that the dispatcher was trying to keep him grounded by giving him something to focus on. But it wasn't working.

"Clark, take one or two slow, deep breaths. But if you start to feel dizzy, sit down slowly and put your head between your legs, all right?"

Clark took a moment. Then he said, "I'm all right."

"Knew that. Good job, Clark." The man added, "Any changes in your mother's condition?"

"Dad, any changes?" Clark asked his father.

Jonathan frowned. "No. Tell him to get off the phone and dispatch that damn ambulance!"

"He already did, Dad," Clark soothed him. "It's on the way."

Taking that in, Jonathan looked back down at Martha. He had covered her with a blanket, and he tenderly tucked it under her chin.

"I just got a readout from the ambulance, Clark," the dispatcher said. "They should be there shortly."

Just as he said that, Clark heard the siren and hung up the phone.

Then time sped up, and there were lights flashing outside; a man and a woman in yellow jackets that read EMT flew from the front of the vehicle. In a precision dance, they took over the care of his mother, who still had not regained consciousness. His dad looked on helplessly. If there was anything Clark's father hated, it was not being in control, and there was nothing he could do for his wife, not even ensure that she was getting the proper treatment.

The portable phone rang in his hand, and Clark pressed the talk button and brought it to his ear.

"Hey." It was Lana. "I'm so sorry to call so late, Clark. Please apologize to your parents. It's just, Chloe's really losing it and—"

"Lana." His voice cracked.

"Clark, what's wrong? Is something wrong?" she demanded.

He told her what was happening, and she said, "I'll be right there."

As they were loading Martha in the ambulance, Lana and Chloe drove up. Chloe was wearing a sweatshirt over a pair of pajama bottoms with blue clouds on them, while Lana had on jeans and a white gauze peasant's blouse.

"Clark, what's happened?" Chloe cried. There were shadows under her eyes, and her face was streaked with tears.

He shook his head, feeling helpless, and so grateful that his friends were there.

"We don't know," he said. "She just collapsed . . ."

The female EMT said to Clark, "Do you want to ride with your mother, son?"

Clark hesitated as his father hurried out the door with a jacket in his hand. It looked to Clark as though there was room for only one passenger in the ambulance.

"We'll drive you to the hospital," Lana offered. "Your dad can go with your mother."

"Thanks," Clark said gratefully. He nodded at the EMT as Jonathan drew closer.

"Dad, they've saved room for you with Mom. Lana and Chloe will take me."

"Good." Without another word, Jonathan climbed into the ambulance. The male paramedic trotted to the driver's side door, opened it, and hopped in.

The siren squealed on, and Clark winced.

"It's okay. It's going to be okay, Clark," Chloe said. She seemed to be coming out of her own distress, as if by having someone else to focus on, she could let go of her stranglehold on pain.

The three barreled into her car. Chloe peeled out, following the ambulance, which was squealing down the dirt road off the Kent family farm and onto the road proper.

"Clark?" Chloe pressed, as she worked to keep up with the ambulance. "Did you hear me?"

He stirred, realizing he hadn't even noticed that she was talking.

"Do you think it might be asthma?" Chloe asked again.

"My mom doesn't have asthma." He looked at her in the rearview mirror.

She took a breath, ticking her glance away through the windshield and then back again. "Who was it who said, 'If I can name the monster, I can fight it'?" she asked. "Clark . . ."

"Not a heart attack," Clark blurted, and the sharpest, darkest fear he had ever known rose inside him like a huge shadowed beast. He shut his eyes. *Not my mom.*

"She's going to get the best of care," Chloe consoled him. "Everyone's going to do all they can. It's great that you found her. You've got good friends here, and we're going to help you."

As if to prove her point, she picked her phone up from its cradle above the dash, held it to her ear, and daemon-dialed a number.

"Yeah, hi, Lex. Chloe Sullivan here. Clark's mom is in an ambulance on her way to the hospital. Right. No, we don't know yet. Unconscious in the living room. Good. Thanks. I'll tell Clark."

She disconnected and replaced the phone in its cradle. "He's making calls."

Clark lowered his head, confused by his own reaction. On the one hand, he was glad she'd called Lex. But on the other . . . he didn't know how to describe it . . . embarrassed, maybe. He wanted to say to Lex and her, *We can take care of Mom ourselves.* But that wasn't true. He wanted Lex to make the calls, get the best doctors. But a small part of him insisted that this was Kent business.

After a time, he said, "Why'd you call me, Lana?"

Chloe shot Lana a look. Lana moved her shoulders, and said, "I was worried about Chloe."

Chloe huffed. "And Clark could fix Chloe? Fix what I did?" she demanded.

"No. I could talk to him about being worried about you," Lana said a little defensively. "That's all, Chloe."

They were tense. Everyone was. Too much happening, too much to deal with.

Without realizing what he was doing at first, Clark slowly began to shut down, as if, one by one, all his power switches were being turned off. He fell into the center of himself, tuning everything else out. He couldn't feel anything, not the jostle of the car, not his own heart pounding; he couldn't really hear Chloe mutter, "Great," when a flicker of lightning gave scant warning and a thundershower broke overhead. He couldn't really see anything, either. But in his mind, the image of his mother lying unconscious on the floor was all too clear.

It was very odd. He didn't feel connected by his senses to his surroundings. As if his whole world had shrunk down around him and gone inside his body.

At that image, his heart skipped a beat, and it was as though someone had pushed "reset." He shook his head. His vision was a little blurry, and he felt strange, almost as if he weren't quite *inside* his own body.

It's just nerves, he told himself, but he wondered . . .

Thunder rolled over the top of the car like a tank as the skies cracked open and rain pummeled the top of Chloe's car. The force of the downpour rocked the vehicle. Lana held onto her side armrest. Chloe muttered, "Just let's not have an accident."

Lana glanced over at Chloe. "I'm sorry I snapped at you."

"Me too," Chloe said tersely. "I mean, I'm sorry too. That *I* snapped at *you*."

The windshield wipers became the only sound in the car—they and the heater. They were comforting sounds, and Clark tried to concentrate on them, and on the fact that two of his best friends were with him.

"Should I call Pete?" Lana asked, turning to Clark. Her question startled him, and he nodded.

She gave Chloe a questioning glance. Chloe gestured to her phone and Lana picked it up.

"Daemon-dial," Chloe said. "Punch two."

Lana did, then said, "Hi, Pete. Listen."

Clark felt like a spectator on his own life as Lana filled Pete in. He lost track of the conversation until she hung up and turned to him, saying, "He'll meet us at the hospital."

"It's the middle of the night," Clark said weakly.

"Yeah, so?" Chloe retorted, giving him a patented frustrated look in the rearview mirror. "Clark, we're your friends. Your mother's in trouble."

Heart attack. He didn't want it to be something like that, something so serious that friends of his were calling each other to meet down at the hospital. He remembered an old saying, that bad things came in threes. First Mr. Hackett; now his mom . . .

"Clark, we don't know what happened yet, okay?" Lana asked him. Her eyes were luminous. She was truly the most beautiful person he had ever seen. Her features were soft, and there was a gentle, reassuring air to her words. He wished they were in a place relationship-wise where he could hold her, and not just for the sake of solace. But they weren't.

"We're almost there," Chloe told him. "Hang on, okay?"

I don't have much choice, he thought, then the temptation to shut down swept over him again. If only he could just stop everything for a while. Stop thinking. Stop worrying.

But he couldn't. This was his mom they were talking about.

When they got to the hospital, Clark marveled at the sense of unreality about it. Pitch-dark outside, bright lights inside. The thunder rolling and lightning snapping versus the squeal of soft-soled shoes on tile; the PA system paging doctors; now and then a little child yowled and someone else coughed.

"I hate hospitals," Chloe muttered. She pointed toward the reception area. "Come on."

She took over, asking about Martha Kent's whereabouts. The nurse ushered them through to the ER wing, which lay beyond her desk and to the right.

Clark took off with a jog . . . not a superfast run that would have alerted the others that he was something other than he appeared to be, just a regular-paced one, although it took everything in him not to move more quickly.

Curtains were draped everywhere like big sheets of ice; almost more by luck than chance, Clark found his mother's little sectioned-off area.

Martha lay in a hospital bed, a sheet draped over her up to her chest. She was still unconscious, hooked up to machines that blinked and beeped. A man in scrubs was examining her, and a woman also in scrubs stood by with a clipboard.

"Clark." That was his father's voice. Jonathan was shielded from Clark's view by the man in scrubs.

"Dad . . . ?"

Jonathan shook his head. "They don't know what's wrong yet."

"I'm guessing not an MI," the man in scrubs said to his colleagues. "Guys, you need to go to the waiting room, all right? I'll let you know how she's doing once we stabilize her. But we have to focus on what we're doing here."

Jonathan hesitated. Clark said, "Dad, he's right. Let's give them some room."

Reluctantly, Jonathan followed his son, still looking over his shoulder at his wife.

As they entered the waiting room, Chloe stood anxiously waiting. Lana had just finished filling the second of two cups of coffee from the vending machine, which she offered to Jonathan and Clark as they came in. Jonathan thanked her and took one, while Clark silently shook his head.

"They don't know what's wrong yet," Jonathan said. "But they don't think it's a heart attack."

"So we can't name the monster yet," Clark murmured, hardly relieved that it wasn't a heart attack. "Which means they can't fight it yet." He knew that in situations like this, seconds mattered.

Chloe came over and gave him a hug. So did Lana. Then Lana touched Jonathan's arm and said, "I'm sure she'll be all right, Mr. Kent."

He nodded gratefully. "Thank you." It was clear that he wasn't as sure about that as Lana was.

"When will they know what's going on?" Chloe asked.

"We don't know that either," Clark told her.

"Time to hurry up and wait," Chloe said. She gestured to herself. "In my pajamas."

The four sat. Clark fidgeted. His father's eyes were closed, and Clark wondered what was going through the older man's head.

A few minutes later, Pete walked in. He crossed over to Clark and clasped hands. "Hey, Clark," he said. Pete took the second cup of coffee that Lana had bought and joined the anxious vigil.

Clark nodded at him, grateful beyond words for his presence. Pete remained silent as well, but his company spoke volumes: Here was a truly good guy who cared about Clark and his family. He knew Clark's deepest, darkest secret, and he had kept and honored it.

Clark didn't know anyone else in Smallville he could trust like that.

Lana would never tell, he thought.

Then he felt a pang of sorrow.

But Lex might.

On his way to the massive garage where he kept many of his finest cars, Lex paused before Maria del Carmen's door. He listened for sounds that might show that she was still awake. But there were none, and he moved on.

Martha Kent was in trouble.

He flipped open his cell phone and began punching in numbers, calling doctors and specialists. He wondered briefly if the ER doctor who had advised against his father's operation after the twister would be on duty. They'd gone out a few times, and it had been pleasant. But no sparks.

Now take Maria del Carmen . . . there's sparks, all right.

He smiled faintly. Then the reality of his evening's mission wiped the smile off his face.

Martha Kent is in the hospital.

There, thought the thief, spotting the window of the guest room as he compared it against his map. The map was encased in a plastic sheet; it was raining, but he had come prepared.

Maria del Carmen was most likely asleep in that room, if he had triangulated her position correctly from the sensorial output he had received on his headset. Like Lex's office, he had managed to bug some of the rooms. This guest room was one of them.

He threw a grappling hook expertly into the ivy-covered wall, checked the tension, and started climbing. It was easy. He'd done this kind of thing dozens, if not hundreds of times, and thanks to the weight room in prison, he'd kept in shape during the long years of his incarceration.

He'd brought a glass cutter, but to his surprise, the window was ajar. All he had to do was push slightly, and it opened with ease. Gingerly, he climbed through it, collapsing his bulk into a ball to avoid making any noise.

One boot down, then the other, and he was standing in her room.

He drew a pair of night scopes from his black jacket and

pulled them over his eyes. He could see everything in the room even though it was pitch-dark.

Pretty girl. Bit boyish. Got that short hair they like these days.

She was sleeping the sleep of the dead, completely out of it, in a large canopy bed fit for a princess. He wasn't too worried about her. In fact, he found this part of his mission exhilarating. The realization that he might get caught was a rush—always had been, always would be. He'd already planned an escape route, and he'd be out the window before she could do much more than let out a scream.

He continued to survey the area. She wouldn't have much with her; she'd been traveling like a refugee . . .

. . . . Hmmm . . .

On the ornately carved dresser lay a beat-up fanny pack, the only object in sight.

He picked it up and sniffed at the contents, rubbed some between the fingers of his latex gloves.

Bingo.

He was back out of the window in seconds.

Like a cat.

In her room in their small apartment, Rebecca Morhaim woke suddenly. She thought she had had a bad dream, but as sleep evaporated, so did the memories of any nightmares.

Still, it had been an upsetting day; she deserved to have a few nightmares.

And a bowl of ice cream.

Smiling in anticipation, she got up, slipped her feet into her slippers, and padded down the hall. She tiptoed past her father's door, not wishing to awaken him. His new job was going well so far, but he came home tired, didn't say much, and went to bed early.

There was a new half gallon of store-brand chocolate chip in the freezer of their small refrigerator. *Someday we'll be getting the expensive brands,* she promised herself. *But for now . . . it's the cheap stuff.*

She got out a bowl, a spoon, and a scoop. Carrying her bounty to the table, she had just pulled out her chair and sat down when the knob to the front door twisted.

She jumped back up, frightened.

Someone's trying to break in!

And then the door opened, and her father walked in.

He was wearing all black, like a ninja or something, and he didn't see her at first. She called out, "Daddy?" and he started.

Then he laughed. "Hey, sweetie."

"Where were you?" she demanded. "I didn't even know you had left!"

"Sorry. Insomnia." He shrugged. "I took a walk. I still have those dreams . . ." He left the rest unsaid. They were dreams of prison, of being caged up. When he had them, he usually woke up in a cold sweat and couldn't get back to sleep. He'd been to see a therapist courtesy of a Kansas state felon reentry program, and she had suggested that when it happened, he ought to go out, get some exercise, and clear his head.

"What are you eating?" he asked, coming into the kitchen.

"Food of the gods," she replied.

"Ice cream. Yum," He got out a spoon and a bowl. "Mind if I join you?"

"I'd love it."

Father and daughter got down to the serious business of life, each with a nice big bowl, each smiling at the other almost shyly. They hadn't actually known each other for all that long. Been in each other's thoughts, yes, but as for living in the same house, talking every day about things . . . Rebecca was still adjusting to that.

"How do you like your job?"

He kept his gaze on his ice cream. "It's all right."

"Kind of boring?" she ventured, and when her father smiled up at her, Rebecca was a little surprised at how old he looked.

He had been in prison for so long. When she was nine, her mother had died, and she'd been placed in foster care. It had been horrible; her foster family hadn't wanted her, only the stipend her presence brought into their home. They'd finally decided that she cost more to take care of than they were bringing in, and "relinquished" her. It was put into her records that someone had brought her back, and that made her next placement difficult. When she finally was placed, that family moved out of state, and she bounced back into the system. The fact that she had two foster families in such a short amount of time made her look even worse.

Rebecca never wanted to be parted from her father again. Sometimes, she woke in the night in a cold sweat, worried that she had dreamt his return and that he was still in prison.

She would do anything to keep that from happening.

Anything.

CHAPTER NINE

It was nearly dawn, and day would break soon. Already, the sky over the fields of Smallville was beginning to lighten.

Ten minutes longer, and Field Operative T. T. Van De Ven would have scrubbed the mission and attempted it again the next night. He would have been far too conspicuous.

"Insertion complete," he said into the wafer-thin mic sewn into his balaclava. "Over."

"Roger that, sir," said the voice on his headset beneath the knitted mask. "Over."

"And out," Van De Ven said.

He unhooked the umbilical around his waist and gave it a tug. It began to rise as, above him, the helicopter glided upward, its blades whirring silently. The machine was state-of-the-art, the finest money could requisition.

He was dressed in black, but to-blend-in-with-the-civil-ians-black—turtleneck sweater, black jeans, and his boots were not standard issue. The only remarkable part of his appearance was the black balaclava over his face.

And the submachine gun slung over his shoulder.

He had authorization to shoot to kill if he was spotted. So far, it was everyone's lucky night.

He and his superiors had chosen a fallow field not far from the Smallville Hospital to infiltrate the small town. His fellow field operatives had traced Maria del Carmen Maldonaldo Lopez to its borders, and he was here to stop her from disclosing what she knew about the Project.

It had taken a while for Van De Ven's superiors to realize

that she had not been eliminated in the shutdown of the AYUDO compound. Her remains had never been recovered—unlike those of Dr. Ribero and another worker named Marco Taliaferro—and another operative had traced her to Port-au-Prince, where she had successfully arranged transport off the island of Haiti.

They'd lost her after that, but then a colleague had intercepted a phone call made in Cuba to Mexico City. A friend wired her some money. That had gotten them back on her trail, although she seemed to have incredible luck staying one or two jumps ahead of them. Van De Ven doubted she knew she was being followed, but he did know she was afraid for her life, and that made her cautious. She was a clever woman, and he was sorry he was going to have to take her out.

But she knows way too much to be left alive.

He pulled off his balaclava and stuffed it into his black field jacket. Then he trotted from the field toward the hospital. He'd go in there, use the bathroom, then see if the cafeteria was open so he could get a bite to eat. It was one of the least conspicuous places he could go to reconnoiter—strangers were always going into and out of hospitals, no matter how small the town—and he needed to figure out where Maria del Carmen was. He had his suspicions, but they were yet to be confirmed.

If she had gone to Lex Luthor's mansion, the mission was already severely compromised. It might be necessary to take Luthor out as well.

He took a deep breath, savoring the fresh night air. He had grown up in the Midwest himself, and he loved to be among vast fields of growing things. It made him feel alive in a way that running covert operations never could . . . and his job was, to him, the closest thing to heaven that existed.

It was a pleasant early morning, far cooler than back in Haiti. It didn't stink like Haiti, either. Haiti was a hellhole, as far as he was concerned. He hated his rotation there, couldn't wait to leave. He had never seen so much grinding poverty in his life, and he had lived all over the world.

There was nowhere else the Project could be conducted, however. The cooperative *voudon houngan*—the local Voodoo priests and priestesses, as eager as any other Haitian to make some money and gain some ground with the ruling elite—had given the department invaluable information about how they created actual, living zombies. Some of them had wanted only money, while others lusted after the magic powder the department was using in its own zombie experiments.

They would have been surprised to learn that blended with the datura was a common herb called milk thistle. The plan was to make the zombies more active, to give them strength and power so that they could become supersoldiers—secret weapons for the US Armed Forces. Milk thistle did that. The mixture was concealed in fertilizer that was being shipped to the vast cane plantation that was the cover for the Project.

How Dr. Ribero had heard of that fertilizer—much less stolen some—was a matter of utmost concern. Given Haiti's leaky economy and the many shades of gray that made up the market system, skimming imports was a way of life. But the Project had watched the LuthorCorp fertilizer like proverbial hawks at every juncture of transfer. No chain of custody had ever been more rigorously kept.

Yet, somehow, Ribero had managed it.

Too bad we killed him before we found out how he did it.

To complicate matters, the batch Ribero lifted had been bad. There was too much milk thistle in it, and the excessive amount had made the zombies go berserk after a while. First they were docile, like traditional Haitian zombies, then they slipped into overdrive. They became ravening monsters, their killer instinct outweighing everything else.

The two zombies who had attacked Maria del Carmen had reached overdrive. The third didn't go crazy until after Van De Ven had contained it. Its time had come on the way back to the lab.

Ribero might be dead, but the pretty AYUDO team member was not. And given the fact that she had done everything she could to get to Lex Luthor, it was likely she had discovered that it was something in the stolen fertilizer that had created a new kind of zombie—one that was fast-moving, aggressive, and unpredictable.

As soon as she had escaped, they were after her. Trouble was, she had a head start. Van De Ven had assumed she had died in the fire along with Ribero and Taliaferro, and it wasn't until two days later that the forensics specialists informed him that her remains were not among the ruins of the AYUDO compound at Cap du Roi.

It was very bad that she had come to Smallville. It was even worse if she had convinced Lex Luthor that fertilizer from his plant was being shipped to Haiti as part of a clandestine government plot to turn ordinary soldiers into ravening monsters.

Lex was not the Luthor who had authorized LuthorCorp's participation in the Project. Lionel Luther was . . . and he was in so deep that if he ever told a living soul what he had consented to doing, he would probably be assassinated before the next morning.

We'd be first in line for the kill if he breaches our security, Van De Ven thought angrily. *And we'd be justified.*

A lot of people in this world have no idea of the kind of

evil we're up against, the things we have to protect them from. For the kind of commitment to freedom we have, we have to accept that there are going to be some casualties along the way. Necessary losses. But all those bleeding hearts—same ones we protect day in, day out—would throw up their hands in horror if they heard about the Project.

Same as if they ever saw one of the slaughterhouses where the leather to make their fancy shoes was retrieved . . . or a sweatshop where some six-year-old boy was forced to work a sewing machine for fourteen hours a day.

Lionel Luther understood these kinds of things—he wouldn't have become a billionaire if he didn't—but Lex . . . Lex Luthor was a loose cannon. It was hard to figure him out. He claimed to be an altruistic liberal, but lately, he'd been coming down pretty hard on the side of might. He bore watching, perhaps cultivating. But at the present time, he could not be trusted.

Especially given his love of the ladies . . . and Lopez is one lovely lady.

One lovely soon-to-be-dead lady, that is.

Farmers can't call in sick.

Cows need milking and chickens need feeding no matter how bad one feels.

So it was that Jonathan told Clark to go home and try to get some rest while he stayed at the hospital for news of Martha's condition. After some shut-eye, Clark would have to do all the chores—not that difficult a task for someone with special gifts like his.

Clark protested because he didn't want to leave his parents, but Chloe put her hand on his shoulder, and said, "Your dad's right. Besides, you two should work in shifts. While he's up, you should sleep. And vice versa, until you guys find out what's going on with Mrs. Kent." She looked at Clark's father for agreement, which he gave with a weary nod.

At least it's a Saturday, Clark thought. It was four in the morning, so, technically, they were into the weekend.

Sensing his surrender, Chloe said, "Lana and I will drive you home, and—"

"I'll do it," Lex said. He had arrived about forty-five minutes before. Jonathan's back had stiffened at the sight of him, but the older man had managed to remain icily polite to the younger one. They had an edgy relationship, Jonathan and Lex, with Clark planted firmly in the middle of it.

Lex gave Clark a knowing smile. "I drove my Porsche," he said, tempting his friend.

Clark glanced at his father, who muttered, "Just don't speed."

"If you hear anything . . ." Clark said to his father.

"I'll call you," Jonathan promised.

"I can give you my cell phone number," Lex offered.

"I'll call the house," Jonathan said to Clark. "You'll be home soon."

"Up to you, Mr. Kent," Lex replied. He fished in his pocket for the keys.

"Hey, Clark, you need company at your house?" Pete asked, half-rising.

"I'll be okay," Clark told him.

Pete looked a little hurt but said nothing, only nodded as if to say, *Can't compete with a Porsche.* "I'll be by later, help you with the chores."

"Thanks." Clark knew that Pete was aware that he didn't really need any help—that he would only be coming by to check on him.

He's a really good friend.

Lex and Clark walked outside to the hospital parking lot.

Lex's car sat beneath one of the parking lot lights, gleaming like a beautiful spaceship. Pressing the key, Clark deactivated the security system while Lex observed, smiling, and the two walked around the car, Clark to the driver's side. He sank into the low-slung seat and put the key in the ignition. The vehicle purred, ready for zero to a hundred and sixty in sixty seconds, and they took off.

Lex gave him a look. "I should have asked if you're okay to drive."

Clark nodded. "Gives me something to think about besides my mom." He wrinkled his eyebrows and took his gaze off the road for just an instant.

"Can you think of anything she ate at your house that might have done this to her, Lex? The doctors can't figure it out."

Lex shook his head. "We had some fruit and cheese. Just like we always have."

Something in his tone caught Clark's attention. There had been a hesitation just before Lex had answered.

Does he know something he's not telling me?

Clark was shocked. He was so upset he missed a shift up and ground the gears. Lex was supposedly one of his best friends. He wouldn't hold back anything that would help his mother, would he?

"Clark, you want me to drive?" Lex asked, sounding a little nervous.

Clark shook his head. He glanced at his friend, "You'd tell me, wouldn't you, Lex? I mean, if something happened . . . if she accidentally ate something that was off . . ."

"You think that I'm not telling you something," Lex said slowly. He blinked. "Do you think I'm afraid you'll sue me or something?"

"It's my mom, Lex," Clark pressed.

"Clark." Lex kept his voice low, kind, and patient. "I don't know what's wrong with your mother. But whatever it is, I sincerely doubt it has anything to do with me, my house, or my food." He raised his hand. "I ate everything she did, and I'm fine."

Clark exhaled. "I'm sorry, Lex. I didn't mean to . . . I don't know what I'm doing."

"You're right there!" Lex shouted.

He grabbed the wheel and pulled hard to the left, where the road dipped off the tarmac into a cattle guard in a dry creek bed. The Porsche cornered beautifully, but the turn was too extreme, even for the precision machine. The sports car angled downward toward the cattle guard, hit something, and then rolled.

"Lex!" Clark shouted.

There was chaos inside as the car tumbled over and over and over. Clark was tossed hard like rag doll, but he felt no pain. He was certain Lex was not as lucky.

Finally, the car rocked to a stop. They were hanging upside down; with an easy yank, Clark freed himself and got to pulling Lex out of his harness. The odor of gasoline permeated the air like an oiled tarp.

His friend was unconscious. Clark shook his head to clear it from panic. *First Mom, and now Lex. Did someone curse Smallville or something?*

Lex came to as Clark was yanking the straps out of the seat. Realizing his friend was awake, Clark refrained from his next move, which would have been pushing the door off the hinges with a brush of his hand.

"Lex, I smell gas," Clark said urgently. "We've got to get out of the car."

"Oh, my poor Porsche," Lex said with irony dripping in his voice. He moaned. "Next time, I'm driving."

Clark got out of the car and ran around to the other side. Though the door hung open, it was slightly jammed. Clark gave it an extra pull—from his vantage point, Lex would never be able to tell that Clark had had to use his super-strength on it.

"Hang on, Lex," Clark said.

"I'm okay," Lex replied. "Do you smell all that gas?"

"Yeah. I'll have you out of there in no time," Clark assured him.

Lex broke into one of his enigmatic smiles. "I know, Clark."

Clark worked the seat belt, wishing Lex would slip back into unconsciousness so he could perform his rescue more easily. For all he knew, the car was going to blow at any moment.

Maybe now he gets to find out about my secret, he thought. *If I have to let him find out who I am to save his life, I'll do it.*

"Who are you?" Lex slurred.

"Lex, it's me, Clark." Clark was concerned. Confusion was often the symptom of a concussion—a bruise on the brain, which could be life-threatening.

"No," Lex said. "Him."

Clark looked over his shoulder. In front of the car, a grim-faced man was sprawled on the ground. His face was illuminated by the headlights, and Clark saw with great relief that his eyes were open, and he was blinking. That meant he was alive.

Did I hit him? Clark wondered uneasily.

He finished easing Lex out of the Porsche, helping him to climb out and flop onto his stomach. Lex appeared to be in good shape, his eyes open and focused, his coordination good as he rolled back over.

"Thanks, Clark," he said. "I'm okay."

"Good," Clark replied. Then he hurried over to the other man, assessing the damage as best he could. "Are you all right?" he asked.

"Yes." The man spoke tersely, gritted out the one-syllable word. He seemed more angry than hurt, and Clark was confused. "No thanks to you, son. Out joyriding? You two boost a car?"

"No," Clark said, shocked at his question. "This is our . . . his car." Then he realized how strange it must seem for two young guys to have a car that cost over a hundred thousand dollars in rural Kansas.

Ouch. What a waste of a great vehicle. Of course, Lex can buy another in a hot minute.

The man appeared startled as Lex lifted his head. The car's headlights illuminated his features . . . and his bald head.

The man's voice stayed calm, well modulated. "Lex Luthor?"

"In the flesh," Lex said. "What's left of it. And you are?"

"Just passing through," the man said easily. "Now I can tell the grandkids I almost got run over by Lex Luthor in his Porsche."

Lex chuckled wanly. "That's a good title for a children's book. Or a Christmas carol. 'Grandpa Got Run Over by Lex Luthor.'"

The man squatted and looked inside the car. "Fine piece of craftsmanship."

"Used to be." He fished in his jacket pocket and brought out his cell phone. "I'll call for some help. You should get checked out at the hospital just in case. Clark, you okay?"

"I'm fine," Clark said quickly. "Not even a scratch."

"I insist." Lex was firm but pleasant. "Clark, have you got the number written down anywhere?"

He had been taking a sheaf of papers home for his father—when someone was checked into a hospital, there were enough papers shuffled back and forth to fill a file cabinet, all because of liability and insurance. And Clark figured that was why Lex was being so insistent about calling to make sure the man was all right. In a lot of ways, it was more complicated being as rich as Lex was. Clark could never get over how many lawsuits were filed against the Luthors, and many not even because billionaires did things that were . . . questionable. Some people saw suing a rich man the same way they viewed the lottery—a way to get rich, overnight.

"All the papers are in the car, Lex," Clark told him. "Why not call 911?"

"Good idea! Why didn't I think of that? Must be the blow to the head!" Lex said, and punched in the triple-digit number.

Just then a siren wailed in the background. Clark and Lex looked startled.

"Someone must have heard the accident and alerted the hospital," Lex guessed. He flicked the phone shut. "They should be here soon," he assured the man. "The hospital's just down the road, so it's not a long drive."

"I'm fine," the man said. "And I'm in a hurry."

Lex said to Clark. "I'll call for another ride home." He dialed a single number.

To the surprise of both Clark and Lex, the man got to his feet and began loping away.

"Wait!" Clark called to the retreating figure. "You might need help! You might not realize that you're hurt!"

The man waved a hand as if he had heard Clark but was

dismissing him. Then the siren grew louder, drowning out anything the man might have yelled to Clark in return.

Soon a Smallville Fire Department truck screeched to a halt behind Lex's Porsche and four or five firefighters leaped out of the vehicle, one of them stumbling as he blurted, "Awesome car!"

One circled around to Lex and Clark and shouted, "Two males out!" He said to Clark, "Anyone else inside?"

Clark shook his head while Lex said mildly, "It's a Porsche. There's no room for anyone else."

"Hell." The firefighter stared at it. "What a damn shame."

"We're all right, too," Lex said. He gestured in the direction where the stranger had run off. "We swerved to avoid a man who was crossing our path. I told him to wait for you. He should be just up ahead."

"Stranger? Ran in front of you?" the freckle-faced firefighter said. "I'd sue his butt!"

Lex smiled politely but said nothing. Clark guessed that this was not the time for Lex to be talking about lawsuits.

"I'm not seeing any danger here," said another of the firefighters, this one wearing a name tag emblazoned with the word CAPTAIN. "Would you like me to call a towing company?"

"Got my own," Lex said.

The captain nodded. "Well, we need to fill out a few papers."

Clark silently groaned.

More papers.

Lex said, "Of course," and walked with the captain to the fire truck. More than once, Clark had watched Lex handle these kinds of situations with total calm and self-possession. He knew demons haunted his friend, but when he had on the Luthor "game face," no one would guess that Lex Luthor was anything but a self-assured billionaire with the world by the tail.

"Who was driving?" the captain asked.

"I was," Lex said quickly.

He gave Clark a look. Clark didn't like lying, but he remained silent. There was nothing to be gained by correcting Lex, and it wasn't important.

But one never knew, in the grand scheme of things . . . did maintaining one's silence on the little things become so habitual that it became the first reaction to whatever life handed one? To keep silent, pull back, see if someone else stepped forward? As someone with special gifts, Clark couldn't let that happen to him.

I have to remember that sometimes it's my duty to act, not react. I don't have that luxury.

"And that guy who just appeared?" the captain was asking Lex, frowning slightly. "Who was he?"

"I have no idea." Lex cocked his head. "Who called in the accident?"

"Let's see . . . it was anonymous. Cell phone." The captain shrugged. "It happens out in these fields. Someone on a farm hears a crash, phones it in, doesn't want to get involved for some reason. You know, country folk."

"I know," Lex said. "Actually, it's the same in the city. Hard to get citizens to get involved."

The captain looked appreciative that Lex understood the complexities of his job. "People get spooked. Don't know if they should say anything or stay out of it."

Clark raised his brows, wondering if the fire captain could read minds.

Then the man said, "Son, a word with you as well?"

"Of course," Clark said.

T. T. Van De Ven had jogged on ahead, then dived into a cornfield and carefully made his way through, an expert at making his presence nearly undetectable.

Except when I dodge out in front of my subject's luxury automobile, he thought, beyond irritated with himself.

Scowling, he turned on his headset and contacted the helicopter.

"Who the hell authorized you to contact the Smallville Fire Department?" he demanded, dispensing with protocol.

"Sir, we saw you go down. We thought . . ."

"You aren't paid to think. I am."

"Yes sir, I'm sorry. Won't happen again."

"Go back to base," he ordered the chopper. The Project had a secret base near Metropolis. There was one in each region of the United States.

"Yes sir."

"Over," Van De Ven snapped, and disconnected.

Moron.

Ought to be shot.

Stealthily as the helicopter, he made his way through the cornfield. Now he had to add an unintentional contact with Lex Luthor to all the strategies he planned from now on.

Then it dawned on him: for the time being, Lex was away from his mansion. If his target was there, he could take her out with a lot less fanfare than if the young billionaire was in residence.

I don't know if I'll make it there before he does, but I've got nothing better to do. Completing my mission is my only priority.

The zombies were marching. Torchlight flickered on their faces, drawn and confused . . . some were rotting and dead; but others were still alive . . . and their eyes were screaming.

Help me, help me, help me, I'm in hell . . .

Marica ran from them, ran for her life. But they were screaming.

Help us, help us, we're in hell . . .

She reached the edge of a cliff and looked over. Below, the thick tropical foliage of Haiti was blazing. Smoke boiled up from wave after wave of flame. Birds and animals screamed.

Help us, help us . . .

It was the cry of Haiti, a country brought so low that the rest of the world had given up on it.

The cry of the zombies left back in Haiti, people she had known like Baby Loa . . .

We're in hell!

Marica woke with a start. She bolted upright, confused for a moment about where she was. The things hanging down around her—*snakes! Hands!*

She lay back down, trembling, staring up at the hangings draping the beautiful canopy bed in one of Lex Luthor's guest bedrooms.

Only a dream.

A dream that had been the nightmare that was Haiti. That still was Haiti, for the people trapped on it.

She wiped tears from her eyes—she had been crying in her sleep—and rolled onto her side. What a strange journey she had been on. Last night she had hoped it would all end here, and now she wondered what strange compulsion had prompted her to confront Lex Luthor so fearlessly . . . and stupidly.

He claims he doesn't know a thing about the fertilizer. But if he's involved, he's not going to admit it to me. And if he is, he's not going to be happy having someone around who can point a finger at him.

People were murdered in Cap du Roi. Did I somehow as-

*sume that because he and I come from the same social class,
that I would be immune to being eliminated if I pose a threat
to what is going on in Haiti?*

*I don't even know if it was because of the fertilizer. I don't
even know if it really did turn people into zombies. For all I
know, Dr. Ribero had his own agenda, and he showed me a
faked slide. I don't know anything, really.*

I've been running on sheer terror.

She slung her legs over the side of the bed, smiling
weakly at her long LuthorCorp T-shirt. Lex had offered her
any number of exquisite nightgowns, explaining that he kept
a few in the guest closets "in case someone decides to stay
over." There had not been a bit of shame in his voice or his
mannerisms; it was a known fact in the upper circles of society that Luthor men had . . . appetites.

Not my concern, she reminded herself. *I'm not here to
begin a romance with Lex Luthor.*

Stiffly she stood, sore from her travels and her injuries.
She hobbled over to the dresser where the fanny pack lay,
and . . .

It was gone.

She whirled around to see if she misremembered where
she'd put it . . . but it was nowhere to be seen.

She opened up all the drawers of the dresser, dropping to
her knees with a grunt to look beneath the nightstand beside
it. She crab-walked to the bed and lifted the sapphire dust
ruffle, feeling around on the spotless hardwood floor.

Nothing.

She rifled through the other nightstand, then the closet.
She raced to the bed and pressed her palms into the bed-
clothes, ripping them away. She picked up each of the large,
goose down pillows and shook them hard.

When she stood in the center of the demolished room, she shouted, "Damn it!"

He had taken it in the night . . . or had it taken.

How could I have been so stupid? she thought to herself. *I walked right into the lion's den with a big chunk of fresh kill . . . and expected him to leave it alone?*

She threw open the door and stomped into the hall.

"Lex!" she bellowed.

There was no answer. Then Lex's assistant, Drew, glided down the hall like a windup toy and smiled at her politely. Despite the early hour, he was dressed in black trousers and a white T-shirt, ready for the day.

"Yes, Ms. Lopez?" he queried.

"Where is my pack?" she demanded, then shook her head. "Where's Mr. Luthor?"

"He's not home at the moment," he said, all smoothness and polish. "He should be returning shortly. Is something missing from your room?"

She wasn't about to go into it with the hired help. "Are my clothes finished?"

The man looked mildly apologetic. "Sorry, but they came apart in the wash. They were pretty worn."

That rang true. She really wasn't surprised that her old khaki shorts and the ragged T-shirt hadn't made it.

"Mr. Luthor pulled together an outfit for you," Drew continued. "I'll go get it. Would you like something to eat? There are fresh croissants."

"Fresh . . ." She was startled by the juxtaposition of her year in Haiti with the realities of life among the wealthy . . . no matter where they lived.

"There was something in my room," she began, then realized that it made no sense at all to go into this with him.

He looked concerned. "A spider? Would you like me to come check?"

She snorted and whirled on her heel, half-running down the corridor.

"Your room is in the other direction," Drew told her.

"I'm not going to my room," she announced. "I'm going to Mr. Luthor's office."

"It's also in the other direction."

"Oh." She turned back around. "Where's a phone? I need to make some calls."

"I'll bring you one," he offered. "Would you like me to bring it to your room? For privacy?"

She thought about the T-shirt she was wearing and the lack of clothing beneath it, but she didn't really care at the moment what he or anyone else thought of her.

"*Sí,*" she said imperiously. "With coffee. And one of the fresh croissants."

She raised her head and went back into her room.

She slammed the door and crossed to the windows. Pulling back the drapes, she stared out at the beautiful garden behind the house. So incongruous, this huge Scottish mansion in the middle of Kansas. It was like a fortress, an island to get away from all the cares of running a huge empire. She did not deceive herself; the life of the ultrarich was certainly comfortable, but it was not without its own set of stresses. It only looked that way from the outside.

But no matter how much stress there may be here, it's nothing compared to watching your child die of starvation. Or having your parent dragged away by soldiers in the dead of night to never come home again.

Or becoming a zombie . . .

Those are the stresses of Haiti.

She paced, furious with herself for being so trusting. She had let down her guard.

I have got to get my evidence back. What am I going to do?

Her mind raced, but she had no answers.

By the time Lex's assistant had brought her the phone and a breakfast tray, she had calmed down enough to realize that if she phoned home in the excited state she was in, her parents would insist that she return to them. In their world, such matters were left to others to deal with. The police and the politicians were looked upon as hired help, charged with keeping things going. They wouldn't dream of becoming involved in a situation such as she was in now.

So she took a long moment to compose herself before she took the phone and dialed her parents' estate in Mexico.

"*Bueno*, Residencio Lopez," came a voice. Marica smiled.

"Chana?" she asked the housekeeper on the other end of the line. "It's Marica."

"*Señorita* Marica!" Chana cried. "How are you? Are you well? Your parents were so glad to hear that you had decided to visit the Luthor family. Are they treating you well?"

Marica bit her tongue. Then she managed to say, without tripping on the words, "Oh, yes. Very well." She reached for her cup of coffee and sipped it. It was excellent. "I'm eating fresh croissants as we speak."

"That is wonderful. I'll go get your mother. They're so glad you're out of that terrible place. They'll be flying out to get you, and—"

"No!" Marica blurted, then caught herself, and said, "Ah, Lex is here, and we're off to go . . . to admire his fertilizer factory," she finished lamely. "I wouldn't want to keep him waiting."

"Well . . ." Chana sounded torn.

"I'll call back in a couple of hours, Chanita," Marica said playfully, taking advantage of the old housekeeper's affection for her. "Lex is so busy . . . he's taking so much time out just for me."

"Ah." The housekeeper's voice dropped. "Is he single, Marica?"

"For now."

The two women giggled.

"Take care, *mi hija*. You know those men, they are playboys."

"I know. I will take care. Don't worry. Give *besitos* to my mother for me. And keep many more for yourself." *Besitos* were little kisses . . . and Chana had always loved receiving them from her favorite girl in all the world.

"You're such a good girl, Marica." Chana sighed. "I'm so glad that nonsense with Haiti is over. You were wise to leave. You need to come home. Your mother is such a fine lady, helping with the church orphanage. You can do things like that."

"Of course," Marica soothed.

They hung up, and Marica shook her head. Chana and her mother lived in a different era, when wealthy Mexican women did the kind of "good works" that did not interfere with their endless rounds of teas, fashion shows, and shopping.

I'm a different kind of Mexican lady, she thought. *I can't tell them what's going on here or they'll just make me come home . . . or try to. And if I step outside this house . . . it's possible I'm not safe. I don't know the whole story, but I do know I cannot assume anything.*

I can't trust anyone.

I'm going to have to be careful around here, monitor how much I tell, and stop telegraphing my plans.

She looked out the window again, feeling lost and afraid.

Supremely frustrated, T. T. Van De Ven lowered his field glasses and took out his earpiece. There was far too much activity on the Luthor compound for him to take out his target. He was not pleased; and confirmation that the Lopez woman had lost possession of the fertilizer sample displeased him even more.

Sighing, he pulled out his secured field-worthy phone and called his superiors. As he anticipated, they told him to lie low and wait for further orders.

CHAPTER TEN

In his rathole apartment in Metropolis, Shaky wadded up the latest rejection letter, taking extra time to compact it tightly, the thicker paper from this one making even the simple task frustrating.

He took the paper and slammed it against the Formica top of his ancient steel desk, letting kinetic energy and the hard surface do the work for him.

—*Wham, wham, wham,* went the paper.

Dammit! I was sure I had this one.

The letter was the latest in a series. Shaky tossed it in a high arc over the top of his somewhat battered lab table, strewn with reports and beakers. The piece of paper bounced off the far wall and fell through a tiny basketball hoop he'd stuck over the huge wire basket he used as a bin.

He shoots, he scores!

Even with the bad news, his own abilities cheered him.

No biggie. There will be other grants.

The down-on-his-luck scientist tried to be optimistic. Yet even as he sat there, sweating slightly in his chair, his polyester shirt not wicking the sweat away as well as he would have liked, his mind added the score like beads on an abacus. *Tak-tak-tak.*

That was the last one.

He'd sent out seven letters, and he'd gotten seven rejections. No one wanted to fund his experiments, no one had a sense of *vision.*

He sometimes felt he understood what it might have been like to be one of the scientists in the old B movies he'd loved as a kid. The actors in their roles would bemoan about how no one understood them, how no one else could see what their works would do to benefit mankind. But he, Charles "Shaky" Copper understood what it was like to *be* the man they only pretended to be.

His ideas for immunotherapy treatment, his suggestions at wakening latent psi powers through the use of chemicals and altered consciousness . . . those were only his less controversial ideas, and they still scared people too much.

You'd think people would be more daring in the twenty-first century.

But no. They were limited, blind idiots and only *he* could see. He stared at the pile of paper in the basket across the room. There it was: empirical evidence of their lack of vision.

Oh well. Things were bad, and he'd have to see what he could do. He still had that pad, didn't he? Shaky reached into one of the big side drawers of the desk, scrabbling past several candy-bar wrappers, some throat lozenges, and fast-food napkins.

Aha!

He still had it—the pad he'd swiped from the hospital, right before he'd been fired. He could write up some prescriptions, employ a few homeless men to get them filled, and through good sales technique, gain rent money and enough capital to keep operating for a little while.

Guess I'd better get on it.

He had a good work ethic, even if he applied it to strange ends, so he was hard at work on a prescription for a new name-brand muscle relaxant when he heard the knock at the door.

"Come in!"

Well! Business at last.

Shaky tried to think. What was the latest flyer he'd put out? Was it the "Spanish Fly for Real," advertising his own homemade roofies, or perhaps the "Memory Potion Will Help You Ace Tests—It Worked for Me!"

Periodically he'd plaster the local college with signs and had sold a number of tonics and knockout drugs to some of the more adventurous kids there. It wasn't much, but every little bit helped, particularly when things got tight. Some of his wilder customers had been involved in his prescription drug racket as well, which had been lucrative.

The figure in the doorway didn't look like a student, though. He wore a matching jacket and jeans, and he had a backpack slung over his shoulder. In his right hand he carried a clear plastic carrier full of . . . *dirt?*

Shaky gave it a try anyway. "How can I help you?" He'd spent a summer as the assistant manager for an apartment complex, working his way through school. He had loathed learning the people skills the job required, but they came in handy now: helped him sell himself—and get himself out of trouble. Too bad he hadn't learned how to *write* that well.

The stranger scowled. "I don't want any of your mumbo-jumbo crap. What I want is for you to help me with this."

He indicated the container.

He wants me to help him with that? thought Shaky. *Dirt?*

"Ah, I don't really work with earth. There is a potter next door who might be able to help you . . ." Shaky let his voice trail off, hoping the guy would get the picture.

He did.

A fresh scowl and another shake of his head. "Look, pal, I *know* you're the kind of guy to help me out with this."

Setting down the backpack, he reached inside his pocket and threw down several of Shaky's flyers, including some that he hadn't circulated lately—an old one talking about the juice of youth, and yet another about a superexfoliating foam Shaky had done some experiments with, hoping to be the next Ron Popeil of chemistry, with his own hour-long infomercials full of pimply teens.

But underneath them was a copy of the paper. The one that had been the beginning of the end of his time at college, the one that had separated the scientists with vision from those without. He'd been on the way to his master's degree and he'd written a paper called "Mad Scientists—Not so Mad?" The paper had focused on the concept of scientists as visionaries, as agents of change. One of the teaching assistants had thought it was so funny that he'd distributed a copy to his friends.

The fact that the paper had been backed up by several experiments—descriptions of providing electric shocks to dead animals, suggestions that the fictional character created by Mary Shelley in *Frankenstein* had perhaps not been so off base, or that Robert Louis Stevenson had been far ahead of time in his portrayal of Dr. Jekyll, reverting intellect to ancestral memories—had made the ridicule worse.

Shaky could tell that he'd made a mistake when he'd started hearing the snickering. Other students had called him names, had not *seen* what he was truly getting at.

The paper in the dirt-man's hand was well worn, and looked like it had been thumbed through many times.

"I don't know where you got that—" Shaky began.

"Hey, you don't have to worry about me—I've been a fan of yours for years." The stranger lowered his voice, looking around. "I'm here to give you a chance—a chance to work with the stuff that your wildest dreams are made of."

Shaky tried to keep his anger in check. Some guy coming in, messing with his mind, wanting him to play with *dirt* for Pete's sake. Saying it was some kind of weird science!

"Look, Mr. . . . Ah . . ."

The scientist waited, giving the pause some weight. People always wanted to leap into pauses, hated uncomfortable silences. This guy was no different.

But he surprised Shaky.

"Sorry, no names just yet. This stuff is too hot."

Shaky frowned. This idiot just wasn't making it easy. *Go away,* he thought. *I've got illegal drug prescriptions to write.*

"Look, I don't know who you are, but I don't play with dirt, haven't since I was a kid, and I'm not interested in running any soil samples for you."

Shaky expected the man to get tense, yell, or react strongly. Instead, he laughed.

"Okay, okay. Sure." He chuckled again. "You're a man of science! And you haven't seen any *proof* yet. I can dig that."

The man reached down and unzipped the backpack. He reached in and withdrew a tiny cage; within it was a mouse. Nothing special, just a little lab rat, nose quivering.

The man set the cage down on Shaky's desk, moving aside some old canary yellow paper pads that sat there. Then he put on a rubber glove and grabbed some of the soil from within the clear container, careful not to get it on his hands.

Shaky took a closer look at the stuff and could see that it was too processed—too refined to be just simple dirt; the stuff looked more like fertilizer.

His irritation notwithstanding, Shaky was curious. What was the guy going to do next?

It is that very curiosity that gives me vision.

Too bad it made him patient with strangers who were messing with his schedule, but then, who knew?

The man put some kind of clear liquid over the fertilizer. The stuff was pungent, smelling like old cheese.

"This is a chemical I learned about in . . . my last living situation. They put it in junk food. Makes animals—and people—eat just about anything. Boy, I love chemistry."

Shaky watched the man place the mixture in front of the mouse, who sniffed at the mixture, then began nibbling it.

"He hasn't had anything for a while; I wanted to keep him hungry."

The mouse finished eating, but was clearly still hungry. He kept looking for more, little head moving, eyes darting, animated whiskers quivering. He looked outside the cage, over toward the legal pads, then the other direction, peering up at Shaky.

Suddenly, the poor little thing went into horrible convulsions, twitching and jerking, then collapsed onto the floor of the cage.

Shaky grimaced. Though he was a scientist, he did have feelings. He didn't like to see anything suffer, despite the need for lab trials.

Then the mouse trembled all over, and slowly got to its four feet. And then it stopped. The little nose still quivered, the eyes still peered, but it was as if the mouse had been completely anesthetized, a veil of disinterest put between him and the world. There was no more *life* in his motions.

The stranger pulled a wedge of cheese from his pocket and put it in front of the mouse.

The creature didn't move. It stood there, alive, yet somehow *not* alive, dead to its own desire to eat . . . to survive.

Shaky felt a chill. This was eerie, *spooky*-cool. He couldn't take his eyes off of the rodent, which stood there, hungry, yet not going for the cheese.

It was as if its will had been taken away.

"Look, it's like this. This stuff"—Shaky saw him indicate

the soil out of the corner of his eye—"has some kind of way—"

Here the man paused.

"—of creating zombies."

The scientist's eyes widened as he added the evidence he was seeing in front of him with the man's statement. Could it be? Was this guy messing with him, jerking him around?

"Ah . . ."

"It's real," the man assured him. "This isn't the first thing I tried it on."

Shaky stared at him in wonderment.

The man chuckled. "You're wondering why I came to you?"

"Yes," Shaky said, his eyes still on the mouse.

"It's worked on a cat, and a dog, and a couple of mice. But I'm running out of it. And let's just say I want some help extracting the, ah, *active* ingredient. Not everyone wants to eat dirt, you know.

"I'm thinking . . . more than one," the man continued. "I'm thinking you and I could make . . . several of these," he said as he gestured to the mouse.

A thrill ran up Shaky's spine. He pulled his gaze from the mouse and looked up at the man standing in front of his desk. He didn't look like a mad scientist, a world conqueror, or a man who wanted to create legions of zombies.

Zombies!

The very word resonated in his soul. To do this for *real*.

If it *was* real.

"This is commercial fertilizer," the man continued. "I stole it. It's got the zombie-making stuff hidden in it, so they could conceal what they were doing."

" 'They?' " Shaky asked anxiously.

"Slave labor. Foreign country," the man assured him. "No one in the States knows I've got the stuff."

From then on, Shaky thought of the man as "the thief."

"It's for real," the thief continued. "Works great. But all I have is this little batch of it, and I can't get any more from my, ah, supplier. So I'm thinking, figure out the formula, distill it . . . and let 'er rip."

Let 'er rip.

Shaky started thinking about how he might analyze the soil, run pH checks, put some in a 2:1 soil-to-water suspension, maybe see if he could get access to the U's gas chromatograph. He still had a friend in one of the lab guys there, got him a few bottles of pills now and then—

His eyes sharpened on the man. Maybe this guy was DEA, messing with him before he busted him. Or what if he was a nutcase and there was just some kind of dope on the smelly stuff?

A knock came at the door.

Both Shaky and the thief looked annoyed.

An elderly man stood there, dressed in a ratty old army coat. He had an anxious, ingratiating smile on his face.

"Sorry, boys, din't mean to wake yez," he said in a high-pitched, whiny voice.

Shaky relaxed. It was old Willie Thorpe, one of his partners-in-crime in the drug racket. Shaky would give him a prescription, send the old man to a local pharmacy, and wait outside for him to come out with the drugs.

Willie came by now and then to check and see if there were any more prescriptions in the offering, or if there was other work he could do. Once or twice, Shaky had asked him to deliver stuff, giving him a semireliable cutout in his drug delivery service; not that the old man wouldn't give him up if it came down to it.

The scientist hadn't used him for a while—there had been a matter of a few uppers going missing in one of the man's last errands. The kid who'd bought them had called Shaky on it, demanding his money back. Only two pills had been missing, but it had put the old man off Shaky's useful list for a while.

But now . . .

Now I need proof before I get involved. Mice are one thing. Men are another. If Willie counts as a man anymore in the state he's in.

So what are you, Mr. Thorpe, a man or a mouse?

Shaky hid a grin. "Sure, Willie," he said. "Glad you showed. I could use your help."

The old man's rheumy eyes brightened slightly, a smile passing across his face like a drop of water in the desert. Something was up—maybe it was his itch for some booze, maybe he was lucid enough to realize that he was hungry. Whatever it was, desperation had brought him to Shaky's door, and desperate men did desperate deeds.

Willie nodded eagerly. "Yeh, yeh, I hoped yew could."

"But first I want you to do something for me," Shaky said, holding up his hand. "Something you're peculiarly equipped to help me with. Because you know, Willie, there are times I need you."

The old man's face grew wary. He'd been on the street for years, had seen and had things done to him that Shaky didn't even want to guess at.

"What?" he asked. "What do you want me to do?"

"Try this new vitamin sample I've made," Shaky said offhandedly. "See if it tastes any good. My friend here, Mr. Smith, is going to try to sell it through health food stores. We're wondering if the taste is too off-putting."

He nodded at the thief, who looked back at him and

grinned a cruel, thin smile. The thief took the fertilizer and put in on Shaky's desk.

"Running low," he said to Shaky.

"That don't look like no vitamins to me," said Thorpe. He had stepped forward to look at the sample, and was edging back, now, toward the door. "I dunno, Mr. Shakes. It don't even look like it would taste good. I don't think even them health nuts would eat it."

"Willie," said Shaky. "It's really, really good for you. You can't believe what a boost it will give your immune system. I think you owe it to yourself to try this."

The old man gave the guy a reproachful look. "I hain't done nothin to deserve any tricks, Mr. Shaky."

"But I know you have, Willie," said the scientist. "Like maybe taking a few of the goods we sent to the U?"

Thorpe looked scared and headed for the door.

"Do it, Willie," Shaky said. "And . . . maybe I'll forget the whole thing."

Willie paused.

Gotcha.

Shaky set the hook.

"But I tell you what. I'll give you this"—and Shaky held up the prescription he'd been working on—"and some cash to get it with, and . . ."

The old man's eyes were on him, wide. He hadn't gotten any deals that sounded like this in a while, ". . . you get a nice beer to wash the vitamins down with."

Thorpe hadn't survived as long as he had by being stupid. But he was thirsty. Very thirsty. His eyes raked across the so-called vitamins and the prescription.

"Where's the beer?" he asked, suspiciously.

Smiling, Shaky reached into the minifridge he kept to the right of his desk, under the printer. He pulled out a beer and felt the pull it had on the old man, who unconsciously licked his lips.

Shaky kept up the polite smile, setting the drink down on the desk next to the other items. He watched Thorpe's face as he did so, enjoying the vacillation between fear and lust. Oh, how the man wanted that beer.

And how he feared what Shaky might do to him for stealing the pills.

Finally, a look of sadness came over his face, a grim acceptance of his weaknesses, and the old man came forward, shuffling slightly.

"Yew drive a hard bargain, Shakes," he said, "but I'm a man that likes a bargain, so let's see what you got."

He grabbed the prescription, looked at the writing on it, and nodded.

Then he opened the beer and took an appreciative swig.

"Got to get my mouth a little wet 'fore taking your vites," he said, smacking his lips. This close, his skin was a patchwork of webbed veins and blocked pores.

Shaky kept his smile; his sense of curiosity was alive as he watched the old man eat the fertilizer, scooping it up with his knobby hands. He gulped it down in several fast chomps, doing his best not to taste it. Then, as Shaky had suggested, he took several pulls on the beer to wash it down.

"Tastes like *crap*," he said with a grin, confident that he'd gotten the better end of the deal. Sure he'd had to eat some dirt, but that was nothing. He had drugs on the way, and a beer to keep him company.

Shaky let out a sigh. "Yeah, we're working on that," he said. He raised his eyes at the thief, who gave him a barely perceptible nod.

Shaky turned back to the homeless man and looked. Thorpe was standing there, just looking straight ahead. The beer bottle was held cradled in his left arm, and the prescription in his right. His eyes stared at nothing.

Too damn cool, thought Shaky.

Then, like the mouse, Willie went into convulsions. He dropped to the floor and went fetal, his legs kicking backward, his hands balling against his stomach as he contracted and heaved. Shaky was so astonished he bent to help, but the thief waved him away.

So Shaky stood by and observed, taking mental notes. How long it was lasting, what kind of injuries Willie was inflicting on himself, and so on. He thought about grabbing a notepad, but he was too mesmerized, wondering if Willie was going to up and die in his apartment. That would be really bad. And if it happened, he was going to give the thief holy hell.

Willie was in such bad shape to begin with that the damage he inflicted on himself caused severe consequences— his nose began to bleed, and bubbly blood foamed on his lips. He made a strange, whirring noise like an overheated engine. His eyes fluttered open, then closed.

The thief began to look concerned. He determinedly avoided looking at Shaky, which scared the scientist.

He's thinking the old bastard's gonna eat it, too. What have I gotten myself into?

Strangely, his agony didn't affect Shaky the same way the mouse's had.

Then Willie went limp. Shaky heard him panting, then an odd groan.

He leaned over the old man, whose eyes were open, and very blank. So he was going to live after all . . . at least for a while. Shaky was flooded with relief. He had never had to think about how to move a dead body out of his place before, and he hoped he would never have to again.

He gave Willie a little longer to recuperate. Then he waved a hand in front of the old man's eyes.

Willie was still breathing, but he didn't blink. His lips parted slackly.

The man glanced at the thief, who gestured at him as if to say, *Be my guest.*

Shaky stared at him a moment. Then he said, "Willie, sit up."

Willie did so, raising himself off the floor with great difficulty. He hunched over, hands dangling in his lap, looking like a lumpy old stuffed animal someone had just plopped on the floor. It was a wonder he didn't sag right back over and collapse.

Shaky stared at the thief, who chuckled and folded his arms, cocking his head as if he didn't quite believe what was happening, either. Shaky's world was shifting upside down, and his mind was whirling. His heart pounded. This was too amazing! If he didn't know better, he would have sworn that the thief had set this whole thing up, paid Willie to knock on the door and go through with the charade. It was the kind of thing Shaky himself would do . . . if he had the resources.

I have the resources now, he thought. *Oh, my God, do I.*

He said more steadily, "Willie, stand up."

The poor old man had to work very hard to fulfill the command, but it was obvious that he really, really wanted to do it. It was all he wanted to do—he completely ignored the outstretched beer in Shaky's hand.

"So," Shaky said to the thief.

The thief waved an imperious hand at their . . . at their *zombie.* Shaky wanted to pinch himself. Their zombie!

"Pick up the bottle and the prescription, Willie," he said, indicating the desk.

Without acknowledging him, the old man did just that.

"Put them back down."

Willie complied.

Wow!

"You see?" said the thief. "You *can* see, can't you?"

Shaky felt his heart thudding in his chest as he nodded eagerly. Oh yes, he could see all right. He could *see*! The possibilities of a psychotropic like this, of something he could use, learn, expand on . . .

He wondered how far he could take it.

"Go downstairs," the thief said to Willie. "And step in front of the next bus you see."

"Hey, wait," Shaky said, horrified. "Wait just a minute."

The man gave him a tired, cynical look. "You wait. This is my gig. Unless you're fond of the old guy? Sounds to me like he ripped you off. Don't you want to take it to the limit? See how far we can push him? Cuz if you ain't got the stuff, there's a dozen more like you. All I have to do is spin a dial and take my pick of partners."

"No, wait," Shaky pleaded. "But . . . they'll—they'll autopsy him. They'll find the . . . stuff."

The thief chuckled. "Not in this town, Dr. Innocent. They don't cut open homeless derelicts. They don't have the money or the manpower. Autopsies are expensive. Unless there's foul play involved, they'll throw him in a box, run it through the crematorium, and forget about him."

While they were arguing, the old man turned and walked toward the door, his eyes focused on a far-off place.

"Wait," Shaky whispered, but the thief held up his left hand. His right went into his jacket, and Shaky thought, *Oh, my God, does he have a gun?*

Willie turned the knob. The thief looked challengingly at Shaky.

Willie opened the door and paused on the threshold.

"Walk in front of the first bus you see," the thief repeated calmly.

Willie, don't do it, Shaky thought; but another part of him was urging Willie on. This whole deal was evil and exciting and beyond anything he had ever imagined in his life. It was exactly what he'd been writing grants about, trying to keep body and soul together with writing his stupid fake prescriptions; wondering each morning if he was going to get busted—*again*—and sent away—*again*—and never see anything more exciting than the cracks running down his walls and the cockroaches skittering across his floor.

Without a single look back, the old drunk exited, and the scientist heard him clumping down the stairs.

A thrill raced up his spine as he and the thief moved to the window.

In silence they watched.

Willie exited the building and walked toward the street. Shaky's heart caught. He found himself whispering, "Go, go, go," like an armchair quarterback glued to the set.

The bus that ran from the university to downtown zoomed around the curve.

Oh, God, no, don't do it. Don't, Willie!

He opened his mouth to warn off the old man. Just as spontaneously, he clamped it shut.

"Go," the thief whispered. "Do it."

The bus rattled closer. The old man stared straight ahead.

Shaky watched as the old man looked over and saw the bus coming.

As it neared the front of his building, Willie took a sudden step forward.

The bus hit him square on.

Willie's body was tossed forward like a baseball from a

pitcher's hand. Then the wheels on the bus rolled over his old body.

The scientist let out a breath he didn't realize he'd been holding.

"Cool," the thief said.

Shaky turned from the window. True to his name, he was shaking.

He went to the fridge and bought out a bottle of vodka, which he liked to drink chilled. He unscrewed the cap and took a hefty swig, then handed it to the thief.

"Cool," Shaky agreed, trying very hard to smile. "Very cool."

CHAPTER ELEVEN

About half an hour after the crash, Lex's personal mechanic rode along in the flatbed truck that came to pick up the Porsche and supervised the loading of the once-beautiful car with a crane.

A driver had come with a Mercedes—*one that has lots of metal,* Lex thought, amused. *In case we have another crash. When it comes to me and cars, it's safe not to make assumptions that lightning—or car wrecks—won't strike five or six times in the same place.*

Taking one look at Clark, who appeared to be drained and tired, Lex told the driver they would take Clark home first.

Clark protested mildly, but the truth was that he was exhausted, and he wanted to see if his father had phoned to report on his mother's condition. By the time they got to the Kent farm, Pete was there. He was milking Mary and Elizabeth, two of the dairy cows. A large woven basket of chicken eggs sat on the ground beside him in the barn.

"Hey," he said, as Lex and Clark walked up. "What happened, man? I thought you'd be here hours ago."

"We had a little accident," Clark began; then at his friend's look of alarm, added quickly, "but we're both fine."

"Well, I got the eggs, and I'm working on the cows," Pete said, wiping his forehead. "Takes me back to the days when my family had more livestock." He grinned. "And reminds me that I don't miss 'em."

Clark smiled.

Lex rubbed his hands together, and said, "I'll make some breakfast."

"That's okay," Clark said. Then he realized that Lex wanted to stick around, help out in some way. He hid a smile, unable to imagine Lex doing farm chores. "Thanks." Clark picked up the basket of eggs and handed them to Lex.

Lex glanced down at the eggs, then up at Clark. "Can't say they're not farm fresh," he said. "An omelet good with you both?"

"Sure. Thanks," Pete said gratefully. "I've been working up quite an appetite."

"Okay. I'll get started." Lex looked at Clark over his shoulder as he began to walk out of the barn. "You wanted to check your phone messages?"

Clark paused, feeling a bit awkward. In an effort to save a few dollars—the farm, as usual, hovered on the brink of insolvency—his mother had canceled their voice messaging service and bought an old answering machine at the Smallville Hospital thrift shop. There was no way to listen to the messages without playing them back on the speaker. If his father made any reference to his special gifts on the message, Lex would hear it. On the other hand, Clark wanted to know if he had called in to report on his mom.

Unaware of Clark's dilemma, Lex glanced expectantly at Clark. Clark licked his lips, and said to Pete, "I'll be right back."

The phone machine was in the kitchen. The light was blinking, signaling that someone had called.

Lex set the basket of eggs down beside it and picked an egg up in his hand. He smiled faintly.

"Amazing," he said. "They're still warm. I had an omelet in France once that was to die for. My father bribed the chef to give us the recipe, and I swear he lied when he wrote out the ingredients. We could never duplicate it."

The phone machine sat waiting. Clark finally said, "Uh, Lex? I . . . I'd like to listen to my messages in private."

Lex blinked, then said, "Of course, Clark." But his voice was a little strained.

Uncomfortable and a little defensive, Clark mentally cataloged several times in the last month that Lex had wandered off with his cell phone while in Clark's company, taking and making calls.

I guess I'm not as important as he is, Clark thought, then caught how petty that sounded and flushed, as Lex wandered out of the kitchen.

Turning down the volume, Clark hit REWIND and waited while the answering machine chugged along.

Then he heard his father's voice.

"Son? It's Dad. She's a lot better. Sitting up . . . hold on."

"Clark? Hi." It was his mother. Warmth spread through his body, and he smiled as he listened to her weak but steady voice. "Don't forget Elizabeth's antibiotics. And we should probably throw away her milk."

He nodded. The vet had been out to see Lizzie, and declared that she had a bit of a bovine sickness that was not harmful, but needed seeing to.

"I'm better, honey. It was something I ate, apparently." She sounded almost chipper. "I'm on a liquid diet right now, so your father is going to sneak me in a sandwich from the cafeteria."

"Oh. I guess he's not home," she continued. Then she said away from the speaker, "But Jonathan, I'm starving!"

"Doctor's orders," his father said in the background. Then Jonathan said into the phone, "I guess you're out doing the chores. Call us, son. Your mother misses you."

The call ended. It was followed by another one . . . from Chloe.

"Hey," she said. "Your mom's better, so Lana and I went home. Take care. Give us a call."

There were no more calls. Lex must have been nearby, for he came into the kitchen and said, a bit brusquely, "So. All done?"

"Yeah. Thanks." Clark moved away from the phone machine.

"Good. Because I have an omelet to cook." He opened up a drawer and pulled out a wire whisk. "Any word on your mom?"

"She's awake. And much better. They still think it was something she ate."

"Not at my house," Lex said tersely. "Which reminds me, I have a call to make, too." He paused.

Private, too. Clark said, "Mom wants me to check on Elizabeth. Our cow." He gave Lex a wave and went back out the door.

The day was fresh and clean, the kind of day that made him understand why his parents worked so hard to keep the farm going. Sunlight glittered on tidy rows of vegetables in his mother's organic gardens. The aroma of damp earth and fresh produce was heady and good. There was no city job that could compare with the sense of satisfaction one could get from walking on one's own land and seeing the efforts of one's labor. As his father liked to say, "It makes perfect sense to me that the Garden of Eden *was* a garden."

In the barn, Pete was hefting a pail of milk. Clark rushed over to him, and said, "Did you put both the cows' milk in there?"

"No. Your mom said something the other day about Elizabeth being sick." He handed the pail to Clark. "This is from Mary. So, how is your mom?"

"Talking. Razzing my dad." A wide smile split Clark's face. He hadn't really felt the tension in his body until now, when it was a little safer to relax. A suicide, a funeral, the hospital, a car wreck . . . everything had mounted up. But it felt as though the bad times were beginning to end.

"That's awesome," Pete said. "I'm really glad, Clark."

They smiled at each other. Then Clark said, "You know, with that phone machine my mom bought . . . I was worried that my father might say something . . . that he shouldn't."

"Got you." Pete walked back toward the barn door with Clark. "Especially with being up all night and so worried about your mom. He could have easily forgotten to be careful." He looked at Clark. "So, what happened with this car wreck?"

Clark flashed him a sheepish grin. "I rolled his Porsche."

"Get out!" Pete stopped walking. "His *Porsche*?"

"This guy was running across the road . . ." His grin faded. "Man, Pete, I could have hit him. Lex turned the wheel just in time."

"Whoa."

The reality that he might have killed someone this morning finally hit home.

There's a lot of dying in Smallville, he remembered one of them—someone in the group—saying to that new girl, Rebecca. She had looked really freaked out.

"Well, Clark, you *didn't* hit him," Pete finished. "And your mom's on the mend. It's all good."

"Yeah. Back to normal."

Pete slid him a sly glance. "Which means that you can spend today working on your farm implement report."

Clark winced and groaned. And then nodded.

They dumped Elizabeth's milk, washed up at the sink next to the barn, and ambled into the farmhouse.

Lex had just finishing scooping two halves of a fantastic-looking omelet onto two plates. As the guys sauntered in, he gestured to them, and said, "Your timing couldn't be better. *Bon appétit.*"

"Aren't you joining us?" Clark asked.

"Can't," Lex replied. "I have a houseguest. She's waiting for me."

I'll bet, Clark thought, grinning to himself.

"Don't worry, Clark. Someday you'll have a 'house-guest' too," Pete drawled. He washed his hands and dried them on a towel.

"She's a good Catholic houseguest," Lex drawled.

Then, as Lex picked up his black leather jacket, which he had slung over one of the dining room chairs, he saw the wadded-up sheaf of papers that comprised Pete's first draft of his pesticides report.

"What's this?" Lex asked. He chuckled. "The word 'fertilizer' jumped out at me."

"Go ahead and read it. It's for a history project we're doing," Clark told him. It was only then that he caught Pete's anxious expression.

Lex looked interested. He bowed his head and began to scan, then frowned and read aloud.

". . . 'commercial fertilizers such as those produced at LuthorCorp's factory in Smallville release significant amounts of lead, cadmium, and arsenic into the ecosystem, causing equal or greater harm as is generally associated with pesticide use. But while the creation of the multibillion-dollar pesticides industry has received much criticism for the unhealthy effects of its products, fertilizer development has grown alongside it without as much public outcry. Yet the fact remains that commercial fertilizers can and do cause serious diseases in humans and animals.' "

He looked up at Clark. "Are you writing some kind of exposé piece on my factory, Clark?"

Clark's lips parted. He was shocked. Pete had assured him there was nothing in there that would slam Lex's business.

"I wrote it," Pete said.

"But it's got Clark's name on it," Lex said slowly. His eyes were clouded with questions . . . and anger, too. "And as for your research, it's faulty at best."

Pete reached out his hand for the report. He said, "I'm just reporting what I found."

"You've drawn some fairly dramatic conclusions," Lex argued. He looked over at Clark. "So, you're putting your name on this?"

"I . . . I don't know," Clark said. "I'll have to read it."

"I thought you had by now," Pete said irritably. "It's getting pretty close to the deadline for you to expect me to take another tack. And besides, this is what I found to be true." He frowned at Lex. "I didn't make up the statistics on page two, Lex. I'm sure you know by now that a lot of dangerous chemicals go into the process of making your fertilizer."

"There are standards, and we meet them," Lex shot back. He thrust the report at Pete.

As he slung his jacket over his shoulder, he said to Clark, "I thought we were friends."

"We are," Clark said, bewildered by the turn of events, the sudden, thick tension in the air.

"Oh," Lex said coolly.

He headed for the door.

"Lex!" Clark called after him. "Wait!"

Clark looked through the kitchen window at the retreating figure. He was very familiar with the hunched, squared way Lex was holding his shoulders, the way he was stomping across the field. Lex Luthor was pissed off.

He turned to Pete, and said, "You told me you're weren't going to get into his face."

"He shouldn't be surprised by what I wrote in there," Pete rejoined. "These are commonly known facts."

"You've said that about three times now." Clark turned away, not sure what to do or say next.

"There's no getting around the fact that the fertilizer factory isn't that great for our environment." Pete looked at Clark as if he were insane. "Or have you rationalized that because you like Lex?"

"That's just . . . strange," Clark said. He picked up his plate. "I'm hungry," he announced.

Pete followed him to the table. "Are you going to put your name on this? Because I'm not rewriting it, Clark. You've taken so long to get around to it, and—"

"I've been a little busy. My mom is in the hospital," Clark reminded him.

There was a long silence between them. Then Pete put the paper down on the table.

"Pete," Clark tried again.

Pete sighed heavily. "I guess I knew you wouldn't like it. That's why I got so defensive. But it's all true. You should read some of the environmental briefs that were filed when the town tried to stop the Luthors from building the plant. It's scary how toxic some of that stuff is."

"Not the whole town. And lawyers always exaggerate."

"Even if they did, they can't alter the basic facts." Pete held out his hands. "What do you want me to do, Clark, not tell the truth? Not mention things that might hurt Lex's standing in Smallville? Because it won't affect his bottom line. Nobody cares what kind of garbage he makes down at the plant, as long as the yield per acre stays solid."

We're having almost the same conversation we had with Chloe, Clark thought. *This is so weird.*

"I don't know," he said honestly. "Let's eat."

"Okay," Pete grumped.

The two friends sat down. Pete picked up his fork. Clark followed suit, and they both dug into the omelet.

It was incredibly salty. Way too salty.

Clark glanced over at Pete, and they both burst into laughter.

"Okay. If he'd been here, would you have told him his cooking sucks?" Pete demanded, cracking up. "Or said nothing and eaten it?"

"We'll never know," Clark said archly.

They both carried their plates to the sink. Pete leaned against the counter while Clark scraped their breakfasts into his mother's portable composter.

"Careful. There's so much salt in that stuff, it might hurt her garden," Pete said.

"I was just thinking the same thing," Clark admitted.

They both started laughing again, harder and harder. It was pure tension release, and it felt great.

Lex pondered Pete's report on his drive back home; he was still thinking about it when he let himself in.

Drew met him at the door, a sharp expression of concern on his face, as he said, "Mr. Luthor, there's been a burglary."

"Burglary!" Marica shouted as she stood on the stairs, gazing down at the two of them. She was wearing black

leather trousers and a scarlet blouse, and she looked amazing.

As she came down the stairs, she launched into a barrage of Spanish, some of which Lex actually understood. He spoke passable French, and Spanish was in the same class of languages—the Romance languages—although it was clear she was not discussing anything good, she stomped toward him.

"I don't think it can be called a burglary when the man who owns this house took it," she said. Fuming, she planted her hands on her hips as she glared up at Lex. She was so close to him that he could smell the scent of French-milled lavender soap on her skin. He was distracted by her fresh beauty and the astonishing force of her indignation, and he simply stared at her for a few moments.

"You stole my fertilizer!" she snapped at him, and it sounded so comical he almost laughed aloud. But he understood that someone had actually gone into her room and taken it, and that was a serious breach of security.

Lex glanced at Drew, silently asking him if he had figured out the details. As Drew raised his brows and shook his head, Lex politely took Marica's arm and led her into the library.

He closed the door. "I didn't steal it," he said flatly. "Are you sure Drew didn't move it for safekeeping? Put it in the safe? Maybe it was the maid when she was cleaning. After all, it was just dirt." He avoided the temptation to remind her that he had suggested she put it in his wall safe, and she had demurred. She hadn't wanted to let it out of her sight. Without waiting for her to answer—his question was rather inane—he picked up the phone and called Security.

"Your guy already did that," Marica said over his voice as he instructed the two house guards to meet him in the library immediately. "And they said they couldn't find anything."

"That's ridiculous." He gestured for her to have a seat, but she remained standing.

"Someone came into my room while I was sleeping," she said, as if that had not occurred to him. "Was it you?"

"No, Señorita Lopez. I assure you it was not," he said. He thought a moment. "Tell me again what you told me last night."

She shook her head. "I will not," she informed him coldly. "You are not to be trusted. I will inform the authorities and . . ." She trailed off, looking confused.

"No proof," he said, practically reading her mind. Her eyes flashed, and he held up his hand. "Hear me out," he said, then gestured to two chairs by the leaded-glass windows.

There was a soft, polite knock on the door.

"Come in," Lex said patiently.

It was Drew. "Would you like some coffee?" he asked.

"Very much." Lex smiled at Marica. "Miss Lopez?"

"No, *gracias*," she snapped.

"Just for me."

"There are croissants," Drew added. "I'll bring some. Miss Lopez likes them very much."

He shut the door. Lex shrugged as if to apologize for his staff, then folded his hands and made a steeple, thinking through what he was about to tell this woman, who was, for many intents and purposes, a virtual stranger. And someone, for all he knew, who had made up this entire story in order to extract cash or something else from the Luthor family.

"As I mentioned last night," he began, "my father and I have a . . . complicated relationship. And as you know,

LuthorCorp is an enormous conglomerate. A lot goes on that I don't know about. But my father always knows about everything."

"And you admire him for that," she shot at him.

His smiled faintly, but didn't respond. "It concerns me greatly that someone came into your room without your permission."

There was another knock on the door, and Drew reappeared with the coffee. Two of Lex's burly security men were with him.

Without preamble, one of them came to Lex and asked to speak to him . . . alone.

Lex said to Marica, "Pardon me a moment," and walked with the guard to the window.

"The window in the lady's room wasn't completely closed," the guard said. "We're wondering if someone came that way. Scaled up the wall. There are no footprints in the mud, of course, with the rain."

"Of course," Lex said smoothly. "How about the doorknob? Could you find anything there? Any prints?"

They discussed their investigative methods at length; Lex was pleased to see that they had already gone through their paces, yet very angry that someone had walked into the room of a guest and taken her belongings. The other man appeared to read Lex's expression, for he stammered an apology before he left the room.

After the two men were gone, and he and Marica were alone again, Lex said, "When I was a boy, I had a pet spider monkey named Coconut. I don't think he ever stole fertilizer, but we did find a pair of my father's diamond cuff links in his bed."

Marica shook her head and began to rise. "There's no point in my staying here any longer," she said angrily. "As you pointed out, I have no proof, and without proof, there is nothing I can do to stop you from what you're doing."

"I'm not doing it," he said, gazing hard at her. "I swear to you. But if it was my father—and like you, I have no proof of that—I can tell you that he knows some very dangerous people."

"Are you threatening me?" she demanded, her voice rising.

"I'm *warning* you," he replied.

She looked at him, and he saw a flicker of fear.

"I think you're safer staying with me than if you leave here." He moved his shoulders, amazingly tired. "At least you have a home base here. And someone who believes you."

And even then, he wondered if she was setting him up in some complicated scheme.

"If you believe me, then help me look for it," she told him.

Lex poured himself a cup of fragrant coffee and grabbed a croissant. What he wouldn't give for a few moments to put up his feet and read *The Wall Street Journal*.

"Of course," he said. He carried the cup and croissant with him as they left the library.

They scoured the house, and the sample was nowhere to be found. Marica became increasingly angry as they searched, more than once threatening to leave, until Lex reminded her that she might be in danger.

Finally, they took a golf cart to the main warehouse in search of more of the doctored fertilizer. If it was coming from his plant, there was the off chance that the material was just sitting out on a pallet, awaiting shipment to Haiti. At least, that was Marica's hope. He was a bit dubious, but he was glad to accommodate her insistence that they begin a sweep of all the warehouses and outbuildings, just in case.

Turning the matter this way and that had been exhausting; now they began to move onto other topics as they spent the day together. Their current subject was relationships . . . which Lex figured was natural enough, given that they were both young, attractive people used to getting what they wanted.

"Well, there's love, and then there's tension release," Lex observed, as they whirred along in the cart toward the large metal building. The vehicle was an experimental prototype that ran on fuel extracted from corn, and he had high hopes for it.

There was a guardhouse in front of it, with orange-and-white-striped barriers over the entrance and exit for cars and trucks. Lex was having all the plant's security procedures reviewed. He'd never dreamed anyone would want to steal his company's product.

Now, if I ran a diamond mine, that'd be different . . .

"Tension release," Marica drawled. "How romantic."

He sensed that the way to this woman's heart was honesty, and he liked that. Shrugging, he smiled at her, and said, "More often than not, a relationship is really an excuse for the latter, don't you think?"

"Spoken like a man," she pronounced.

His smile grew. "It's true. You've seen the world. You know how it is. Would you rather people keep to the polite conventions, pretend it's always love?"

She had been grilling him about the amount and variety of clothing and grooming items he kept on hand for "overnight guests." He had offered her a choice of black leather pants or jeans, a slinky scarlet top or a peasant blouse. In a way, she found it rather gallant, but on the other, it spoke volumes about his interest in commitment.

She had opted for the black leather and scarlet. They both wore black hard hats, with LUTHORCORP painted on them.

"In my culture, men do keep to the polite conventions in these matters," she informed him.

He inclined his head as he steered the cart, one part of his mind assessing the prototype's performance on the fuel. Smooth ride, no glitches. He might have a winning product on his hands.

"Ah, yes," he said, sliding a glance her way. "The hidden mistress. Why do you women put up with that? Say nothing, and let it go on?"

"I didn't say I would put up with it." She had a faraway look in her eyes as she added, "and I wouldn't keep my silence. I'm rather religious, Lex. You must have noticed that."

"Yes," he admitted.

"I wanted to become a nun when I was a little girl. I've always been interested in helping people who were not as fortunate as I. Then I wanted to become a missionary at one point in college. My parents compromised and allowed me to work for AYUDO. So . . ." She smiled at him. "Just so you know, I won't be borrowing any of your nightgowns."

"My loss," he said. "Truly." Then he cocked his head and gave her an assessing once-over. *God, she's beautiful. I can't imagine her as a nun.*

I can, however, imagine her in one of "my" nightgowns.

"You're big on saying what's on your mind," he said. "I really think you should be careful until we know what's going on. It could get you into serious trouble."

Her smile faded. "It already has."

The moment was lost, the conversation too lighthearted for the matter at hand. He was learning how to read her, and she was more afraid than she was letting on. While that fear lent credence to her story, it made the break-in into her room even more alarming. He had already given Drew the go-ahead to replace the entire mansion security staff. When he and Marica returned from the warehouse, new people would be guarding her room tonight.

He gave the warehouse security guard a wave and the man tipped his own hard hat, raising the barrier across the vehicular entry for Lex's cart.

Then they drove from the bright Kansas sunshine into the dim warehouse. The smell of chemicals hit Marica's nose, and she sneezed. As she surveyed the vast warehouse in wonderment, she said softly, "If something's in here, we'll never find it."

I tried to tell you that, Lex thought to himself, but remained silent.

"Where to begin?" she murmured.

"Exports," Lex suggested. He hung a right and headed for the northwest quadrant of the warehouse. "You are aware that we have off-site fulfillment centers as well?"

"I have nothing better to do," she said, "and I don't care if you do."

Olé, Lex thought admiringly. *Maybe I really* am *in love.*

Row upon row of large plastic bags were piled all the way up to the ceiling. There were towers of fertilizer as far as they could see, and Marica was taking it all in with an air of mild astonishment.

Yes, it's all mine, he thought, with no small measure of self-deprecation. *I am the king of fertilizer.*

She looked at him with a little grin, as if she knew what

he was thinking. Then, growing more serious, she said, "They could use this in Haiti. The good stuff, I mean."

He nodded, wondering if he could arrange some shipments as a humanitarian effort . . . after this current situation died down. It would be a nice write-off . . . and she would appreciate it.

"Do you ever think you'll go back?" he asked her. "Work on a different project in Haiti?"

She shivered. "I haven't even thought about it. I have a mission now. This is life and death, Lex."

I'm beginning to believe that, he thought.

He steered the cart around a corner, where he caught sight of someone run-walking from one aisle to the next in an almost furtive motion, and he gave the cart horn a little beep.

The figure stopped as if he had been pinned to the wall by a searchlight and slowly turned.

It was Tom Morhaim, the new hire with a police record. Was it Lex's imagination, or did the guy look guilty about something?

What's he doing in the warehouse? His job site's on the third floor of the main building.

"Hey, Tom," Lex said easily.

"Mr. Luthor." Tom gave his boss a nod. "Mr. Hamilton sent me to see if we have any spare fertilizer for your tiger orchids."

"Tiger orchids? What are those?" Marica asked.

"I grow them. As a hobby," Lex said. "I have a few specimens in my private office in the building. As a rule, they're only cultivated in Indonesia." So it made sense that Jack Hamilton had sent Tom to check in the export area.

Still, it's pretty interesting that we're looking for something that's been stolen, and we've come upon a thief . . .

"Have you seen any containers marked for delivery to Haiti?" Marica asked, bulldozing over Lex's authority. "Specifically Port-au-Prince?"

"No, ma'am," Tom said. Lex watched him carefully for signs that he might be lying. There were none.

"But I haven't been looking for any. I'm here for the stuff for tiger orchids."

She looked dispirited. "As if it would just be sitting out," she muttered. "This is ridiculous."

"That's often the safest place to hide something," Lex observed. "Out in the open."

She humphed and said nothing.

They drove around the stacks, but after an hour, she turned to him, and said, "Let's go back to your house."

I did have a full day of meetings scheduled, he thought. But instead, he said, "All right."

She looked around anxiously as the cart shuttled back out of the warehouse and into the sun.

"I'm a sitting duck," she said.

Lex replied, "Don't worry, *señorita.* I'll make sure you're safe."

She looked at him anxiously. "Will you really, Lex? Or should I be afraid of you?"

Their gazes locked. He found her an intriguing mix of real bravado, false courage, and an honesty that was rare these days. He really liked her.

"You have nothing to fear from me," he said. "I promise you. I'll protect you from whatever comes."

She looked unconvinced. "You didn't see what I saw," she told him quietly.

"And what was it that you did see?" he asked her.

She looked him full in the face. Her dark eyes were

troubled; tears welled, and he was astonished at the misery written across her face.

"Hell, Lex. I saw hell." Tears slid down her cheeks. "I'm scared," she admitted. "So scared."

"Marica . . ." He took a breath. What was happening here? "Marica, I'm here for you."

She closed her eyes. "I've been so tired."

"I'm here," he said softly.

CHAPTER TWELVE

Clark did the best he could on the farm implements report, but he kept looking over the paper Pete had written. It was extremely critical of both pesticides and fertilizers, and it was well researched. Pete had worked hard.

Clark still couldn't help wondering if his mom had suffered some kind of reaction to something at Lex's house, something that had to do with his business. There were probably traces of chemicals in the mansion that Lex's system had gotten used to. She was known for her organically grown produce, and she had spoken many times against the amount of chemicals put into the earth by commercial agribusiness. She had not wanted the fertilizer factory, either, even though she had eventually gone to work for Lionel Luthor. When she married Jonathan Kent, she married the land he loved as well.

He finished the paper and did some more chores. He was about to call Chloe when his father came home, looking tired but far more relaxed than Clark had seen him in days.

"She wants to come home," he told his son, "but they're going to run a few more tests."

"Can I go see her now?" Clark asked.

"She can't wait," Jonathan said.

"Did you really sneak her in a sandwich from the cafeteria?"

Jonathan smiled. "Now, Clark, your mother and I have to have *some* little secrets just between us . . ."

Clark chuckled. "You didn't," he guessed.

Feigning innocence, Jonathan raised his brows, and said,

"Ask her when you see her." He fished out the keys to the truck and handed them to Clark. "Drive carefully, son."

Clark decided that now was not the time to tell his father about rolling the Porsche. Feeling a little guilty about concealing it, he took the keys and headed for the door.

Clark drove to the hospital, remembering the man who had darted out in front of the car. *How would I feel if I killed somebody?* he thought. *Because I'm strong enough to do it without sitting behind the wheel of a car. I'm going to have to be careful all the time . . .*

His gloom dissipated as he drove into the hospital parking lot and entered the hospital. On impulse, he stopped at the gift shop and looked around for something to buy her. He saw a picture frame surrounded by sunflowers on sale.

An older woman behind the cash register smiled at him. She said, "This for your girlfriend, honey?"

"My mom." He flushed.

She beamed at him and carefully wrapped the frame in pink tissue paper. She added a bow and handed the package back to him.

"She's lucky to have such a nice young man for a son," she said. Then her face turned wistful. "My grandson was diagnosed with multiple sclerosis recently."

He glanced down at her name tag. It read MATHILDE BROOK. Jake Brook was her grandson.

He swallowed hard, and said, "Thanks, ma'am. And I'm sorry."

She looked sad. "He's such a good boy. You wonder why these things happen . . . well." She changed her tone of voice, brightening up. "Go and give your mom a kiss."

"I will."

And he did, when he came into the room and found her reading a book about edible landscaping. Her glasses had slid down to the end of her nose , but she didn't seem to notice. When she saw him, it was as if the sun had risen in her face. She positively glowed.

"Clark." She held up a hand.

"Hi, Mom." He bent over and kissed her. Then he said, "I brought you a present."

"Oh, Clark. You shouldn't have." She looked enormously pleased. She looked at it for a moment, then handed it back to him. "Could you unwrap it for me? I'm pretty tired."

That scared him a little. The thing was only wrapped with tissue paper and Scotch tape. Concealing his unease, he smiled at her, and said, "Sure."

He unwrapped it and handed it to her. She beamed at him. "Oh, honey, it's lovely." She held it against her chest.

"Dad told me he really did sneak you a sandwich," he tested.

She winked at him. "Now, honey, married people need to have a few secrets."

He was astonished. Sometimes his parents really were like two halves of the same person.

They talked for a while, watched a little TV together, then the nurse shooed him out because visiting hours were over.

It was dark. He was surprised so much time had passed, and he wondered if his father had been able to get the basic chores done without him.

He got into the car and turned on the radio, then decided to swing by the minimart to grab a soda. Soon he was trundling down Main Street, glancing over at the Talon and wondering if Lana was working, and remembering that he had never called Chloe back.

He hung a U to go into the drive-through when he noticed a flash of light in the alley next to the sporting goods store.

Curious, he skipped the entrance to the drive-through and turned into the alley.

Someone was crawling into the store's transom window.

When Clark's headlights shone on the person's body, the man fell back out of the window and landed on his butt in a puddle.

It was Marshall Hackett.

"Hey," Clark said. He got out of the truck and hurried over to Marshall, who was trying to wipe muddy water off the sleeve of his letterman's jacket. His jeans were wet around the thighs.

Marshall glared blearily up at him. "Kent," he said with derision. "You in love with me or something? You're always around."

The smell of alcohol hit Clark full force. Marshall was very drunk. He said, "Let me help you up."

"Go 'way." Marshall flailed at the window. "Gonna steal a shotgun."

"Come on." Clark helped him to his feet and guided him toward the truck. "I'll drive you home."

"Oh, God, don' do that," Marshall pleaded, his face betraying panic and despair. He pawed at Clark like a wounded animal. "We're all dead there. We're zombies." He burst into tears. "How could he do that? How could he?"

"I don't know," Clark said honestly. "I'm sorry, Marshall. I really am."

"Didn't he love us?" he wailed, stumbling. "How could he kill himself?"

Clark was at a loss. There were no answers, and saying he was sorry only went so far. Of course he was sorry. Everyone was sorry. But that didn't bring Marshall's father back to life, or make Jake Brooks well.

"Why?" Marshall asked again, stumbling. "Just tell me why!"

Then a voice behind them said, "Because he couldn't get past his own pain. It doesn't mean he didn't love you. He just hurt too much."

Clark wheeled around, taking Marshall with him.

Silhouetted beneath the streetlight at the other end of the alley stood a girl with her hair piled on top of her head. A decoration of some kind was stuck in it—like a Chinese chopstick, and she had on a black V-neck sweater and faded jeans. Heavy makeup, big earrings. She looked very arty and exotic.

It was the new girl, Rebecca Morhaim.

"Rebecca, hi," Clark said. "What are you doing out here?"

She hesitated, twisting her hands together until she seemed to realize what she was doing and dropped them to her side. "I . . . Chloe dropped me off and . . ."

Marshall stiffened. "It was because of *her.* That Sullivan bitch." He staggered; Clark kept him upright as he began to cry. "I'm gonna kill her!" He tried to push Clark out of the way. "Gonna steal a shotgun!"

"Marshall, you're upset," Clark said, restraining him, mindful of his own strength. "You don't know what you're saying." *And you shouldn't be saying it, at least not around strangers.*

"Be careful. Drunks are trouble," Rebecca said to Clark. Then she looked flustered, as if she realized she was in the middle of a situation that had nothing to do with her, and said, "I—I have to go."

"Wait." Clark glanced back at the truck, trying to figure out how to take care of both Marshall and her. He couldn't just leave her there without a way back. "Do you need a ride home?"

She hesitated, scanning the area. Beneath the streetlight she looked lost and alone. She was very small, and the harsh light gave her the appearance of being trapped in the glare. Without completely understanding his reaction, he felt for her, sensing that she was troubled about something.

"I'm . . . I was supposed to meet my dad here," she said. "Pretty soon. Um, he's . . . he'll be here soon, I mean."

In an alley?

Red-faced, as if she realized how implausible that sounded, she put her arms around herself and smiled weakly at Clark. Her black sweater was thin, and a slice of her belly was showing above her jeans. Clark was impervious to temperature, but he figured she must be awfully chilly.

"I don't think he'd want you out here by yourself," he told her. "It's getting late."

She looked left, right, and the expression on her face reminded him of a lost child. There was definitely something up with her. Then she said, "Maybe we got our wires crossed. Maybe he's waiting for me at home." She unwrapped her arms from around her waist, and said, "Yeah, maybe I would like a ride home after all. Thanks."

There was an edge to her tone that Clark didn't understand, but he led the way back to the truck, Marshall in tow.

They had to sit three abreast, Marshall shotgun and Rebecca in the middle. She smelled good, of makeup and perfume, and Clark thought of Lana.

Why can't I just move on?

Rebecca was checking him out, too; he could tell, could feel her eyes on his profile. He wondered what she saw, what she thought of him. He knew that if he turned his head now, their gazes would lock.

He kept his eyes on the road.

She's pretty, she's nice . . . what is it about Lana that keeps me there?

Then the moment passed. Marshall's head fell back, and he started to snore, and she and Clark chuckled. Rebecca gently nudged his head toward the window so that it wouldn't end up resting against her own head. She pressed her hand against his head for a moment, then pulled it away experimentally, apparently satisfied when it remained where she had put it. Marshall murmured something, then began to snore again.

"I thought about putting him in the back," Clark told her. "I'm sorry. I should have."

"No. This way, he's safe. In his condition, he might have decided to see if he could fly," Rebecca said. "I had a foster brother . . ." She caught herself. "I knew someone who saw *Mary Poppins* and jumped off the roof of his house with an umbrella. He broke his arm, but he was more upset that it hadn't worked like in the movie. 'It didn't work! It didn't work!' "

They laughed together.

Then she grew serious, and said, "What I said about drunks. That had nothing to do with my dad. I . . . I lived with relatives for a while, and one of them . . . he drank a lot. It was pretty scary."

He knew she had distinctly said "foster brother," and he knew that had nothing to do with living with relatives, but he didn't press for an explanation. He only nodded, and said, "That must have been tough."

"Yeah. I learned to handle myself around him." Then she gazed out the window for a moment, and said quietly, "Everything in my life is different now." She moved her arm to pat her hair, brushing his as he drove, and then she murmured, "Sorry," and put her hand in her lap. He ticked his glance over to her and saw her flushing in the lights from the dash.

I wonder what she thinks of me, Clark thought. *I wonder if Chloe and Lana have talked about me around her. If she knows about how things are among the three of us.*

Heck, I don't even know how things are among the three of us.

"Well, unless you're psychic," she said, "you don't know where I live."

"I'm not."

At least, not that I'm aware of. My powers have been developing as I age . . . Is that something I have to look forward to? Because from what I've seen of telepathic ability, it's not something I'd like to have to deal with.

Rebecca gave him directions, and he was still curious why she was waiting for her father in an alley instead of meeting him at home. The question hung between them, making him feel awkward, but he didn't ask it. It seemed like prying, and she was so edgy he didn't want to add to it.

She lived in a run-down apartment building in town, and it was obvious that she was embarrassed for him to see it. That might have explained her hesitation in accepting a ride from him. But on the street she had looked cold, tired, and a little frightened, and he figured those factors had mentally canceled out her shame, and so she had let him take her home.

He pulled up to the curb and saw that there were no lights on in her apartment.

He said, "Your dad's not home yet. Do you have a cell phone?"

She chuckled and said, "We can't afford something like that. He probably left me a message on the answering machine," she said, too brightly. "I'll bet he forgot he was supposed to meet me. You know how single dads are . . . Well, I guess you don't know. You have two parents." She sounded wistful, a little envious.

"I'm lucky," Clark agreed. He opened up the truck door. "I'll walk you in, make sure everything's okay."

He walked her to the door and stood by her while she fumbled with her key and finally got it into the lock. The screen door was ripped, and the hinges were rusted and needed to be replaced. He thought about how Marshall had terrorized Chloe, and for a moment anger and frustration swept through him that someone as nice as Rebecca had to live in a place like this.

After she opened the door, she reached around and switched on a light. Her look of discomfort spoke volumes: She didn't want him to see how she lived. Clark couldn't avoid a glance as she stepped inside, turning to face him as if to block his view.

"See? Everything's fine," she assured him.

He could see the living room. There was a big, ugly sofa, a cheap coffee table, and a TV on a stand. That was it. He compared the stark room to his own family's living room. His mother had worked hard to make it warm and inviting, and there were days when he walked into it that he felt the safety there, the sense of sanctuary. He doubted Rebecca felt that way in this room, especially when she had to come home to it alone.

"Want me to check the rest of your apartment for you?" he asked. Without waiting for her answer, he focused his X-ray vision and swept it through the other rooms. There was no sign of another person. No sign of much at all, in fact. The two bedrooms were very sparsely furnished, like the living room. He saw no pictures on the walls.

Well, she did say that they just moved here . . .

"No, that's fine," she answered, unaware that he had already searched her place for intruders. "But thanks. You're very gallant."

He smiled. "Chloe would probably say I'm a chauvinist."

"I like it," she admitted. Then she blushed again.

She likes me, he realized. He was flattered and embarrassed at the same time.

"Okay," she said, brightly. "I'm good." She kind of stood on the balls of her feet as if for emphasis, like a little cheerleader jump, and for a second he thought she was trying to kiss him good night. He wasn't sure what to do. She was so much shorter than he that he had to crane his neck to look at her.

Then the moment passed, and they were simply smiling at each other again.

"Okay." He nodded at her, waiting a beat. "If you're sure you're okay here by yourself."

For a moment she said nothing. It was almost as if she were holding her breath. Her eyes glittered, and her smile faded just a little as he took a step away. She wasn't okay alone.

If I didn't have Marshall to contend with, he thought, *I'd stay with her until her father got here. Maybe I should call Chloe.*

Then she said clearly, "Yeah, I'm sure. You'd better hurry. Marshall might decide he can jump out of there in one giant leap for mankind or something."

"True." He glanced over his shoulder at the truck. Marshall's head was back, his mouth tipped open. No doubt he was still snoring. "Well . . . see you Monday."

She gave him a little wave. "Thanks, Clark. If you see Chloe or Lana, please say hi for me."

He smiled at her in return. "Sure."

She waited until he was in the truck to shut the door, giving him one more wave. Clark put the truck in gear and drove off. Marshall was still passed out, still snoring, with his head tilted way back. Clark felt sorry for him, but he was also alarmed at what Marshall had said about getting a shotgun and going after Chloe.

I'd better tell Dad about it, see if we should get the sheriff involved . . .

As he was thinking about it, he saw a flash of white across the street. He leaned forward to peer through the windshield. There it was again, catty-corner, lurching past the minimart where Clark had planned to get a soda.

It was a very pale person, dressed in a navy blue sweatshirt and a pair of jeans. The way he was walking, Clark figured that, like Marshall, he had to be drunk.

It was none of Clark's business, and yet he felt strangely drawn to the stumbling man, so obviously out of control. The guy was disheveled and very disoriented, jerking forward, then stopping, then jerking forward again. He was like a battery-operated toy that was running out of juice.

Clark drove up abreast of him and looked out the driver's side window. It was dark on that side of the street, and Clark couldn't get a very good look at him. He considered using his X-ray vision but refrained, waiting to see if he could make contact by normal means.

"Hey," Clark said, rolling down the window.

The guy didn't react. He didn't even seem to notice that the truck was there. He just kept walking and stumbling on down the street. He looked drunk.

He's so white. He doesn't look real.

"Are you sick? Do you need to go to the hospital?" Clark tried again.

The guy shambled on, then jerked, stopped, and disappeared into an alley.

Okay, that was weird, Clark thought uneasily.

Then Marshall raised his head and muttered, "Kent, gonna be sick."

Great.

Marshall had the decency to wait for Clark to pull over and let him out; then Clark waited inside the truck. In less than a minute, Marshall was back inside, looking miserable.

After a few more minutes of driving, Clark pulled up to the Hackett residence, a pleasant gray two-story house with a wraparound porch. The porch light was off, but the streetlight glowed on weedy grass and a pile of newspapers beside the front door. It was as if no one had been living there. Perhaps no one was. Perhaps the best they could do was simply exist, make it from one day to the next, one hour to the next . . .

Clark was as reluctant to leave Marshall there as he had been to leave Rebecca at her house. But he hoisted the football player out of the truck and half walked, half carried him up the three cement steps, then to the front door, where he hesitated, reluctant to ring the doorbell.

Marshall slurred, "Key's in pocket."

Clark felt in Marshall's jacket and found a ring of keys. He searched through them, looking for a likely candidate, and came upon a small family photo encased in a plastic frame. From behind her husband's wheelchair, Mrs. Hackett was leaning forward, her arms draped around her husband's neck, her face pressed lovingly up against his. The boys were grouped on each side, apparently sitting on chairs. Portrait of a happy, loving family. He could almost hear the photographer ordering them around, telling them how to pose, hear the Hacketts laughing as they took their places.

Now all those faces were silent . . . and at least one of them would never laugh again.

Letting the picture go, he found the right key and opened the door, easing Marshall inside, half-expecting Marshall's mother to call out, "Where have you been?"

But there was no sound other than the *tick-tock* of a clock in the hallway. His and Marshall's footfalls provided a counterpoint as Clark turned to him, and said, "Where's your room?"

" 'Stairs," Marshall slurred, and Clark walked him to the stairs. Expecting Marshall to negotiate them was hopeless, so Clark put his arm around him and did almost all the work himself by hoisting Marshall up, so that his feet barely touched the stairs. The football player didn't notice. In his condition, there wasn't much he would notice.

Clark's efforts made considerably more noise than if a single pair of footsteps had sounded on the stairway, and he kept waiting for Mrs. Hackett to call out. Growing more concerned, he swept the Hackett home with his X-ray vision, and found two figures in two different rooms. In the largest of three bedrooms, a woman sat, clutching a photograph and weeping. In the other room, a male figure sat at the window, unmoving. Mrs. Hackett and Jeremiah. Both were awake, and yet neither called out to Marshall.

Clark found that very sad.

"Left," Marshall rasped, and at first Clark thought he was saying that he had been left, as in abandoned. Then he realized that Marshall was indicating that the door on his left was the door to his room.

Clark pushed it open and Marshall lurched forward,

falling onto the bed. Clark stood awkwardly, wondering if there was anything more he should do.

Then he turned and left, going back the way he came. As he walked down the hall, his elbow brushed a sideboard and knocked over a ceramic vase. It made a loud clatter. He grabbed it and righted it, thinking that surely now Mrs. Hackett would come to check on what was going on in her home. For all she knew, they were being burglarized.

Silence reigned through the house, except for the incessant ticking of the clock.

He thought of the saying, "Let the dead bury the dead." These people were not dead. They would come back to life, once their grieving was done.

At least, that was what he told himself as he went down the stairs and through the front door, vastly relieved to be out of the house.

When Clark got home, his father was in his robe, drinking a cup of tea and watching the news. He smiled at Clark, and said, "Did Mom finally get tired or did they throw you out?"

"Dad, the strangest thing happened," Clark replied, filling him in about Rebecca, Marshall, and the pale man who had seemed to vanish before Clark's eyes.

"Smallville. You gotta love it," Jonathan said. Then he laughed wryly, and added, "Though I'm not sure why." He looked hard at Clark. "Do you think Marshall Hackett might actually harm Chloe?"

"I don't know," Clark said truthfully.

"That family's been through so much. I'd hate to put any more pressure on any of them." He sighed, then regarded his son with an intensity that caught Clark up short.

"If anything ever happens to me, you need to stay strong. For your mother," he said levelly.

Clark raised his brows. "Of course I will."

Jonathan ran his hands through his hair and sighed heavily. "When I saw her lying there . . . I never want to feel that way again." He looked away, lost in a mix of emotions. Clark swallowed hard, remembering the panic he himself had felt.

What if I hadn't found her? What would have happened?

"The Hacketts must have been under a lot of stress, keeping a family secret like that. Always having to be careful of what they said, doing their best not to let on." As if Jonathan realized what he was saying—and drawing the same parallels Clark was drawing—he smiled wryly, and said, "But I guess every family has its secrets."

Yeah, but rocket ships in the barn probably aren't on most people's lists, Clark thought.

"Marshall was really drunk," Clark told his father. "He probably didn't know what he was doing. He didn't even get inside the sporting goods store. He couldn't possibly have taken anything."

"Then maybe we can leave it alone," Jonathan ventured. "He'll probably have forgotten all about it when he wakes up."

Clark grimaced. "I wouldn't want to be him when he does wake up. He's going to have a terrible hangover."

"This just in from Smallville," said the news anchor on the TV. *"The police have reported a rash of burglaries that have swept through the center of this small farming community. Over a four-hour span tonight, all three of the town's jewelry stores were burglarized, with sizable amounts of merchandise being stolen from each store."*

There was a shot on TV of Kendrick's, the oldest jewelry store in Smallville.

"In each case, entry was accomplished at the back of the store, through a transom window or, in one instance, by forcing the back door."

The camera traveled up the door of Kendrick's to show a small window above the doorway.

"That's how Marshall was trying to get into the sporting goods store," Clark told his father.

"Was he carrying any jewelry?" Jonathan asked his son. "Anything bulky?"

"Nothing," Clark replied.

They looked at each other. Jonathan sighed.

Clark said quickly, "Dad, we don't have any proof."

Jonathan's brow furrowed, and Clark knew he was weighing what to do. Clark's father had always stressed that justice must be tempered with compassion . . . and they had both learned that there was no such thing as black and white, right and wrong. The context of a situation could change its tenor; what might look wrong to one person could feel right to another. A military general might look upon him as a threat to national security—and on his parents as criminals for harboring him. But someone else . . . someone who loved him—would see them as Clark's true family.

On the other hand, if someone who loved him, or someone whom he loved, found out that he was an alien from outer space . . . would that person still love him? What context would she put her feelings in?

Chloe had felt that he had abandoned her at the prom to dash off on a hopelessly romantic quest to save Lana from the twister . . . when the truth was, he had been able to save Lana; if he hadn't left the prom when he did, she would have died in the storm.

"Do you want to watch any more of this?" Jonathan asked Clark. When Clark shook his head, his dad clicked off with the remote.

"We'll talk about what to do in the morning. From what you told me, Marshall's not going to be going anywhere tonight."

"That's right," Clark insisted.

Jonathan sighed. "We're going to have to get serious about helping that family out, son. They're in distress. That boy is sending out SOS messages so loudly the whole town should be able to hear them."

"Then we won't tell the sheriff?" Clark prodded. "We won't say anything?"

"Now, I didn't say that," Jonathan reminded him. "But don't dwell on that tonight. Get some sleep."

"Okay, Dad. You, too."

But Clark sincerely doubted either of them would be able to stop worrying about what to do about Marshall.

A few hours later, the sun rose, tinting the walls of Marshall Hackett's room with rosy light. He woke up slowly, groaning. His head felt as if someone had ripped it off his neck, turned it inside out, and stuffed it back onto his body. Everything hurt; everything felt sick.

He couldn't remember a thing he had done. And when his mother told him that Clark Kent had practically carried him into the house, he was both humiliated and ashamed.

"I watched from my doorway," she said. "I saw him take you into your room."

"I'm sorry, Mom," he told her, looking at her tear-streaked face, her gaunt cheeks and hollow eyes. *You jerk,* he railed at himself. *She's going through enough without you screwing up, too.*

"I know, baby," she murmured, and she took him in her arms and held him tightly. They stayed that way for a few minutes.

Then his mother said wearily, "Drink some water and go back to bed, honey."

As he turned to go, she touched his face. "You know your father loved you, don't you?" She searched his eyes. "Just as much as Jeremiah."

Even though I was adopted, Marshall filled in. He nodded, even though he was still reeling from the shock of the discovery. It was all too much: Chloe blowing their cover and his father telling him something in death that he should have told him in life.

"Why . . . why didn't you guys tell me?" he asked in a small voice.

She flushed. "Your father . . . he was afraid you would feel different. But I . . ." She let the sentence trail off.

But her unspoken message was clear: She had wanted to tell Marshall. She hadn't in order to please her husband.

Neither spoke of it, and Marshall realized with a start that there were still lots of secrets between them.

He drank the water and dozed. The afternoon shadows dragged across the walls of his bedroom as he lay still, listening to the dull thumping of his heart. Now and then, he imagined he heard his father's comings and goings. He could almost hear his voice.

He finally managed to eat some dry toast and drink some ginger ale—his father's prescription for nausea. Moving slowly, he was standing at the kitchen sink, munching on the toast, when he heard his mother weeping in the hallway.

"Monica, get your mommy, will you honey?"

She was on the phone with his little cousin in Arkansas. Monica's mother was Marshall's aunt Maryellen. Had she known that he'd been adopted and never said a word all those years? Had the whole family known? He thought of all the family gatherings he'd attended, assuming he was just a regular Hackett . . . how many of them had promised not to tell him the truth?

"Maryellen? They won't give us the life insurance money," his mother said brokenly. "Because of the way . . . because Sam killed . . ." She began to cry harder. "Self-inflicted."

Marshall went numb.

"I don't know what we're going to do. All the medical bills. The mortgage. I don't make anywhere near enough to carry it all." She sounded terrified and alone. "I'm so scared, sis . . ."

Marshall started to go to her, but he figured she would clam up and stop talking with Aunt Maryellen.

We're broke. We're going to be homeless, he thought. *I can't let that happen.*

He set his jaw.

I won't *let that happen.*

CHAPTER THIRTEEN

The thief smiled at his partner-in-crime, and said, "This town is too small. We're running out of places to rob."

"Guess that's why they call it Smallville," Shaky replied.

They were walking the streets together, casing various businesses to burglarize, when Shaky added, "I don't think it's such a good idea to pull any more of these right now. It's on the news. If someone sees one of our . . . creations . . ."

The thief laughed. "Relax. I've got someone right here in town I can pin the blame on. An old friend."

"Wh-what?" Shaky asked, even more freaked out. "What are you talking about? I thought we picked Smallville so we could test out the zombies. I didn't know you had something else to . . . deal with."

"An old score to settle," the thief said. He scratched his head, pointed, and said, "What about that electronics store? Let's do that one."

Shaky looked across the street at the place the thief had indicated. Beside a row of storefronts, an alley cut back into what he surmised was probably a parking lot. It was the standard configuration for commercial buildings in Smallville.

"I think we . . . we should lie low," Shaky said.

The thief just laughed.

Shaky hid his trembling. He was very, very sorry he'd hooked up with this guy.

Not that I had much of a choice.

◆◆◆

That evening, Marshall didn't drink, but he did take a tranquilizer from his brother's new prescription. Since their father's death, Jeremiah had been put on so much medication he could probably open his own pharmacy.

At midnight, Marshall began to feel woozy, and he wondered if he was going to be able to stay awake long enough to commit his crime.

He wasn't after a shotgun this time; he was after money. After his mother had hung up from her conversation with her sister, she had begun phoning all the places they owed. It had taken her a long time. She'd started arranging for ways to make the payments smaller, or to delay them for a while. Some of their creditors had been accommodating. But others had made his mother cry fresh tears.

He would not let that happen again.

With his father dead and his brother out of commission, it was up to Marshall to shoulder some of the burden of providing for the family.

I just never thought I'd do it like this.

In his pocket he carried the handgun Samuel Hackett had kept locked in a drawer in the desk in his study. It was a heavy, alien object. In his other pocket he had stuffed a ski mask.

His destination, an all-night grocery store, gleamed in the distance. Marshall's heart pounded at the sight of it, and more than once, he thought of turning around and going home. His mother thought he was at the Talon. He could be, within ten minutes.

The memory of the desperation in her voice strengthened his resolve.

He walked on for a few more minutes. Yawning, he tripped on a crack in the sidewalk and the world wobbled. He realized he was getting sluggish from the tranquilizer.

Gazing at the moon, he saw it as a blur of nearly two moons. The streetlights were diffuse yellow globes that seemed to move as he ticked his glance to them.

He chuckled bitterly.

No way am I robbing anybody tonight.

He turned around to go home, glancing left and right, as if to assure himself that no one would guess that he had nearly committed a crime. Home was not that far away—nothing in Smallville was—and he hoped he could keep himself together until he got there.

Then, from the corner of his eye, he caught the movement of something white on the other side of the street.

Slowly, becoming more unfocused, he turned his head to check it out . . . and his mouth literally dropped open.

Am I seeing things?

It looked like a dead person. It moved like a mummy. Staggering down the street, staring straight ahead, it was dead white, its unkempt hair sticking out around its head like a fright wig.

As Marshall gaped, it was joined by a second one that lurched out of the nearby alley. It moved like a windup toy.

A man carrying a black leather bag came up behind the pair of nightmares. He sauntered along as if he hadn't a thing on his mind. There was something very wrong with his face . . . was it a mask?

Marshall spotted a Smallville community trash receptacle. With great effort, he crept behind it, lowering himself to a squat as he peered around it at the three figures.

Shortly after that, a van pulled up to the curb. The man skirted around the two white figures, pulling open the rear passenger door. Once they were inside, he slid it shut, opened the passenger door at the front, climbed in, and closed it behind him.

The van squealed away.

Marshall murmured, "What?" He was almost completely overcome by the drug he had taken. He fell to his knees, his head bobbed forward onto his chest, and he tumbled face-first onto the pavement.

After a while, he became aware that someone was shaking him.

"Mom," he slurred. "I'm up."

"This is the Lowell County Sheriff's Office," a voice harshly informed him. "You're under arrest."

Dressed all in black, T. T. Van De Ven sauntered into the Smallville Grille and was escorted by the hostess to a booth. A waitress made her way to his table, sparkling and eager to please. She flirted a little, and he smiled back. He knew she liked what she saw: He worked out, and he had big, dark eyes that drew women in and made them want to listen to his troubles.

Stay out of the limelight, he reminded himself. He didn't need any civilians remembering him later. He politely ordered a steak, and toned down the charm as he waited for his meal to arrive.

Then, as was his custom, he discreetly inserted his omnidirectional earphone into his left ear and started eavesdropping on those around him. The snippets he overheard painted the usual word pictures about the locals. Small towns were all the same. Hell, people were all the same: He heard businessmen cheating on their wives, people sharing worries about their jobs. The weather, the crops, what Lex Luthor was up to . . .

Hmm. He focused in on that, ignoring the other conversations.

". . . Luthor shouldn't have fired us," a man's voice was complaining. "For what? A bag of dirt?"

Van De Ven raised a brow and glanced idly around the room. Two burly men were seated approximately eight feet away from him, and by the looks on their faces, they were extremely upset.

"She probably lost it herself," the taller of the two men said to the others. "You know how rich chicks are. Think they own the world. They never keep track of anything. She probably threw it out and forgot."

Dirt? They had to be talking about the fertilizer. She had lost it?

"Luthor won't even write us letters of recommendation," the shorter one groused. "How are we supposed to get new jobs?"

"Guess His Royal Highness figures we should eat cake."

"Frickin' Lex Luthor," the short one grumped. "I'm gonna sue him for false termination."

"You and what lawyer?"

"Yeah."

Van De Ven was thunderstruck. They *had* to be talking about the sample Lopez had on her. The one he had been sent to retrieve.

It was *gone*? Who had it?

"It was probably Blanca," the short one said. "That maid from the agency? She's a kleptomaniac."

"Yeah. Probably so. Hell of a maid, though," the other one replied. But there was no real conviction in his voice. He was just helping his friend blow off some steam. "Man, I can't get over it. He fired us because of *missing dirt.*"

"Yeah, well, I never liked him. The Luthors are rich snobs, and that's all there is to it," the short one rejoined.

They continued talking for about thirty minutes. T. T. Van De Ven listened to every word.

And then he walked outside "to have a cigarette," so he told the waitress, and contacted his superiors. His line was as secure as if he'd been inside Air Force One, but he was cautious all the same, avoiding using any names and keeping to their strictly enforced code.

"This will change your mission parameters," came the reply. "Stand by for further orders."

"Standing by, sir," Van De Ven replied crisply. He felt a small thrill; maybe instead of all this waiting-around crap, things were about to move into high gear. He hoped so. He was getting incredibly bored.

"Good." The man on the other end of the line disconnected.

And T.T. got back to his listening.

CHAPTER FOURTEEN

A week passed, and Rebecca grew more and more confused about what her dad was doing when he thought she wasn't looking.

He kept leaving, and she had only managed to follow him twice. Each time, he'd wound up here, at the cemetery. It creeped her out.

What is my father doing in the Smallville cemetery? Rebecca wondered, as she hid behind a tree and watched her father pacing among the headstones. *Why?* It was Saturday night, and all the other kids in Smallville were hanging out—Chloe and Lana had invited her to the Talon—but here she was, spying on her father in a boneyard.

She had been grateful to Clark Kent for giving her a ride home the other night, and even more grateful that he hadn't asked her any questions about why she was searching for her father in the middle of the night. She felt stupid now for lying to him about getting a ride from Chloe. All he had to do was mention it in front of Chloe to discover that she had lied to him. She'd actually been following her father on foot like a spy.

She didn't mention that she had long before lost track of him, and had gotten so lost that she'd wondered if she'd ever find her way out of the maze of the town. That in itself was embarrassing enough; Smallville proper was a tiny place. But she'd been so preoccupied with trying to keep up with her dad that she'd completely ignored the route she had taken.

Then he had turned into an alley and seemingly disappeared.

Something had happened to her father since they had come to Smallville, and she was scared. Tom Morhaim kept leaving when he figured she was asleep, and staying out for long hours at a time. If he was going on long walks, as his therapist had suggested, then he was more troubled than he had been back in Metropolis. Because the walks kept getting more frequent, and lasting longer.

. . . and now these walks are taking him to a graveyard. What's up with that?

She peered around the trunk of the tree. Her father kept walking up and down a particular row, staring down at the names as if he were searching for a particular gravesite. Fog was wisping along the ground, then rolling upward, wafting around his knees as he moved. More fog billowed behind him, like skeletal hands sliding up his back and resting on his shoulders. It was an eerie sight, as if ghosts were winding themselves around him and trying to pull him down into the very graves themselves.

She shivered. She was cold, and frightened.

He walked on. Then he stopped abruptly and shined his flashlight on one grave in particular. He stood motionless before it and dropped to his knees.

Rebecca craned her neck, but she was at the wrong angle to see much more than the top of his head and the glow from the flashlight, which was illuminating him from below. His features were cut into sharp sections of yellow light and muted shadow; he was like a jagged Halloween pumpkin. He was like a stranger.

His head dipped, and she could no longer see him. Her heart pounding, she moved around the tree, clinging to the trunk, and found a space between overhanging branches of lacy leaves to observe him. Part of her was deeply ashamed that she was spying on her own father; but another part was wounded to the core that he had not confided in her, told her what was troubling him . . . and what he was looking for among the dead of Smallville.

She took another step forward. He didn't hear her, only kept his head bowed, as if in prayer.

Is it someone he knows? she wondered. As far as she knew, he'd never been to Smallville before in his life.

She took another step.

And a distant step answered hers.

The hair rose on the back of her neck. She and her father were not alone.

"D-dad?" she croaked, but she was so freaked out that she couldn't make a sound. The word came out as a breathy whisper, nothing more.

Then there was another footstep, and the crack of a tree branch under someone's foot.

"Dad!" she called. But again, her voice was a sandpapery rasp.

Then a bone-chilling fear swept over her, an icy net that fanned over her body and caught her up; she was so afraid she went numb from head to toe.

Someone was standing right behind her, and ready to put a hand on her shoulder—

"Daddy!" she shouted.

Her father leaped up from the grave and whirled around.

"Becca!" he shouted.

She ran toward him, flinging herself into his arms. But he pushed her out of the way and raced toward the tree, pulling a gun from his jeans pocket as he did so.

"Come out of there!" he shouted.

"Daddy, no!" Becca cried.

Her father disappeared into the darkness; she heard him thrashing through the overhanging tree branches, and she covered her mouth with both hands and whimpered, not really aware that she was doing it.

Oh, God . . . please, don't let my dad get hurt . . .

She took a step forward, then another, then she was galvanized into action. She raced toward the trees, shouting, "Don't hurt my father!"

"Rebecca, stop!" he bellowed.

She didn't listen. She ran straight into the thick foliage, panting, flailing with her arms . . .

. . . until someone caught her wrist and dragged her back the way she had come.

To her relief, it was her father.

"Oh, Dad!" she cried, and threw herself against him. "Who was that?"

"Nobody. I don't know," he amended. "Probably just some homeless drunk." Then he looked at her strangely. "What are you doing here?"

"It felt . . . evil," she said. She glanced in the direction of the trees and felt her stomach do a flip.

"It was just some guy," he said again. "Rebecca, I asked you why you're here."

"I . . . I followed you," she admitted. Then she looked up at him. "I'm sorry, Daddy. It's just . . . you've been going out so much, on these walks. I was worried."

He frowned at her. "Then why didn't you just tell me? Why did you sneak around behind my back?"

"I—I don't know," she admitted. She looked down, embarrassed. "I'm sorry."

"No need to be sorry." He cupped her cheek. "We have to be honest with each other. We're all we have, you know?"

She blinked back tears as she gazed up at him. "It was so hard, while you were . . . away. Mom . . ."

He swallowed hard. "That should never have happened,"

he said. "Your mother was a good person. I know it was hard on you, baby."

She closed her eyes as grief washed over her. The loss of her mom was a wound that still hadn't healed.

"It was hard on you, too," she said.

"She died believing in my innocence," he told her. "I know you were awfully young when it happened . . ."

"She told me about it," Rebecca said.

"I was only there to drive the car." He sighed and shook his head. "I certainly didn't expect anyone to get hurt."

"You were young," she said loyally.

"Thank you, honey," he said.

He pulled her against his chest and leaned his head on the crown of her head. She could hear his heartbeat and listened to it, finding refuge in its calm steadiness. This was her father, her only living relative. This was the man who had come for her when he'd gotten out of prison, like a knight in shining armor . . . her father.

"We have a chance to start over here in Smallville," he told her. "I know you had a rough road too, honey. Bouncing around from foster home to foster home . . . it's hard to trust anyone. And it shouldn't have happened.

"There are nights it upsets me so badly that I can't sleep. So I go on walks."

"But . . . why here?"

He sighed, and shook his head. "It's a little weird," he warned her. Then he took her hand and walked her toward the grave she had seen him kneeling in front of.

On the headstone were the words, MICHELLE MADISON, BELOVED WIFE AND MOTHER. 1935–1978.

She caught her breath. Her mother's name had been Michelle, and the double-M initials had been her mother's, too.

He said softly, "This lady was only forty-three when she died. Pretty young. So it was a little like visiting with your mother." He gazed at the headstone, sorrow sharpening his features.

"Oh, Daddy." She sniffled.

"I didn't want to upset you," he said. Then he flushed. "I actually thought you might worry that I'd gone a little nuts."

"No." She shook her head sadly. "I have a doll that doesn't look a thing like her except that it has blue eyes, like Mom did. And when I miss her a lot, I get that doll out. I was embarrassed to tell you that. I mean, I *am* in high school now."

His features softened. "It's not fair, what you've gone through. I'll make it up to you, Rebecca. I promise. Right now we have it tough. I have a low-paying job and we live in a dump."

"Oh, Daddy, it's not that bad," she cut in. "And we're to-gether."

"You deserve a lot better," he insisted. "And you will have a lot better." He cupped her chin with his hand and gazed into her eyes. "But you're going to have to trust me, all right?"

"All right." She smiled at him. "I'm sorry I didn't tell you I was scared."

"In prison, you learn to hide your feelings from other peo-ple," he said. "You wall yourself in and learn to take care of yourself. I'm still pretty rusty at letting you know what's going on with me." He gave her a wink. "But I'll do better on that score, too."

As they hugged, she remembered that he had gone into the stand of trees with a gun. He was not supposed to have a gun. It was a violation of his parole.

Be honest with him. Ask him about it, a voice inside her head prodded her.

"Let's go home," he said, taking her hand.

But she didn't want to lose the warmth between them, this special moment where after so long, they had really connected. They had a lot of time to work out the kinks, figure out all the details . . . not for *anything* would she say or do something to shatter the mood.

She smiled back at him . . . and kept her silence.

They went home, had some hot chocolate, and watched a little TV together. As they were gazing in companionable silence, she snuggled against her dad and thought about all the burdens he was trying to carry—still adjusting to life outside prison, working a job, trying to pay the rent and buy food, and taking care of her. All she had to do was go to school.

I'll get a job, she decided. *An after-school job, so Daddy won't worry about me being alone, and I can make friends, and make my own money.*

Shaky was having a nightmare.

In his anxious, fevered mind, buses zoomed back and forth; buses flew; buses honked and slammed on the brakes; but each one of them hit Willie hard enough to shatter him into pieces that spun and danced like comets. The wheels boomed as they spun in a rhythm like heartbeats, then like a death march prior to an execution.

Willie was dead, and the wheels pounded words inside Shaky's head, *Your fault, your fault, your fault.*

Then another bus hit Willie and his head shot off his body, soaring into the air, end over end; until it floated toward Shaky, and that ruined mouth opened and said, in the snaggle-toothed old man's voice, *You did this to me!*

Shaky woke up with a start; and from the other room of the thief's Metropolis apartment, the thief himself appeared at the threshold in a pair of sweats and a T-shirt that said, ironically, "DARE to keep kids off drugs."

"Would you stop that?" he snapped. "Night after night you go into this routine . . ."

Shaky raised a hand to his damp forehead, and said, "Sorry."

The thief grunted in disgust. "Medicate yourself or something. We need to be fresh for the morning. We got business down in Smallville."

More robberies, Shaky realized. He felt sick and tired and scared. His partner was crazy. And evil.

"Okay," he said, and wondered how on earth he could ever get himself free—free of the waking nightmare, and free of the guilt.

I killed that old man, as sure as if I'd shot him.

"So, no more moaning?" the thief said, regarding him closely. "Right?"

"No more," Shaky murmured. Tears welled in his eyes. "No more."

The next morning was a Sunday, but Rebecca had already noticed that all the shops on Main Street were open on Sundays. She went down the rows of stores asking for job applications.

When she got to the Talon, she discovered another world inside—this was where all the kids from school hung out—and Lana Lang was behind the counter.

Rebecca approached her shyly, and said, "Lana, I was wondering . . . if you need any new waitresses?"

"As a matter of fact, I do," Lana replied, smiling pleasantly as she put several frothy cups of coffee on a tray. She sprinkled some chocolate on top of one of them and added nutmeg to another. "Are you looking for a job?"

Rebecca licked her lips. "Yes. I don't . . . I have a little experience doing waitress work . . . well, no, I don't. But—"

"Do you know how to run an espresso machine?" Lana asked, gesturing to the ornate brass object glittering against a larger mirror that reflected back the bustling interior of the coffeehouse.

"No," Rebecca admitted, discouraged.

"Would you like to learn? It's really cool when the steam kicks in."

Lana was grinning at her. A little shy, a little eager, Rebecca said, "I've always wondered what the difference between espresso and cappuccino really is."

"Espresso is black—cappuccino's got steamed milk. You're not a coffee drinker, I guess? That's okay. Around here, you'll catch on quick," Lana told her. "What schedule were you thinking of? After school? Can you do the occasional weekend?" She laughed. "Well, most weekends? Especially after football games?"

"Sure. I'm not exactly doing anything else at the moment." She took a breath. "So, do you think you could use me?"

Lana beamed at her. "I know I could." She held out her hand. "Welcome to the Talon."

Rebecca was thrilled. "Thanks, Lana."

Lana hefted her tray. "My pleasure. I was just about to advertise for more help. You saved me the effort."

"Thanks so much," Rebecca blurted, still amazed that someone so young was running a business . . . especially a thriving business like this one.

She looked around, impressed. *She's probably making*

more an hour than my dad is. She seems so happy. Life can be good.

It really can.

"It'll be great to have another pair of hands around here," Lana added kindly. "We've been shorthanded this semester. A lot of family farms are really struggling. The kids have to pitch in."

She smiled, and said to Rebecca, "Well, let me take this order to its final destination and I'll help you fill out your paperwork. You can start today, if you want."

Rebecca was stunned. And moved. "Thank you . . . for your faith in me," she said, having a little difficulty getting the words out. She wasn't used to things turning out like this. "This is great."

"Hey, guys." It was Chloe, who came up to the counter holding a newspaper. It wasn't the one she edited at school, but the regular Smallville paper, the *Gazette*. "There were two more burglaries last night."

"What?" Lana frowned at Chloe. "I thought Marshall Hackett had been arrested."

"He was." Chloe opened the paper and showed Lana and Rebecca the headline.

SMALLVILLE CRIME WAVE.

"The bookstore and that little store, Fair Notions, got hit," Chloe continued.

"Fair Notions." Lana shook her head. "I don't know that store."

"The new yardage shop. They've got that cool Goth fabric I made my Halloween costume out of last year. It's over by the cemetery, fittingly enough." Chloe considered. "The bookstore's over there, too." She made a scary face. "We're being robbed by ghosts!"

Rebecca blanched. She had found her father by the cemetery, and he had had a gun with him. What if the person in the bushes had been a security guard, searching for him? Or a cop?

Trying not to be conspicuous, she sank down on one of the barstools. Her legs simply wouldn't support her.

"You okay?" Chloe asked.

"Yes," she said brightly, covering up her reaction. "Guess what! Lana just hired me to work here!"

"Oh, cool," Chloe enthused, her green eyes sparkling. "Congratulations! You're on the caffeine train now."

"By the way, you get to drink all the free coffee you want," Lana said. "And at night we usually divvy up the pastries that are too old to sell."

"Wow, that's great," Rebecca continued, smiling a huge fake smile.

"It says here that some woman saw one of the burglars. She said he was dressed in white, or glowing, or wearing a mask or something." Chloe bobbed her eyebrows up and down. "That should be helpful."

"The ghosts of Smallville," Lana said.

"It's probably true." She smiled in Rebecca's direction. "I still haven't shown you the Wall of Weird, have I? Why don't you come to the *Torch* office after school tomorrow . . . unless you're working?" She gazed questioningly at Lana.

"How about you start at four?" Lana suggested.

"Great," Rebecca said again. Then she blurted, "My dad's going to be so proud of me."

It was a little bit of a geeky thing to say, and she was immediately mortified. But the other two girls just smiled at her, sharing her victory, and she thought, *Wow, they really are nice. Maybe we'll become good friends. Friends I can confide in . . .*

Then the walls her father had been talking about went up. There was no way she would ever tell a soul in Smallville about what had happened to her father back in Metropolis. More than once, a girl had assured her that the fact that her father had been to prison didn't bother her in the least; that of course she loved being friends with Rebecca. But after a time, that girl—and the next girl, and the next—stopped hanging out with her.

It bothered most people that he had been convicted of a terrible crime. And it bothered them even more that back in Metropolis, a man who had once supported five children, a wife, and a mother-in-law on a security guard's salary was now stuck in a wheelchair for life, collecting disability. The last mayoral race, the victim had been on TV in a political commercial endorsing the candidate who was toughest on crime. That had dredged everything back up, and school had become unbearable.

"Oh, we're going to have Punk Day on Friday," Lana told her. "We're all going to do our hair the way they wore it back then, and dress up." She wrinkled up her nose. "It's going to be a lot of fun. Do you think your mom might have anything in her closet you could wear?"

They don't know about us. They really don't. I'm safe.

"My mom passed away," she said, using the old-fashioned term because it seemed just too harsh and pathetic to say, "died."

"Oh, I'm sorry, Rebecca," Lana said. "I didn't know."

"That's okay," the girl replied, feeling even more uncomfortable now that she'd told them the truth. "It happened a long time ago."

"We don't have mothers, either," Chloe said. Her voice was edgy, tinged with bitterness. Then she relaxed a little and added, "We take care of each other."

She smiled at Rebecca, and so did Lana; and Rebecca thought, *If they ever find out about Dad, I'll just die. I couldn't stand not having friends again.*

When Rebecca got home from the Talon, there was a note on the table that said, *"Gone to the store. Back in a bit."* Rebecca set it back down on the table and wandered to the fridge. She got out a diet orange soda and moved to the well-worn sofa they had purchased from the Salvation Army and sat down. She turned on the TV and something caught her eye.

"*. . . woman told police who arrived on the scene that she had discovered a man with slack features and a pale complexion loitering in the supply room of Smallville Drugstore near the locked cabinet holding controlled substance medication."*

The screen showed a woman with blue hair and enormous, frightened eyes. She said, "He just stared at me. I told him to leave or I was calling the police, that's what I said, yes sir!" She had a heavy Southern accent. "He didn't move a muscle. I swear he was on something.

"Then when I went to call y'all, he turned around and left. Just like that!" She snapped her fingers.

Then it wasn't Dad after all, Rebecca thought, and she was ashamed for thinking it might have been.

Howard Ross, Pete's uncle, was coming back from a nice evening at the Smallville Pizza Palace, where he'd eaten some pie and swapped some tall tales with a few of the farmers he sold feed to. The men around here were anxious—family farming was a tough way to make a living—but they were honest guys, and friendly, too.

Of course, Howard made friends wherever he went. He liked people. Liked to yak with 'em and yak at 'em. Drove his nephew crazy with all his yakking.

He chuckled, thinking fondly of Pete. The kid didn't know it, but Howard was considering giving the boy his teal Lexus when Pete graduated from college. Hell, he could afford it. Even when times were tough, farmers still needed to buy feed for their livestock. Couldn't exactly skimp on that.

He motored along, admiring the way the moon hung in the clouds, whistling along with the radio.

Then, to his right, he saw a clump of white figures staggering out of an alley. He raised his brows; they looked terrible. They were the palest, whitest people he had ever seen.

Must be the light, he thought. *Maybe they're in a punk rock band or something.*

He drove on.

Yeah, he thought, switching radio stations, his mind returned to the Pizza Palace and his customers. *I think Pete will get this car. Man needs a fine automobile once he's grown-up.*

CHAPTER FIFTEEN

In the middle of the night, the zombies of Smallville walked. Six of them, they swayed on holy ground, the dead of Smallville slumbering beneath their feet.

These zombies—homeless men no one would miss—were in better condition than the zombies of Cap du Roi. The poison that had distorted their nervous systems and harnessed their wills was more refined than what had been used on the living dead of Haiti. If the Project had had Shaky on their team, it was likely that no one would have ever learned of the Project. At least, that's how the thief saw it. He'd done a little background work starting with the information the Latina had given Lex Luthor—information he had heard over his headset prior to stealing the sample. He knew what the government was up to . . . and who was involved.

He hadn't shared this information with Shaky. There was no need. They were partners, not friends.

The thief had no friends.

Fog boiling up around them, the zombies stared at the face that filled their souls, giving them the only direction they had. Beneath their seemingly mindless attentiveness, their silent voices were screaming, *Help us! Save us! We're in hell!*

But the thief held some terrible power over them, as surely as if he had some kind of remote control hidden in the pocket of his navy blue windbreaker. As he looked on, surveying their condition, they were forced to stand stock-still as he instructed each of them on their tasks for the evening: more burglaries, with just enough mayhem thrown in to distract anyone who got in the way of successfully lifting credit card numbers and cash from the tills of the businesses of Smallville.

The scientist was dressed similarly to the thief, in jeans and, in his case, a burgundy sweatshirt.

Though they usually kept the zombies rounded up in an abandoned warehouse just off the interstate, the two men had assembled their zombie patrol in the cemetery, which seemed a good place to begin the night's wild work. They had agreed that if anything went down—such as the law catching up with them—they would simply leave the premises, abandoning their creations. If anyone figured out what was going on, that would be tough luck for the creatures who would have no way to describe their captors, nor to explain that somewhere inside the apparently mindless shells of their bodies, their conscious minds were drifting below the surface, struggling for release.

But these zombies weren't going to be talking anytime soon. They couldn't even speak if they were tortured—the thief had already experimented in that direction, and he was positive of that. They were silent witnesses, and silent accomplices. Their lips were sealed—with drugs and maybe even a little Voodoo magic somehow loaded into the formula.

"By the way, do you need any more lab equipment?" the thief asked Shaky. "You mentioned a lab supply store in Metropolis that you like. We could take some of these guys up there, snag whatever you need. Want an electron microscope?"

Zombie eyes watched. Zombie eyes listened. Shaky shook his head. His dark eyes were troubled. He pulled out a cigarette and lit it, taking a deep drag. The zombies stirred, the smoke stinging their eyes. Shaky took no notice, but as he began to pace away from them among the headstones, they found relief. They still breathed, still needed food and water.

And they needed marching orders. They needed to be told what to do . . . or they would stand in the cemetery all night, without volition, without direction. That was the real curse of the living dead.

"We need to cool it," Shaky said. "There's been too much news coverage. We're doing too much, committing too many burglaries. There have been sightings."

The thief shook his head. "You're wrong. We're safe as houses."

Shaky flicked ash from his cigarette on a headstone and took another breath. "If anyone connects us to Willie back in Metropolis . . ."

"He was a bum," the thief said, snorting with derision. "That case was closed the minute they found his body. No one gave a damn about him while he was alive, and no one gives a damn now. The Metropolis Police Department has far better things to do than look into the death of a piece of societal debris."

"I can't take any more risks. I got in a lot of trouble when I was younger," Shaky protested.

The other man sneered at the scientist. "You've been clean for years. You've fallen off the law enforcement radar as well, my friend."

"That never happens," Shaky argued. "Once you've been in the system, they never forget you. Especially now, with databases. You're never free. You have to walk their walk until you die. Just like these guys. We're all zombies." He was getting agitated.

"You should be more careful," he went on. "You're fresh out of prison. They're probably watching you."

The thief chuckled. "Calm down, Shaky. It's been over a year. I check in with my parole officer. They have no idea what I'm up to."

Shaky moved his head, and said desultorily, "Everyone leaves a trail. We're not even zombies, man. We're hamsters on a wheel."

"You are really getting boring," the thief said irritably. "You with your nightmares and your whining. I try to be nice, try to get you stuff you need. Listen, do you want out?"

Shaky looked startled. He tamped out his cigarette on the headstone, letting the butt fall into some flowers that were growing in a pot atop the grave itself. His eyes glittered. "Out? How am I going to get out? How are you going to 'let' me out? We're both in this for good."

"'Til death us do part?" the thief mocked.

Shaky had begun to pace again. His back was to the other man, and he was scared. "Something like that."

"Then . . . you could always die," the thief said reasonably. He looked over at the group of zombies.

Shaky raised his brows, backing a step away. "Hey, hold on," he said. "You just wait a minute."

Then the thief reached into the pocket of his windbreaker and pulled out his Anschütz .22.

He said to the scientist, "I wouldn't move if I were you. But then again, I would never be you in a million years. Never let myself be what you've become. I take the next right step, and you just stagger around. And this, my friend, is the next right step."

"Hey!" Shaky shouted. "Don't do this, man!"

The nearest zombie was grizzled and gray-haired, toothless and rheumy-eyed. The thief said calmly to him, "Kill him."

"Hey! Wait a minute!" Shaky cried. "Help!"

The zombie began to advance, raising his hands just like in the old movies, shambling slowly forward. It would have been simple for Shaky to outrun him . . . if the thief wasn't aiming a gun at him.

"Listen," Shaky said, "this is crazy. There's going to be a body if you kill me. There's been enough bodies, man. That's traceable evidence . . ."

The thief considered. "True," he said. "Very true." He reached into the pocket of his windbreaker and produced a vial. It was the distilled zombie formula Shaky himself had devised. There was plenty inside the vial to take away Shaky's life from him . . . and never give it back. In fact, there was enough in the vial for another dozen zombies, at least.

Right now, however, the thief was interested in creating only one.

"Open your mouth," the thief ordered.

Shaky stared at the vial. "Don't do this to me, man. Don't do it! We're partners!"

"C'mon, Shaky," the thief said, grinning. "You know the old saying about there being no honor among thieves. I'll bet you had something planned for me, too."

"No. No, man," the scientist insisted, his face betraying his lie. "No way."

"Hold him," the thief ordered the zombie.

The zombie moved toward Shaky, who waved his arms in terror. The thief advanced on him with the gun, pointing it straight into his face, and Shaky continued to shake while the zombie grabbed him.

"Open your mouth." He waved at Shaky with the gun. "Open it, or I'll have another one of these guys do it for you."

"Oh, God, please, no," Shaky murmured. Tears and sweat streamed down his face. "Please, no."

The thief unscrewed the top and walked toward Shaky. The other man's eyes bulged, and he struggled in the arms of the zombie.

"I'm the only one who can make the formula," he said desperately.

"Wrong, chucko. It's all on the hard drive now. I figured your password out easy. 'Shaky' is not terribly original."

Shaky flushed hard.

He gestured around himself, at the headstones, at the graves. "I don't need you anymore, Shaky, although I was willing to keep you on, at least for a little while longer. Until I was sure I could handle the operation on my own. But you're done. I see that now. As my old man used to say, 'the graveyards are full of indispensable people.'"

The zombies stared at the unfolding drama, heartbeats slow and lethargic, brains unable to process what was happening. They had been given their orders but not given leave to fulfill them, and they were getting anxious and restless, behind their quiescent exterior of passivity.

"Damn it, Shaky, open your mouth," the thief said. "This is the last time I tell you. Next time, I blow a hole in your head and pour this stuff into your brain."

Shaky glanced down at the gun. Seeing that it was equipped with a silencer, he must have realized that his former partner was telling him the truth.

With a groan of utter panic, he opened his mouth.

The thief began to pour the liquid into his mouth. The bitter taste hit Shaky's taste buds, and he hacked, hard, sending the vial spinning into the air. It landed on the nearest grassy grave mound, but did not break.

The thief grabbed the vial, advanced on his victim, held open his mouth, and poured the poison down Shaky's gullet.

Shaky went into a fit of convulsions. The zombie held him fast, since he had not been told to let go of him, and the thief watched in awe . . . and no small measure of amusement. He liked watching the transformation, liked knowing that when it was complete, he'd have another lackey at his beck and call . . . and this one had been somebody once upon a time. In terms of victims, he was moving up in the world.

One day folding blankets in the prison laundry; just a few days later, turning people into mindless followers.

I'd think of myself as a mad scientist, but Shaky had that honor. Until now. Now he's just another dumb jerk who didn't have the sense to give me some respect.

Like the Gadsen flag says, Don't tread on me.

The people who do pay for it . . . one way or another.

The scientist's head slumped forward, and his knees buckled. The thief waited, but Shaky didn't change right away. Sometimes the transformation was rapid. Sometimes it took a few hours.

He looked idly around the graveyard and spotted a crypt on the opposite side of where he was standing.

"Follow me," he said to the zombie who was holding Shaky.

Eerily, the zombie moved forward. He lost his grip on the unconscious scientist and seemed to be unaware of that fact as the man tumbled to the ground. Then he stepped hard on Shaky's arm. The thief heard a crack; Shaky's arm had just been broken.

"Easy, buddy," he said to the zombie. "Stop."

The zombie stopped.

"Pick up your burden."

The zombie bent over and grabbed Shaky by his broken arm. The limb was bent at a bad angle; it cracked again as the thief winced sympathetically.

Was that a jubilant gleam in the zombie's eye?

I wonder if somewhere in there, this guy knows exactly what he's doing, he thought, scrutinizing the zombie. *Maybe we didn't mix this batch right.*

He felt a little uncomfortable . . . until he reminded himself that he had a gun. He wagged it at the walking zombie, who had no reaction at all as he dragged Shaky along after him like a rag doll. He lost his grip again, and Shaky's ruined arm thudded onto the grass.

"Help him," the thief told the others.

Slowly, painstakingly, the others moved forward and glommed on to Shaky's arms and legs. They carried him like a big raft across the graveyard as clouds scudded across the moon. In the distance, a crow cawed, and something rustled in the bushes. The thief was tempted to shoot into the undergrowth, just in case. But just as he aimed his Anschütz in that direction, a possum ambled out, licking its paw without a care, and ambled away.

One of the zombies turned its head in the direction of the possum and clacked its jaw a couple of times. A couple of the others imitated it. The thief watched, intrigued. So far, he and Shaky's experience with the zombies they'd produced was that they were docile, compliant guys who ate regular food and had none of the violent, flesh-eating tendencies like in the movies. Neither one of them had been surprised, chalking all that up to Hollywood invention.

"C'mon, boys, let's go," he said.

They turned back around and shuffled after him, he their

mother hen and they, his fast-moving chicks of the damned.

It was almost dark by the time Rebecca's father came home "from the store." She had fallen asleep watching TV, and when he opened the door, she roused herself and smiled in his direction.

"What did you buy?" she asked eagerly.

"Oh. Not much," he replied vaguely. He was carrying a paper sack, and he reached in and pulled out a couple of apples, a quart of milk, and a loaf of bread.

"That's it?" she asked. He had been out for hours.

He paused, then admitted, "I didn't have enough money to pay for the rest of it, Bec. I had to put it back."

"Oh." She felt an anxious tightening in the pit of her stomach. Then she remembered her good news, and said, "Not to worry. I got a job! At the coffeehouse. You said I was good with coffee, and I got to thinking about that, and I got hired!"

He beamed at her. "That's terrific, honey." Then he frowned. "You won't let it interfere with your schoolwork, will you?"

"No. It's with my new friend, Lana," she added proudly. "She kind of owns it with Lex Luthor."

"That guy's got his hooks into everything, doesn't he?" Tom murmured. "Must be nice."

"Daddy?" she asked.

He shook himself. "Sorry, honey. I'm really happy for you. For us both." He grinned at her. "We'll be eating filet mignon before you know it."

"I don't care if we have meatloaf as long as . . ." She trailed off shyly, and added, "I'm glad we're here, Dad. Together. I like Smallville."

"A change of scene has been good for both of us," he confirmed. He held out his arms. "I'm so proud of you. My smart, pretty girl! This place . . . what's it called?"

"It's the coffeehouse, the Talon." She took his hand. "I'll show it to you tomorrow. I have my first shift then. If that's okay . . ."

"As long as you can manage it all," he said firmly. "Education is your ticket out of this, sweetie. I'm going to make sure you have a good life."

She sniffled a little, glad to have a father around to give her some boundaries and care for her, the way she dreamed he would back when he was still in prison.

We're gonna be all right, she thought.

But that night, her father went out again. She heard him go; she was half-asleep and dreaming about Clark Kent's eyes and his smile and how cute he was. But she was roused by the sound of the door opening and closing, the lock clicking.

She sat up yawning and glanced at the clock. It was almost two in the morning.

When I get my first paycheck, I'll buy him a treadmill, she thought, half-joking. But her stomach was churning. Where did he keep going? Was he really that troubled? Was their situation more dire than she realized?

She lay back down and tried to go to sleep. After a while, she succeeded.

The next morning, as she and her dad ate a quick breakfast of toast, coffee, she idly flicked on the TV. The local news was on.

"*. . . burglary attempt . . .*" the young female news anchor was saying. "*This time, Brian Cienci interrupted what had obviously been an attempt to open the safe of the Smallville branch of Jackson's Auto Body Shop. He saw no sus-*

pects, but he did notice muddy footprints on the floor. Local forensics experts are examining the footprints. Police say this hard evidence represents a break in the case."

Rebecca's hair stood on end. She couldn't help it. She didn't want to think what she was thinking.

But as her father got up to pour himself another cup of coffee, she checked out his shoes.

His muddy shoes.

Then he said to her in a lighthearted tone of voice, "Oh, guess what. My supervisor's wife does beading. She had this neat earring. I thought it would go nice in the new hole you got."

He fished it out of his pocket and handed it to her.

She swallowed hard. *Oh, Daddy, please, don't let it be true that you've stolen this,* she begged him.

"I'll wear it to my first day of work," she told him.

Then she turned away, fighting back tears.

CHAPTER SIXTEEN

Chloe was seated at her computer in the *Torch* office when Clark popped his head in. She glanced over at him and finished her sentence, hit SAVE, and smiled cheerlessly at him.

"Hey," he said. "Mind if I come in?"

She waved him in. "Of course not, Clark. What's up?"

He put his hands in his pockets, took them out again, and finally perched on the edge of her desk, peering at her monitor. "What are you writing about?"

She pursed her lips. "A thoroughly uninteresting story about the upcoming pep rally. Rah," she said flatly. She looked at him expectantly.

Clark regarded his friend. There were circles under her eyes, and her hair didn't have that usual flare. She wasn't putting on much makeup—not that she didn't look great without it. And she was often distracted and listless.

"You're . . . okay?" he asked her.

"Sure. I'm fine." Her eyes wide, she looked confused. "What do you mean?"

He hesitated. "You don't seem fine."

"Well . . ." And then she deflated like a balloon. "I can't stop thinking about the Hacketts," she confessed. "I can't believe Marshall's still locked up. It's not fair, Clark. They didn't have any proof that he robbed that store. Now he's in custody, and Principal Reynolds has asked the school board for permission to suspend him."

"Been talking to eye witnesses?" he asked her.

"No." She crossed her arms in a defensive posture. "I

heard about it in gym class. Clark, I don't mean to be rude, but I've got, like, twenty minutes to finish this thing."

"Sure." He rose. "Call you tonight?"

"Sure." She flashed him a smile . . . which slipped a little as he walked past her.

"Take care," he said softly.

By the time he had left the office, Chloe was crying.

About an hour later, she left the school grounds. Now she stood before Smallville Juvenile Hall, a place she had never been before, and would never have imagined she would ever visit. It was a cheerless place, everything decorated in industrial gray and pale green.

She didn't know what she would say to Marshall. She wasn't sure she should even be there. But she had given her name at the desk with the full understanding that if Marshall didn't want to talk to her, he didn't have to.

The guard walking beside her was stern and unsmiling, and Chloe swallowed nervously as they came to a fork in the hallway, and he said, "He'll come through there. You'll sit in there."

He pointed to a door at right angles with another door. Both looked thick, and both featured a small square of glass in the center with chicken-wire-like mesh embedded in it. Chloe peered through the square to her right but saw nothing beyond it but another door.

Then the guard unlocked the door in front of her, and she went into a small room, dimly lit with fluorescent lights and featuring a single metal table and two folding chairs, one on either side.

At the guard's nod, she sat in the chair on the other side of the table, facing the door, and folded her hands in front of her. She had not been allowed to bring her purse with her—it had been checked into a locker—and the with-drawal of even that little bit of freedom hit home. Marshall was in a detention facility, and he was in trouble.

So she had come to see him. She just didn't know if it was to make herself feel better or to actually help.

The guard said nothing more to her, only walked to the door they had come through and opened it. He spoke to someone in the hall, then he came back into the room and stood against the wall. He looked a little tired, and when he saw her glancing at him, he smiled.

"You'll be safe," he assured her.

She shifted in her chair, "thank you" not quite managing to make it past her lips.

Then the door opened again, and Marshall came in.

He was escorted by another unsmiling man, and he was wearing handcuffs.

Chloe was shocked. She half rose, holding out a hand, but Marshall either ignored it or didn't see it. His eyes were blank. There was no life there, no emotion.

No anger, no hope.

He shuffled to his chair and sat down. He stared blankly at her, as if he had no idea who she was.

"Hey," she said, leaning forward on the table. "Marshall, I . . . how are you?"

He made no response, had no reaction. She might as well have been speaking to him in a foreign language.

"Is there anything I can do?" she asked.

He stared at her. The silence between them was unnerving.

After about a minute, she rose to go.

"My mom," he blurted. "The only reason I'm hanging on . . ." The despair on his face cut her into pieces. "I'm not mad at you anymore, Chloe. I'm . . . nothing."

Her eyes welled. "Marshall," she said, "I can't pretend that I know how you feel because nothing this terrible has ever happened to me. I don't want your forgiveness because . . . because I don't deserve it." She started crying. "I'm so sorry."

He sighed and inclined his head. "It's not your fault. It was nobody's fault. Just a bunch of bad dominoes." He laughed miserably. "That's what's happened to my family."

"Oh, God."

He said nothing more. After a few minutes, the guard crossed to her side, and said, "It's time to go, miss."

Nodding, she rose, glancing up at Marshall through her lashes, hoping he would say something, anything.

But he didn't.

The guard walked her back to the main desk, where the intake clerk had her sign for her purse.

"It's post-traumatic stress disorder," the guard said to her, as she started to leave. "It could go away, or it could haunt him for a long time. He's gotta talk about it, not keep it bottled up the way he's doing." He sighed and scratched the back of his neck. "I've seen kids come in with bad situations. But this . . . this is *bad* bad."

"It's my fault," she said under her breath. He didn't hear her.

"But the doc says he's gotta let it out, or else he's gonna be stuck with it for the rest of his life." He tapped his head. "He'll just relive it over and over. He'll be in hell."

"He needs to bear witness," Chloe murmured. "Maybe he just needs someone who's listening."

She walked back out into her life. She had no idea what she had hoped to accomplish, but she hadn't managed it.

◆◆◆

After school, Rebecca Morhaim came to Chloe, and said, "I think it's time for you to show me the Wall of Weird like you were talking about on my first day here. Because weird things are going on in my life, and I don't know what's really happening and what's not anymore."

"Hey, that's *my* life you're talking about," Chloe said wryly. "Sure. I'll show you."

She moved from her computer desk to the wall where she kept a running clipping service on all the many—many, many—strange things that had happened in Smallville since the meteor shower thirteen years before. As Rebecca gaped, Chloe showed her the guy who had turned into a giant insect, and the plants that grew too fast, and the guy who had killed girls by draining the warmth right out of their bodies. There were hundreds of articles, some with red circles on them, others with penciled notes such as, "For Chloe."

Rebecca stared at it all in total disbelief. Then she said, "So, a lot of things happen here that . . . might not happen anywhere else."

"Nicely put," Chloe drawled.

"Okay." Rebecca's voice sounded small and confused. "Okay."

The new girl turned and left, leaving Chloe speechless.

The thief liked the coffeehouse called the Talon. He liked sitting among the young people; they were all shiny and eager to savor life; they hadn't yet made their big mistakes. Youth truly was wasted on the young.

Mine was wasted in prison.

He did not hold with what his father had liked to say before he'd died three years ago, and that was that getting put away for a decade was probably the only thing that had saved his son's life.

"You were doomed," the old man liked to say. "Born bad. Don't know how, don't know why, but I know it."

When the old man died, the thief did not even shed a tear.

On the table sat a paper bag, and in the bag, what remained of the formula in the vial.

As soon as his business in Smallville was concluded, the thief planned to move to New York, hook up with a chemist he knew, and have some more mixed up. He wasn't sure what he would do after that. Making plans wouldn't be as crucial as they had been up till now.

I'm almost finished here. I've confirmed that my old friend has moved here, and I'm positive it's because the jewels are here. I'm not leaving here without the spoils of war—the bounty we plucked from that jewelry store could set me up for life.

Eleven and a half years, and the bastard's going to pay, that's for sure. With interest.

The thief's name was Jason Littleton, and he had been a member of the gang that had been found guilty of robbing Le Trésor back in Metropolis. Tom Morhaim, now newly relocated in Smallville, had been part of that same gang. However, Jason had also been found guilty of shooting Lee Hinchberger, the security guard who was now poppin' wheelies in a wheelchair.

And that Jason had not done. *I never so much as touched Hinchberger.*

Ol' Tom had pinned that on him, turned witness for the prosecution in return for a lighter sentence, and his accusations had stuck.

Jason had been sentenced to twenty-five years, and the

only reason he was out now was exemplary behavior and an excellent lawyer, who managed to get one of his many appeals to go through. With some doubt cast on the legal niceties of various aspects of his case, the courts had decided to cut him loose after eleven and a half years.

Tom had done his full ten, big deal, and now he was here in this tiny town, trying to make a go of it as a decent citizen.

Jason had initially come to Smallville to confront Tom and make him spill his guts about where he had stashed the jewels. He'd gotten a little distracted when he'd learned that Lex Luthor lived here and had decided to try to rob him just for yucks. That was the night the girl had told Luthor about the doctored fertilizer.

It had been so easy to sneak into her room, lift the package, and take it to Shaky. Frighteningly so. Crime paid, that was for sure. All you had to do was be willing to take a few risks. It was like pitching baseball: one over, one under, one on. Try enough things for a long enough time, and something was bound to pay off.

But now, all he had to do was feed Tom some zombie potion, get him to show him where the jewels were, and take them.

Then Tom will never see me again. Of course, he'll never see anybody again. Cuz I'm gonna tell him to walk in front of a bus, same as I told Willie Thorpe.

Jason smiled at the prospect. Then he returned to reading a science fiction novel. He loved science fiction. It was like his own life.

He sat there reading for another ten or fifteen minutes, when a nice-looking kid about sixteen or so came over and said, "Mind if I grab some sugar packets?"

"Help yourself," Jason said easily.

The kid did so, smiling his thanks. Then he went back to a table a few feet away and dumped them into a large cup of coffee.

Jason's pretty brunette waitress came over to the kid's table with a coffeepot in hand, and said, "Pete, is your Uncle Howard still at your house?"

The kid—Pete—laughed ruefully, and said, "Oh, yeah. He's made some friends at the Pizza Palace. They're going to start playing poker together on Tuesdays. This not being Tuesday, he's home at my house for dinner." Pete sighed. "It's hard to concentrate on my homework with all his talking."

"And so you're staying with us for a while tonight," the girl said.

"Hope you don't mind, Lana," Pete replied. "I'm taking up a table."

"Of course not. And there are plenty of tables," she said generously. "Here, let me freshen that." She poured Pete some more coffee. He took an appreciative sip.

Jason went back to his novel.

Then Pete got up and moved toward the bathroom, and Jason realized that he had been at the Talon almost as long as the kid. That sharp little waitress—Lana—was bound to have noticed him. She would be able to describe him to the police if it ever came to that.

Tall guy, dark, hair with gray in it, just sat in here forever, reading . . .

He closed the book and picked up the sack. Then he headed out the door, not a care in the world.

I don't feel so good . . .

Pete staggered into the men's room, which was deserted. Sweat was pouring off his forehead; his stomach was a churning sea of acid. Then he started to shake. Hard. Harder.

He fell onto the floor and hit his head on the tile.

Again, and again, and again.

The world turned inside out, and Pete with it; he was having convulsions. Every bit of him was contracting, releasing; he was slamming his head, slamming it, slamming it.

Harder.

Then he went somewhere else very far away; somewhere deep inside himself.

CHAPTER SEVENTEEN

From his office in Metropolis at the very apex of his building, his view a sprawling vista of the city, Lionel Luthor connected to his call via the secure line, and said, "Yes, General?"

"We have a situation," the man said without preamble. Lionel appreciated the fact that General Montgomery was not using names on the phone. As sure as he was of his own security measures, it never hurt to be careful.

Something his son, Lex, had yet to learn.

"Our operative at the plant feels that it's time to remove the *item* from its present location and take it to another holding facility," the general went on. "Do we have your consent to do so?"

Lionel frowned. He was being cut out of the loop. "Have you figured out who took the sample from the girl?"

There was a pause. Then the military man said, "That's a negative, sir."

"Which is why you want to relocate the *item*," Lionel drawled, not without some sarcasm in his voice. He was furious: the future of the Project was at stake, and all because the government had been unable to stop this Marica Lopez from seeking refuge at Lex's Smallville home. Lionel and his military partners concurred that Lex had probably heard all about the Project from her by now. The question now was, did he believe her?

He probably does. He's probably fallen in love with her. Men in love will believe anything. He grinned wolfishly as he flipped open Maria del Carmen Maldonaldo Lopez's dossier from a stack of documents on his desk and admired her photograph. She *was* stunning.

The *item* General Montgomery was referring to was the rest of the specially processed fertilizer destined for the secret facility in Haiti, where the government was testing its effectiveness for combat. It was being stored in Lex's warehouse, right under his ignorant and intolerably lax nose. Originally, Lionel had considered letting Lex in on the Project, but decided against it. Lex had a strange moral streak. Sometimes it operated, and sometimes it didn't.

He usually manages to ignore it if my life is in jeopardy, he thought dryly.

But Lex had no particular need to know about the Project, so Lionel had decided to keep it to himself.

"Sir?" The general asked impatiently. "Your permission to extract the item?"

"Covertly," Lionel said. "No fuss."

"Of course not. Thank you, sir."

The general disconnected. Lionel did the same.

Back to work, he thought, moving from the Lopez dossier to a medical report, paging through to the conclusions section. It concerned a drug trial that was being held with two of the subjects having been recruited in Smallville. *Ah, our experimental MS drug looks promising. That's good.* He gazed off in the distance and smiled. *That might eventually give our stock a bump.*

I'll let the governor know we've had some good news. He might want a chance to get in on the action.

Appreciative politicians are a great corporate asset.

Humming to himself, he picked up the phone.

◆◆◆

T. T. Van De Ven had been put back into play. Now he crouched outside the LuthorCorp fertilizer warehouse on the grounds of the Luthor mansion with his team of agents, waiting. He was frustrated, though not surprised, to discover that Lex Luthor had posted extra guards at the warehouse, making a quiet extraction far more difficult.

It was one of several frustrations. He'd located the Lopez girl, but she was sticking close to Lex Luthor, and Van De Ven had been ordered to keep out of the younger Luthor's crosshairs. Since she'd lost possession of the fertilizer that he'd originally been sent to retrieve, she was less of a priority target, but he figured that eventually she would have to be eliminated. She had seen too much back in Haiti to be left alive.

There was one more shipment of doped fertilizer destined for Haiti. Ten crates had already been misaddressed for shipment to a US naval base in Japan by Norman Wilcox, a Project field operative working undercover at the plant. Without the crates, there would be no more tangible evidence, nothing to link LuthorCorp with the Project. If that was what Van De Ven's superiors wanted, that's what he would deliver.

Since it had to be done, it was going to be done by the best.

Van De Ven grinned in the darkness and commed a line-of-site infrared message to the next commando over.

"Five."

He loved this kind of work. It was the mission that made it exciting, the obstacles to overcome. The end result didn't matter to him—he wasn't a big-picture guy. Action was what kept him loving life.

Wilcox had fed him the pertinent data, and Van De Ven was pleased to see that the field operative had been thorough and correct. As he had reported to their superiors, Lex Luthor had gone for redundant systems in a big way. Rather than simply relying on a high-tech sensor net, Lex had employed dozens of guards walking the perimeter, interior, and hallways of his building, which was smart—there were very few devices that would fool a human's senses, but plenty that would confound a machine's.

The strength of all that human security of course, was also its weakness. People got tired and bored, and didn't pay attention all the time. So Lex had compromised, maybe while he waited for even more security personnel to arrive: Each of the guards carried a transmitter which acted like a mini GPS, mapping him into a grid. A team of three watchers kept track of the grid in a small anteroom near the warehouse rest rooms. Wilcox had provided a secretly taken photograph of the room, showing the three men seated at their monitors, making sure that too many of the guards didn't congregate in one place at one time, and that they all kept walking their territory.

If one person stopped moving, or moved out of their established pattern, the guys in the anteroom had been trained to assume that the system had been compromised.

The key to the mission was unobserved infiltration. He and his men would have to get inside and reach the anteroom without being detected.

In an ideal world they'd then take the fertilizer without ever being seen.

But in this one, they had to move ten huge crates of fertilizer. This was not something he or his men could tuck under their arms. So once the trio in the tower was out, they'd have to knock out the roving guards and load up a truck.

Bigger challenge equals more excitement.

The IR receiver in his ear clicked twice, and he commed a reply of a single click. Time to go.

He and his men moved like black shadows across the LuthorCorp landscaping. A drainpipe on the east wall that was well out of the range of the huge floodlights illuminating the lawn provided easy access for Van De Ven to scale the wall.

Just like having a ladder.

He scaled the pipe quickly, and was soon on the roof.

A series of magnetic alarm sensors ringed one of the air vents; in seconds Van De Ven disarmed them, had the vent off, and was sliding down a rope onto a crossbeam.

He took a long moment to examine the room he was in; night-vision goggles gave him an edge than he might not have otherwise had.

He could see two guards from where he was, and in the far corner of the warehouse he could see the upstairs room that the security team used for tracking everyone.

He couldn't see all of the guards, of course—the warehouse was too big.

But the number he did spot was enough.

The rest of his team were each set to locate a guard and track him. Once he'd taken out the three watchers, they had been ordered to put the guards out.

Van De Ven took a small device from his equipment belt and aimed it at the ceiling between where he was and where the office was.

Pop! There was the sound of a compressed air charge, and the camera was on its way.

A buddy of his had designed the thing after seeing it in a *video game* of all things. The brass had checked it out, loved it, and "appropriated" it.

The tiny solid-state camera he'd fired thumped into the

ceiling and stuck, the quickset putty surrounding it activated by the impact.

Van De Ven tapped a switch on the side of his night-vision goggles and his left eye screen displayed what the camera was seeing—a fish-eye view of the entire area between himself and the control room.

Perfect.

Now he could choose his route to the control room. It was like having his own personal satellite.

Van De Ven worked his way across the rafters carefully. The problem at this height wasn't so much the noise, but the dust. He had to work carefully, trying to keep himself away from intersecting paths with the security guards, lest a dust bunny and a sneeze give the game away.

But the camera made it easy.

He slid along the rafters like a black panther in the trees, stealthy, quiet. Within a few minutes he was over the control room. He lowered himself into position, ready to go in.

He checked his watch. *Excellent. Right on time.* The rest of the team should be in place. He toggled the microphone on his regular radio, letting the rest of them know he was going in, and opened the door quickly, stepping inside.

Phat-phat-phat.

The tranquilizer gun he was carrying was a repeater, holding five shots. Fortunately he only needed the three. The curare-based knockout drug was fast and efficient, and the three men dropped like felled apes. He tapped his mic three times; the signal to take out the rest of the guards.

It had gone well. Only one of them, the one who had been walking between the two monitors, had a chance to react before he fell over.

Walking? Why is he walking?

Too late, Van De Ven thought about what having only two

monitors meant. He rushed over to the fallen guard and opened his shirt.

Damn. The homing devices worn by the guards on the floor were also worn by the ones up top. Which meant that one of the guards below had probably triggered an alarm before he was taken.

Van De Ven reached up on his equipment belt and uncovered a transmitter secured with Velcro.

In his research for the mission, he'd learned that all the alarm wires going from the plant ran to the local sheriff's office—not too unusual. But what *was* unusual was that before running to the sheriff's, they all ran through Lex Luthor's mansion. There, the billionaire's son could decide what calls the sheriff took, and which ones he might have taken care of . . . by other means.

Van De Ven had planned appropriately. Now he toggled the mic on his radio again.

"Look sharp. Secondary alarm got sent, but I'm taking steps to slow a response. We've got at least ten or fifteen."

He activated the transmitter's power, then pressed a red button. Miles away, the coded radio signature activated two thermite bombs he'd laid near the comms box for the mansion. Things were going to get hot for old Lex for a while.

That ought to keep him busy.

Unable to sleep, Clark was looking at the stars, which were sparkling and shimmering in the sky like fireflies. He'd read that in space, stars and nebula clusters had colors; he could almost see pinks and turquoises, purples and greens.

He'd always been fascinated by the stars, even before he knew of his own origins. They were incredible glimmering fires high in the sky, on a tapestry of black velvet, so rich you wanted to touch it.

Smallville skies were broad and clear, and the night air was fresh. The world smelled good and hopeful. He couldn't say the same about Metropolis, where the lights on the skyscrapers and streetlamps competed with the stars for brilliance. Exhaust lingered in the big-city air, and there was never a sense of peace there. Busy town, busy people. Same sky, different perspective.

Clark wondered sometimes—like now—what the night sky might be like where he came from. How many moons were there? Was Earth among the pinpoints of light piercing an indigo sky? Did meteor showers pummel the landscape? Did people there stare through their equivalent of telescopes and stargaze, as he did?

Did anyone watch his adopted planet at nighttime, and wonder how he was? And miss him?

He asked these questions in his heart, not speaking them aloud. If there were answers to be found among the stars, they kept them to themselves in utter, serene silence.

He sighed. Silence was not golden. It was frustrating. He felt isolated by the silence of the stars; it punctuated the fact that he was alone on this world, not in the sense of not being welcome, but because he was the only one of his kind. At least that he knew of. If there were other people who had arrived on Earth in spaceships, they, like he, were concealing their identities.

Keeping silent.

He sighed and stretched, moving away from the telescope as he mulled over the events of the past few days. So much had happened . . . and a lot of it was centered around silence. Chloe, accidentally telling the Marshall family's secret. Lex, essentially wanting Pete to suppress the information in his report. And the new girl, Rebecca . . . he was sure she had stories she wasn't telling.

Sometimes it felt as if a secret were nearly the same thing as a lie. He often watched Chloe and Lana exchanging information as if it were some kind of currency, or a present. As far as he could tell, the way girls bonded was through sharing secrets. There were code words: "Don't tell anyone, but . . ." and "This is just between us, okay?" The surest way for one girl to lose a friendship was to violate that trust by sharing a confidence with someone who was not authorized to know.

Breaking silence.

Then he heard a muffled *crump*. Instantly, he knew it wasn't a farm sound or anything that he'd heard before, for that matter. He strained his ears, and listened, directing his focus in the direction from which he'd heard the sound come.

Boom!

Louder this time. And now it sounded more familiar— like that time the gas tank blew up in Pete's car . . .

It was coming from the direction of the Luthor Mansion.

Trouble. I wonder what Lex is up to now?

But even as he thought the words, he was in motion, zooming down the stairs, across the fields, and running to make sure his friend was all right.

As he raced in a blur, Clark tried to think how he could explain his presence to Lex. It was late—past midnight— and a school night as well. What could he say?

Ah, I was just driving by . . .

Why would he be out driving? Getting feed for the animals?

Yeah, Clark, from all the midnight feed stores.

Maybe he could say he was taking a walk.

Sure. Past midnight, on my way to spy on Lex at the mansion.

As he neared the mansion, he could see flames running up the side of the north wall. A window exploded, and a shower of sparks danced along where the sill would have been. One of the gutters broke loose and crashed into a row of bushes beneath it. Smoke boiled up like steam; the sky was blanketed with haze. Crackling bushes shivered as they burned, the energy from the heat making them tremble. The smell of smoke permeated every pore of Clark's body.

Picking up speed, Clark looked hard at the mansion, using his X-ray vision to find people inside.

There.

Two people—Lex and a female—were flailing their arms near the top of the second floor. It was clear they were in distress, shambling through the room, then finding one another and clinging together. The female started to fall, and Lex grabbed her up in his arms and tried to carry her. But he staggered forward, then fell to his knees. Weakening, he lowered the woman to the floor and sagged over her inert form.

Without another thought, Clark dived into the smoke. He worked his way up the stairs, using his X-ray vision to check each step before putting his feet down. He had to go slow or risk missing a hazard.

It was *hot*. His clothes grew singed at the edges, and the air in his lungs grew warm and uncomfortable. Yet he didn't get hurt.

His X-ray vision guided him as he dodged a falling piece of banister. A mirror on the wall shattered, the shards bouncing off him. A wall sconce followed suit.

Nothing slowed him down.

Hold on, Lex, he thought. *I'm on my way.*

Pushing a large chunk of burning wood from his path, he bounded up to the last stair and stepped up to the landing. Flames leaped around him on all sides, orange and red and reddish black, and the air was choked with smoke. He tried to buffet it out of his way, but there was too much of it; it was like pushing at row upon row of blankets strung out across clotheslines.

As he'd been instructed in school years before, Clark knelt on the ground and breathed, unsure if there was a point at which the smoke would be too much for even him. If he had properly surveyed the mansion—and properly visualized the layout in his mind— Lex should be ahead in the next room. Clark moved forward, waving his arms at superspeed, trying again to disperse the smoke out of the narrow corridor area.

Instead his actions fanned the flames, making them burn brighter. The roar around him was startling, but he remained focused.

What if it's too late? he thought. *Bad things are happening everywhere. What if this is one more horrible tragedy?*

He couldn't imagine it.

Scanning once more, he managed to locate Lex behind the next door to his right. He made a fist and slammed it hard on the burning wood. The door fell inward, sending fire and sparks upward.

Clark crawled over the fallen door, ignoring the fact that his clothes were burning. He ignored everything except the fact that his friend was in this room, and he had to save him.

Then he found them. Like two people in a sinking rowboat, they were sprawled on what was just about the only piece of flooring in the room that was not on fire. Lex was curled protectively around an attractive woman with short, dark hair, and both of them were unconscious. Lex looked flushed, and his breathing was shallow. Clark looked deeper, and saw his friend's heartbeat. It was slow, but still regular.

Clark tried to decide what to do. He used his X-ray vision to examine the rest of the mansion, and found, to his surprise, that the room beneath this one was undamaged. He had no idea why, but he could use that to his advantage.

Clark stepped back and used his heat vision to blast an irregular hole in the center of the room, far enough from Lex so that if the wood cracked, it would not weaken the surface beneath Lex and the woman. Then Clark stomped on the floor, driving his leg into it like an axe into a melon. Wood splintered all around him, and he drove the flat of his hand down on it, ripping crossbeams into pieces and shattering subflooring.

There was a cracking and splintering like a hundred branches simultaneously; pieces of wood flew through the air, some catching on fire immediately.

But there was a hole now, a cool, beckoning escape hatch. But pieces of the wood he'd driven through the floor had started to catch fire downstairs. He'd have to move fast.

Clark scooped his friend and the woman up and jumped through, his muscles absorbing the impact easily. He hoped they would be all right as well.

Then he realized he had landed in some kind of tile-enclosed room, something like a bunker, and figured it for one of the many secret places he did not know about in Lex's house. Then he realized that it was really a workout room, which was equipped with a sink, and a pile of fresh white towels; using his superspeed, he soaked them and raced them over to Lex and the woman. He covered them completely, squeezing water from the towels over their hot skin. Then he hoisted them both over his shoulders.

He kicked open the door; the fire raged outside. The only

thing he could think to do was to use his superspeed, dashing as fast as he could so that the wet towels would protect Lex and the woman.

Once outside, he laid them on the grass well outside Lex's mansion. Then he looked down at himself and saw that his clothes had burned so badly that it would be difficult to explain why he himself wasn't injured at all. He thought for a moment, then dashed back through the house and into the tiled room, where, searching through the cabinets in seconds, he located a nondescript pair of gray sweats and a gray sweatshirt. He contracted around them like a quarterback carrying the ball, then dressed in a flash on the lawn, dumping his clothes in the burning bushes.

Then he saw Drew, Lex's assistant, who had not seen him. The man sat on the ground with his head between his legs, coughing hard.

"Hey." Clark crouched down beside him. "You okay?"

"Is Lex all right?" the man asked anxiously.

"Yes. And his . . . friend, too," Clark told him.

Drew closed his eyes. "Thank God. I've called for help," Drew announced, holding up a cell phone. "Did everyone get out? Have you seen any other staff? We have a new security team. There should be six more people inside the house, four security men, my assistant, and the cook."

Clark looked around. In the glow of the house, he saw a huddle of four men in black suits helping a fifth walk among them across the grass. A woman in a bathrobe stumbled along beside them, looking shell-shocked.

"There," he said, pointing to them. "All accounted for."

"Good." Drew slowly got to his feet. "I'll see how everyone's doing."

Forcing himself to move at normal speed, Clark raced

back to Lex's side. After a few seconds a bedraggled-looking Lex flicked open his eyes and stared up at him.

"What happened?" Clark asked him.

Lex squinted. "Clark?"

"Hey." He put his hands in the pockets of the sweatpants. "I happened to be in the neighborhood . . ."

His friend grinned weakly. "Uh-huh."

"Seriously," Clark said. "There was this . . . school event, and . . ."

The woman was slowly stirring; that drew Lex's attention away from his feeble explanation.

Then the pretty woman rolled over onto her side and stared at the fire.

"They did it," she said. "Oh, merciful Mother of Heaven, they did it."

"They . . . ?" Clark asked leadingly.

Lex sighed heavily. "Clark, I think there's something you should know."

Lionel Luthor had been rereading *The Art of War* with a nice glass of burgundy at his bedside in his Metropolis penthouse apartment when the phone rang.

"Sir," a voice said, "there's been a . . . development."

It was General Montgomery again. Lionel listened in stunned silence as the man on the other end described how the "covert" mission to steal a few crates of fertilizer from Lex's warehouse had resulted in half the mansion being destroyed. Though he was relieved to hear that his son was all right, he was outraged by the clumsiness of Project personnel.

"You know this isn't good," Lionel bit off.

"We're aware of that, sir. We're taking steps."

"Roll some heads," Lionel cut in. "Especially the moron

who conducted this 'operation.' And get me out of this mess."

He slammed down the phone.

Surrounded by his own security team, Lex and his guest, Marica Lopez, were treated at the hospital. Unlike anyone else in the ER, the two were escorted to a private room, where doctors and nurses hurried in and out, running tests no one else would have received.

Clark called his father, who drove over; there was some fumbling between father and son about how each of them had managed to have the truck at the same time—Clark had originally told Lex he'd left his truck on the grounds of the mansion when he'd accompanied him and Marica to the hospital in one of the ambulances dispatched to the Luthor compound, but now here was Jonathan saying he had the truck.

". . . because I borrowed it from the Rosses, so we'd have two cars while Martha was here in the hospital," Jonathan finished smoothly, and Clark was taken aback by how smoothly the lie rolled off his father's lips.

After Lex and his friend Marica told Clark and his father everything they could about the fertilizer, they discussed the zombie sightings around town.

Marica had looked at Jonathan Kent, and said, "Whoever stole the sample knew what to do with it. How banal, to create zombies to commit more burglaries."

"It does speak of an unimaginative mind," Lex agreed.

The two smiled at each other, and Clark saw that they were very attracted to each other. Despite the situation they all found themselves in, Clark was touched.

There's all this weirdness and death in the air, but love, too.

Then the two Kent men left together.

"This is all getting very strange," Jonathan said, and Clark found himself bursting out laughing. Sometimes his father had quite the gift for understatement . . .

His father looked at him, then started laughing, too.

It had been a long—*very long*—night.

As Lex and Marica discussed what to do—and where to go—Lex's cell phone rang. It was his father.

"Dad. Yes, hello," Lex said sarcastically. "I'm alive. Is that good news or bad news?"

"Heard you had some trouble down there," Lionel said. "I'm on my way."

"Oh, gee, Dad, want to finish the job they bungled?"

"Don't be an idiot."

Lionel Luthor hung up.

CHAPTER EIGHTEEN

The next day after school, Rebecca went to see Chloe in the *Torch* office, determined to tell her about her father. She was more and more troubled about what was happening. But just as Chloe looked up from her computer screen and smiled at her, Clark Kent strode in.

He saw Rebecca and smiled, then turned to Chloe and said, "If this is a bad time . . ."

"Oh, I was just going," Rebecca murmured.

"No, that's okay," Clark cut in. "I didn't mean that I didn't want to talk in front of you." He came into the office. "Chloe, Lex told me there's some kind of weird fertilizer out there that turns people . . ." He glanced at Rebecca again.

"Go ahead, Clark," Chloe said. "It's all right. Rebecca has been fully initiated into the fact that Smallville is the Twilight Zone." Rebecca nodded.

Clark got down to it. "There's a woman staying with Lex who used to work for a relief project in Haiti. She says LuthorCorp fertilizer turned people into zombies."

The two girls stared at him.

"Her name is Maria del Carmen, but Lex calls her Marica," he continued. "She's terrified. She came to Lex to make him stop the project. They think Lex's mansion was set on fire to kill her."

"What?" Chloe asked, shocked. "Fire? I didn't hear about a fire!" Then, perhaps realizing that she sounded a little callous, she added, "Are they all right?"

"Yes. They had to be treated for smoke inhalation, but they were really lucky," Clark said.

"Zombies from fertilizer?" Rebecca said slowly.

Chloe raised her brows. "There's a new one. And I thought only homework could turn you into a zombie." When neither Rebecca nor Clark responded, she added, "Well, that's certainly Wall of Weird material. And so ripe for sophomoric jokes. Did Lex get a sample analyzed?"

Clark shrugged. "That's the thing. Maria del Carmen—Marica—brought a sample with her for him to look at, but someone stole it."

"Stole it?" Rebecca asked shrilly. Chloe looked at her, and she, in turn, stared back at Chloe.

"In addition to weird people, Smallville does have plain old vanilla bad people," Chloe said to Rebecca. "Lex is rich, so he's a target." She cocked her head, thinking. "And I'll bet someone on his security staff just lost his job, if one of his guests got ripped off."

"Do you think her story's true?" Rebecca asked Clark.

"People have been seeing strangers around town who seem . . . wrong," Clark said. "I saw one."

Chloe nodded. "Could be zombies," she said. "Why not?"

"That's crazy," Rebecca blurted.

"That's Smallville," Chloe retorted, gesturing to the wall of clippings and photographs. "Okay," Chloe said, taking a seat behind her computer. "Let's do a little digging. What did you say her name was?"

"Maria del Carmen. Something and then Lopez."

"Clark," she said impatiently, looking up from her keyboard. "Lopez is as common in Spanish as Smith is in English."

"Sorry." He thought a minute. "I can't remember the rest of her name."

"I'll run it by Lex," Chloe said, then paused, and added, "if it's all right that I know?"

"I think so. I mean, it's pretty wide-open now," Clark replied.

"Well, I have to go to work," Rebecca said. She looked at Chloe. "See you there later, maybe?"

Chloe narrowed her eyes and cocked her head, studying the other girl with frank appraisal. "Everything all right, Rebecca?"

"Sure," she said quickly. "Fine."

Clark turned to Rebecca. "If you see Pete, please let him know I'm working on the implements report." He sighed. "He wrote a pretty harsh paper on the history of pesticides and fertilizers. Lex saw it. Not too happy about it."

"You should show it to your mom," Chloe said pointedly, "especially if it's true that she's in the hospital because of something she ate at his mansion. She'll enjoy a little light reading about the dangers of farming with chemicals."

"There's no proof of that," Clark said loyally.

"Well, I'm really glad that she's okay and that she's going home," Rebecca told him. Her heart leaped a little as he smiled at her.

He is so cute.

Rebecca and Clark both left, and Chloe started researching Maria del Carmen Lopez. Even as she typed in the name, she rolled her eyes, knowing that it was like looking for "Mary Smith" in the Anglo databases of the world.

Sure enough, there were one hundred GoogolPlex matches.

I should have asked for the name of the relief project. I'll make a note of that.

Then she decided to update her files on the Smallville burglaries. She typed in her favorite police files website . . . and sat back to wait for the information to start scrolling.

Then she frowned as a different window popped up . . . and she realized she had typed in the URL incorrectly. She began to hit DELETE, until she began to read the information that was scrolling down her screen: It was a list of people with convictions who lived in and around Smallville . . . and the name MORHAIM, TOM was prominent among them.

Huh?

Chloe didn't know if that was Rebecca's father's name, but she clicked on it and waited to see what popped up.

There were dozens of links, many to front-page stories in the Metropolis papers.

Astonished, Chloe kept clicking.

After only a few minutes, her eyes were bugging out.

Rebecca's father was a convicted felon. He had participated in the robbery of a Metropolis jewelry store, Le Trésor. A security guard had attempted to stop the heist, and he had been shot and wounded by one of Thomas Morhaim's partners—a man named Jason Littleton.

Chloe couldn't believe it. So she clicked on some of the accompanying photographs and studied them, linking up the names with the faces. The first one was of Thomas Morhaim and had been taken shortly after he'd been placed in custody. Then another one, after his trial and conviction. Then his sentencing . . .

. . . and there was a much younger Rebecca in the shot, waving plaintively to her father as he was taken away. The little girl was holding out her arms and crying.

"Oh, my God," Chloe murmured. "Poor Rebecca."

She kept reading the articles. There were pictures of Jason Littleton, a dark-haired man with spinning eyes. He looked mean. She could easily see him putting another man in a wheelchair for life.

Then she moved to more current articles, discovering that

Thomas Morhaim had been released from prison about fifteen months ago. That was the end of the stories about him. He had been allowed to sink into relative obscurity.

And they moved here, and I know Rebecca does not want anyone to know this. In fact, I'm sorry I snooped. Too much information has plagued me lately.

She ran her fingers through her hair, not clear on her next move. There didn't seem to be any reason to tell anyone about this . . . not even Rebecca. If she didn't want anyone to know about her dad's past, far be it for Chloe to bring it up.

Or to let her know that I know. Poor girl . . . no wonder she's been acting kind of squirrelly. She wants friends. She's afraid that if we find this out, we won't want to hang out with her.

That's not true, at least not in my case.

So . . .

Chloe closed all the windows and deleted all the links. She powered down and pushed away the keyboard.

. . . My lips are sealed.

She rose and walked to the doorway of the *Torch* office, paused for a moment, then left for the Talon.

Pete couldn't think, couldn't process. But deep inside him, his consciousness screamed in a constant state of terror, fully aware that something horrible had happened to him.

And so he ran; the adrenaline pumping through his body did horrible things, breaking down the zombie formula and sending it shooting through his body like dumdum bullets. Leaving wounds—by taking away, bit by bit, all the self-awareness that was Pete and leaving . . . something that very badly needed some direction.

He ran screaming, arms windmilling . . . and then he felt an all-consuming, ravening hunger.

He smelled meat and blood all around him.

He dove to the right, and then the left, hands grabbing at the fog in search of something to eat. He ran on, crazed, with no idea that he *was* running.

Part of his brain registered that he was on familiar ground; somewhere the word "friend" registered, but he couldn't put it into context.

Then he saw a figure in the distance.

Food, food, food, came the thought.

He ran toward it, mouth clacking.

When he heard the figure shout, "Pete!" he didn't even recognize his own name.

Clark had to pretend that he had struggled to get Pete bound and into his parents' truck, but he did not have to pretend he was beyond himself with worry as he delivered him to the grounds of Lex's mansion.

Lex and Marica had moved to a small outbuilding pending an investigation of the explosions and the fire. The authorities had asked Lex to leave the property, but he had refused. The compromise was the outbuilding, which he sometimes used to house out-of-town clients or business associates.

They put Pete in a sparsely furnished room. He was still bound, and there was nothing in his dead eyes but fury.

Marica was terrified of him, and Clark didn't blame her. She kept her distance, even from Clark, as if by association he was dangerous, too.

Lex escorted her into one of the two rooms he had had converted into bedrooms for himself and Marica. Drew had accomplished it in record time, and the bedrooms were actually more luxurious than the ones in the mansion, with elaborate wrought-iron headboards, Louis XIV armoires, and, for Marica, an exquisite dressing table.

"You see?" she demanded, as she whirled on Lex in her bedroom. "That guy is a bona fide zombie!"

"Yes, he is," Lex said slowly.

"Do you finally believe me?" she asked shrilly, her eyes brimming with tears.

He nodded. "I believed you before."

"Not entirely." She gave him a penetrating look. "You wanted to, but you weren't positive."

"No," he began, then chuckled softly. "You're right. But now I completely accept that it's real. And that guy is a good friend of Clark's." He sighed. "I apologize for doubting you."

Stymied, she shook her head. "If I had some of that sample left, perhaps we could try to figure out how to counteract it. But without any . . ." She ran her hands through her hair, then dropped them to her sides with a heavy sigh. "There may be more somewhere back in Cap du Roi. We had a lot of it. Dr. Ribero put only that small bit in the pack for me, so that I could carry it easily."

Clark, who had approached the threshold, made a note of that.

He said casually, "Cap du Roi. How do you spell that?"

She told him. Then she said, "What are we going to do? Perhaps we can analyze his blood chemistry."

"I have access to all kinds of experts," Lex offered. "And good lab facilities on-site in our production facility."

"Bueno. Perfecto," she murmured. Clark could practically see her mind racing. "I'll extract some blood, start running panels . . ."

As she planned her strategy, Clark said to Lex, "I'll be in there with Pete," and turned around to go back to his friend.

But Pete was not in the room.

The front door of the outbuilding hung open.

"Pete!" Clark shouted.

He ran out of the building; on either side of a gravel path, four of Lex's security staff lay crumpled on the ground.

"Lex, stay inside!" Clark called to his friend. "Stay there!"

"What's happening?" Marica cried.

Clark bent over one of the guards. The man was still breathing.

Returning his vision to normal, he spied a clump of what looked like small feathers extending from the guard's suit jacket. Clark tugged at it, extracting a small dart.

Clark raced back inside, and said, "Pete's gone. The guards have been knocked out. Call for more help!"

And then he raced off in search of his friend.

With his X-ray vision, he scanned the area. He saw no other people around. No one hustling Pete into a car, no trucks, nothing. He was perplexed.

Then he looked up.

Against a black sky, a blacker shape moved in total silence. It was a helicopter, its blades whirring but making no noise. Focusing his X-ray vision, Clark saw four figures inside. One looked to be Pete, who was bound and gagged.

"Pete!" Clark shouted. "Stop!"

The helicopter rose higher into the sky, and whirred silently away.

Clark was still with Lex and Marica on the mansion grounds when Lionel Luthor appeared in the doorway. The billionaire was surrounded by drama, looming larger than life as he strode into the small building Lex had planned to stay in.

"Son," he said, by way of greeting, "don't you have fire sprinklers installed in the mansion? I specifically order—"

"Yes, I'm fine, Dad," Lex said coldly. He put a protective arm around Marica as she drew closer to him.

The movement drew Lionel's attention to her. "Hello. We haven't met."

She regarded him stonily.

"Don't play games, Dad," Lex said. "You know who she is. Did you come to see if she was still alive?"

Lionel's brows shot up. "Lex, I'm shocked. What are you trying to get at?"

Lex angrily held up his hand. "Pete Ross was just taken away in a stealth copter," Lex continued, "after the poison you helped create turned him into a zombie."

Lionel blinked at him. "Did you have this delusion awake or asleep?"

"Mr. Luthor, Pete is my friend," Clark said, stepping forward. "If anything has happened to him . . ."

Lionel tapped his chin. "One might argue that he will be returned to you good as new. If one knew anything about what was going on here."

"I don't believe you," Marica spat at him. Her dark eyes flashed with fury. "You're a liar and a murderer."

"Hmm. Ouch," Lionel said. He shrugged. "I've booked you into the Smallville Hotel, son. We'll both be in the Presidential Suite. You're welcome, too, of course," he said to Marica. "I believe your home is still intact, Clark?"

"We're staying here," Lex said, raising his chin.

"Here is not safe, son. Here blows up," Lionel replied. "Now, for the lady's sake at the very least . . ."

Lex scowled at his father. Then he smirked. "You've been

reading *The Art of War* again, haven't you? I'm supposed to feel safer because you're with me. No one will try to hurt me because you'll be my human shield."

Lionel smiled pleasantly.

Lex glanced at Marica. He said, "He's right. We'll be safer with him."

She stared at him in utter astonishment and opened her mouth to protest. But Clark could see that she was at a loss to come up with an alternative plan.

"All right, then." Lex's voice was icy. "I want Pete Ross back, Dad. The way he was."

"Lex, I know you think I'm all-powerful. It's flattering, really. But if I were involved in such an all-encompassing government conspiracy, do you really think that I could snap my fingers and the entire Department of Defense would do my bidding?" Lionel intoned. He stepped aside, holding out his arm to indicate that Lex and Marica should leave the outbuilding. "We'll talk more in the limo."

As Marica walked past Clark, she turned to him, and whispered, "All the proof is disappearing. Soon I will, too. Help me."

High above Smallville, T. T. Van De Ven spoke to his superior, General Montgomery, who said, "You have been ordered to stand down. Why are you still in the target location?"

"Sir, I located more . . . proof," Van De Ven said excitedly. "I have . . . living proof, sir. Someone has used the *item* to create that living proof. I captured that proof and it is with me now."

He looked over his shoulder at the young man who was straining at his restraints. He was completely wild. There was nothing human in his actions, no thought, nothing. "My God," the general murmured. "Someone has used the *item*."

"My thinking as well, sir." He paused. "Sir, permission to search the target location for more of the same." Before the general could refuse, he added, "Sir, I am on location and already familiar with the situation. I humbly suggest that I am the best man for the job."

The general sighed. "Permission granted."

Van De Ven nearly whooped with pleasure. He turned to the chopper pilot, and said, "We're going zombie hunting, Johnson."

The pilot smiled back at him. "Aces, sir."

On the ground, Lionel Luthor seethed with fury. He would not tell his son that he had already demanded that he be given the antidote to the zombie-producing formula, and his request had been denied. He was outraged that he was being treated as a lesser player, and there was no reason Lex needed to know that. Not in a million lifetimes.

The best he could do to prevent that revelation was to hold his cards close to his chest and remain detached. Let Lex stew.

And let him and his beautiful new ally find the antidote themselves.

Then Lionel wouldn't *need* to go hat in hand—if ever he needed the antidote. He'd just get it from his son.

CHAPTER NINETEEN

In an atlas in the smoky library of Lex's mansion, Clark found "Cap du Roi" on a map of Haiti.

Then he put on a burst of superspeed that bordered on supersonic, crossing the vast breadbasket of the Midwest, slogging through the swamps of Florida, and racing into the ocean. He swam, too, churning up so much water that he wondered if he looked like some kind of sea monster shooting through the ocean trenches.

The world all blurred past as he raced for the cure in Cap du Roi.

And then he was there.

Clark slowed himself down to what felt like less than a crawl and hunkered low in the darkness of a pale slivered moon, surrounded by the reedy stalks of a sugarcane field in Cap du Roi, opening his senses to the sights, sounds, and smells of this foreign place in an effort to get his bearings. The air felt hot and clammy on his skin, as if a giant, invisible velvet hand held him in its phantom grasp. He shivered in spite of the heat.

A gentle breeze blew, bringing with it the exotic scents of mango and bananas mingled with farm smells that he recognized from his father's and other farms around Smallville; only the dung of these cows, chickens, and other livestock had a more pungent odor than what he was used to. He also detected traces of exotic spices from recent meals and the ash-laden scent of smoldering cooking fires, underlain by the distinctive reek of burned wood, long since extinguished. He could tell by the depth and breadth of this last smell that it covered a large area. A cow bellowed in the distance, followed by the insistent bark of a dog.

Instinctively, he moved quickly through the fields toward the carbon smell of the old fire, skirting ramshackle shanty houses with tin roofs and dilapidated corrals. The bitter scent grew stronger until it overpowered everything else, then he emerged at the edge of a blackened clearing. He stepped gingerly over the charred, skeletal remains of a fence strung with the remnants of broken lights on melted wire just inside the perimeter and followed the fence line, finding sections of it untouched by the fire, all the while watching and listening for signs of activity within. He heard only the rustle, squeaks, and slithering of small animals.

Clark found a battered wooden sign in the bushes beside a dirt road and broken-down gate with the words *"Bienvenue AYUDO"* painted on it and decided to follow the dirt road into the center of the compound. Part of him felt an impatient urgency to rush in and move at high speed, but he made himself go slowly, taking in every detail he could; otherwise, he might miss some small detail that could lead him to the answers he had come here to find.

Dark piles that had been huts with broken frames lined the roads. Collapsed roof supports jutted from them at sharp angles, sticking out like jagged teeth. Many had broken, half-melted metal cot frames. Everything had been burned. No question, this had been intentional—and thorough. *More than burned wood stinks around here,* Clark thought.

The bigger buildings looked flattened under tin roofs. Clark nudged a pile of debris with his toe and turned over a piece of tin from the biggest building, but found nothing except pieces of scorched and partially liquefied metal lab benches and a couple of black, twisted instruments he recognized as microscopes. As Clark pushed aside a piece of tin

at one of the smaller main buildings, a large lizard skittered
out from under it, startling him. He spotted part of a melted
plastic sack with the familiar LuthorCorp logo on it, but it
was only a remnant.

No fertilizer.

That's it, he thought. *I've struck out. Dead end. No trace
of anything. It's all been wiped out.* He closed his eyes and
rubbed his temples, wondering what to do next, thinking
that he had no choice but to go back to Smallville. Maybe
there was something he had overlooked there. *Maybe I
should talk to Lex . . .*

A plaintive, human-sounding screech pierced the air, followed by a chorus of others. Clark's breath caught, then he
realized that the eerie sound came from the wild dogs that
yipped at the moon. The tropical breeze picked up as if in
answer, palm leaves rasped, and tree trunks swayed and
moaned. The effect seemed to ripple outward, causing
snakes to slither in the underbrush and other animals to
scurry in all directions. Clark felt cool sweat trickling down
his armpits.

Then the drums began.

He focused all his attention on his hearing, listening to the
low, insistent, complex rhythms that beat in his ears in synch
to his own heartbeat. The pounding grew in volume, sounding both longer and stronger. The combined effect of hearing and feeling the hypnotic rhythms filled him with a sense
of foreboding, yet he felt drawn to investigate. Pinpointing
the location of the drumbeats, he moved cautiously through
the fields amidst a low, whispering wind that rattled cane
stalks everywhere until he saw a glimmer of firelight coming from another clearing located a mile or so from the abandoned AYUDO compound.

Stopping to take it all in, he scanned the remaining distance between himself and the fire with the full sensitivity of his eyes and ears, checking every inch of the area before him to ensure that no one knew of his presence. He glanced up at the crescent moon looming high above, then, in a momentary flash, he sprinted to the base of a large palm that gave him a clear view of everything that went on in the clearing.

The air hung thick and still. A bonfire burned in the midst of a circle of palms that stood like sentinels, guarding the activity between them. Firelight flickered at the edges of the clearing, darkened from time to time by the formless shadows of the dancers moving around the fire in long, undulating movements. Rattles shook in unison with the drums, adding to the strange hypnotic feeling of hearing and seeing the drums as one.

Two men tossed a log on the fire, showering the night sky with a flurry of shimmering sparks while the tempo of the drums increased and the dancers quickened their pace. The flames jumped higher. A tall, muscular, dark-skinned, bare-chested man wearing a huge feathered headdress, flashing a multicolored robe and a staff with a skull on it, danced wildly in erotic counterpoint to two women who ebbed and flowed with his motion as if all were attached by an invisible cord. Sweat slicked their bodies.

Both women wore nothing but long, flowing, brightly colored scarves. One of them swayed in unison with the other, eyes closed, a huge snake draped over her shoulders, around her waist, and down one leg. Her eyelids fluttered open, revealing white eyes rolled up in their sockets. Her mouth hung open, a sensuous moan oozing from her lips. She seemed to drop lower with each beat, her body shuddering as if physically struck with each thump of the drum.

The second woman moved around her in stagger step, hopping wildly, first on one foot, then the other, all the while holding a chicken aloft by its feet, its wings frantically beating the air. She danced and twirled around her partner like a mad dervish, eyes closed, seemingly oblivious to anyone and everything around her, except the constant pounding of the drums.

A ragged assemblage stood around them, it, too, appearing polarized by opposing forces. On one side, behind the women, a handful of spindly, bedraggled men and women swayed to the music, their eyes wide with fear and amazement, and across from them, behind the man, stood a group that looked even more bedraggled than the first, only this group stood immobile, their eyes fixed, staring straight ahead, glassy and emotionless. Not everyone in this group was dark-skinned like the first. This one had a few lighter-skinned foreigners, either Americans or Europeans. Probably AYUDO workers.

The music, dancing, and drumming rose to a frenzied peak that ratcheted the tension in the air to an almost painful crescendo, then the woman with the chicken gave a sweeping, low dramatic twirl that brought her close to the ground. A knife appeared in her hand as if out of nowhere and in one graceful motion she gathered the chicken to her breast and cut its throat, sending blood spurting everywhere.

She let out a chilling cry that touched something deep inside of Clark, making him feel cold at the core of his being, then she held the chicken aloft again, showering herself and those around her with its glistening blood while the bird beat its wings with renewed vigor and agitation.

The whole scene moved with the life of the bird, keeping the frenzied crescendo vital for a few short moments, then it ebbed with the chicken's life, dance and drum fading with each jerk of the fowl's death throes, until all fell silent. Without a word, the animated people behind the women departed to the left, leaving behind the dancers and their zombie charges.

Once they departed, a lone drummer beat a simple beat that galvanized the zombies. The male priest started down a path off to the right, and the zombies fell into single file, shuffling behind him in a swaying gait, followed by the two priestesses who took up the rear, leaving the bonfire unattended behind them.

Clark waited a few moments before following them, checking in front and behind with his heightened senses to make sure no one detected his presence, then he crept down the trail, keeping the sound of the single beating drum as his guide. They went a few hundred yards before he sensed the sound of the drum shifting. He paused, listening until it quickly faded into muffled silence.

Strange, he thought. *It never stopped. Just faded.* He went a few more steps, seeing nothing but a pile of rocks looming in the semidarkness ahead of him. He climbed on top of them and scanned his surroundings. Seeing nothing, he instinctively looked down through the rocks with his X-ray vision and saw a tunnel leading underground beneath him. Pressing an ear to the rocks, he heard the faint sound of the drum continue on for a few more beats before coming to a halt.

His first instinct was to push the rock aside, but he knew that if they had gone underground and disappeared that quickly, then it had to be mechanical, and if it was mechanical, it had to have some kind of alarm or monitoring system on it. If this was some kind of underground compound, it had to have ventilation. Once more, using his X-ray vision, he checked the ground up and down the path and to the sides, searching for another opening. Sure enough, a few dozen yards behind the rock and another ten or twenty off to the right of the path, he spotted a shaft that came up beneath a jagged palm stump. Clark went to it and discovered that it was in fact hollowed out with a vent grate riveted to its base. He heard voices, the crackle of walkie-talkies, the hum of electronics and other activity coming from the vent.

Gripping the grate with his fingers, he pulled up, slowly peeling it back from its frame. After setting it aside, he eased himself feetfirst into the shaft and worked his way down into the darkness below, controlling his descent by pressing his hands and feet against the sides of the vent shaft. About twenty feet down, he came to a T-section. He eased himself down into it and looked both ways. To his right it looked dark, and to his left he saw light. Dropping onto his chest, he crawled along its length on his belly until he came to another grate. He saw a string of lights running the length of a tunnel on the other side of it.

Working the fingers of one hand into the grate, he pushed out on its edges one corner at a time, wincing at the pop of each rivet. Once it came loose, he remained motionless for a few minutes, listening for any sign that he might have been discovered. When he felt confident that no one had heard him, he lowered himself from the vent into the tunnel and set the grate back in place.

He crept down the hall listening to the voices echoing up the corridor toward him.

"That show they put on is good enough for Vegas," a deep voice said.

"Hollywood," another said. "They definitely have these superstitious locals scared out of their gourds."

"They'll never come anywhere near here, that's for sure."

They both chuckled.

Clark pressed himself close to the wall at the end of the tunnel and peered into a big room. Two men in short-sleeved olive green T-shirts and cammo pants, each cradling a semi-automatic rifle, came walking right toward him, heading for the tunnel. He moved past them at high speed, flashing across the room to a spot behind a desk.

"Breeze coming down the tunnel," the deep-voiced one said after Clark had passed.

"We'd better get up there and check the perimeter," his partner answered. "After that security breach with that bleeding-heart AYUDO woman, we need to keep a close eye on things. We're supposed to shift into phase three any day now."

Clark listened to their footsteps echoing up the tunnel, followed by the sound of hydraulics that he guessed to be the rock doorway sliding open and shut. Looking around, he saw that two airlock-type doorways led off from the room in two different directions. He went toward the one to his left, put his face to the door, and looked through it with his X-ray vision. He saw a wall full of electronic monitors, communication consoles, and computers. Two men manned workstations there. No sign of zombies or the priests and priestesses. They must have gone through the other doorway. Moving to it, he looked through and saw that it led to another corridor. He thought about forcing it open to get in, but feared he might set off some kind of alarm. How could he get in?

While he pondered his next move he heard more footsteps. Looking through the door, he saw another cammo-clad man approach. Clark stepped to the far side of the door and waited for it to open. As soon as the man stepped through, Clark slipped behind him at high speed and made his way down this second corridor, which brought him deeper underground, leading to a complex of rooms that made him think of the ant farms he had played with as a boy, only these ants had a darker purpose.

A horrid stench from one of the rooms assailed his nostrils. Turning his attention toward it, he heard shuffling feet and a strange chorus of wet sounds that went *click clack click clack*. Repelled by the stink and the sounds, yet drawn by curiosity, Clark went toward the room and peered in to see bars like a jail cell enclosing a roomful of zombies. The tall figure of a dark-skinned man, his face half-eaten away, with bulging eyes that looked glassy and empty clutched at the bars, as did others in various states of decomposition. Still others of different races and colors in better shape than the ones at the bars filled the room behind them.

As if sensing him by scent, they looked toward him with unseeing eyes. Arms and legs flopped and shuffled, as a host of drooling jagged toothed jaws moved with increasing frenzy.

Click clack click clack . . .

Followed by animal grunts, agonized moans, and gurgles that sounded far from human. Clark staggered backward in horror. *That's it,* he thought. *I've seen enough. No way I want any of those disgusting things even touching me!*

He backed away from the zombies and scanned the rest of the rooms with his X-ray vision. He saw men everywhere throughout the complex, all armed, carrying walkie-talkies, all dressed in the same military cammo uniforms. Computers had been networked throughout the tunnels and rooms housing command and control centers, and a stockpile of weapons, including semiautomatic rifles and handguns, mortars, grenades, and flamethrowers. Behind one of the doors just off of the room he stood in, he saw a storeroom piled with plastic sacks that had the familiar LuthorCorp logo on them.

Bingo.

He went to the closet, opened the door, and stepped in, closing the door behind him. A wave of nausea swept through him as soon as he entered.

What's happening to me? he thought. *Dizzy. My stomach. I didn't think those zombies spooked me that much.* He took a few deep breaths, but it didn't help. *Better get out of here, quick.*

Fighting the sudden impulse to vomit, he found one of the bags about an eighth full. Tying it into a knot, he wrapped his hand around it and backed out of the room, closing the door behind him. The nausea stayed with him, but the intensity of his sickness lessened some. He leaned against the wall outside the door and, with great effort, tried breathing deep again.

Don't know what's going on here, but I'd better get a move on and get as far away from here as I can.

He turned to run back up the tunnel at high speed. He still moved quicker than any normal man, but his arms and legs felt as though someone had wrapped them in soggy blankets. Every effort took extra willpower, and instead of gaining speed, he found himself slowing. Luckily, no one occupied the room between this tunnel and the last one. By the time he got to the loosened vent he felt winded and ready to vomit again, but this was not the place to slow down or be sick.

Easing the grate out, he tossed the bag ahead of him into the duct and took a moment to try and get his wind again. Sweat poured from him. He wiped it from his face with his sleeve and kept breathing deeply. This time it seemed to work, so he took a little extra time to let his strength return until his nausea diminished.

Whatever it was that made me sick down there, at least it's passing.

When he felt strong enough, he slid the vent grate sideways into the duct, hoisted himself up behind it, and slid into the duct feetfirst, working his way backward past the grate. Once past, he slid it toward the end of the vent until he could fit it back into its original spot, then he inched his way on his hands and knees, moving back toward the vertical shaft down which he had come.

Clark felt more nausea when he slid over the fertilizer bag, but it didn't come as strongly as it had the first time. Dragging the bag behind him, he reached the shaft that led up and out. Not wanting to waste any more time, he tied the bag to the front of his belt and started up the duct, pressing his hands and feet against the sides of the shaft the way he had coming down. He felt his strength diminishing the more he exerted himself with each bit of upward movement, followed by a second, slowly increasing attack of nausea. He barely made it out of the top of the shaft, where he tumbled to the ground in a cold sweat and shivers. Spots danced before his eyes, and he could barely move his arms and legs. Breathing shallowly, he fought to think clearly, trying to understand what was making him so sick.

I don't understand it, he thought, fighting back the darkness that threatened to swallow him. *I can barely move . . . barely breathe . . . no strength. The only things that ever made me sick like this were the meteorites! How in the world?* Blackness washed over him, but he battled it back. *How could it?* Another wave threatened to take him, then it hit him . . .

The fertilizer!

He fumbled with the bag at his belt, trying to untie it while strength ebbed from his whole body, especially his fingers. The more he willed them to move, the less they responded, and his vision blurred at the edges, compressing into a diminishing circle, as if he were being thrust into a narrowing tunnel.

Barely conscious, he loosened his belt, sliding the bag off of it until it fell beside him. He tried pushing it away, but didn't have the strength or the coordination to move any more. In his last moments of awareness, he managed to poke a hole in the side of the bag with the part of his belt buckle that went through the loop.

Green-tinged fertilizer spilled out.

Through a dreamlike reverie, Clark saw a Haitian woman wearing a long, flowing dress and a kerchief around her head appear as if from out of nowhere. She seemed to float toward him, making the sign of the cross over him when she drew close, then she smiled, flashing brilliant white teeth that stood out from the light brown skin of her face and took the bag of fertilizer from beside him, before rolling him over onto his back.

She made a gesture and two dark-skinned men hurried toward them. One took Clark under the shoulders and the other grabbed his feet, then they swiftly followed the brown-skinned woman through a grove of trees and across a few fields to an old shack where they laid Clark down.

"I am known as Mama Loa," she said with a Haitian-French accent.

Clark struggled to respond, but couldn't muster the strength to speak. She put a finger to his lips and her face grew serious.

"Don't try to move or speak right now. You need to get your strength back."

She made him sip a bitter liquid, then lit a cigar and blew smoke over him from head to foot. After shaking a rattle and stroking his head, arms and chest with a feather, she leaned in close.

"I was the head of the village until they came and changed everything," Mama Loa said. "They turned all of my people into zombies. I alone have escaped the Voodoo curse."

The drink jolted Clark wider awake. This wasn't a dream. The Haitian Voodoo woman with the bright dress was real, but she was helping him. She wasn't one of them.

"How did you find me?" he whispered.

"My guides told me you would come. They told me where to find you."

"Guides?"

She made the sign of the cross. "My spirit guides. My *loa.*"

He gaped at her. "Um, ma'am . . . I'm not sure I believe in spirit guides."

She held her arms wide and smiled beatifically. "Magical beings are everywhere. Just because we cannot see them does not mean that they do not exist."

His strength and clarity were coming back more strongly by the moment, and, he had to admit, the drink she had given him seemed to help. "No disrespect intended, but I'm not sure I believe that magical beings told you where to find me."

She arched her eyebrows. "You are magical, are you not?"

Instantly on guard, Clark was at a loss for how to answer her.

She smiled. "What is magic but a result for which there is no discernible cause? Is it magic if I call upon my guides for help, but science if you are sent to Earth to help?"

He swallowed.

And she burst into delighted laughter.

Clark sat up under his own power, propped up against an angled plank that leaned against a wall inside the dilapidated shack. A brightly colored woven blanket covered him. Mama Loa's bitter tea had worked wonders, making his recovery swift. He still felt weakened, but the chills and fever had passed, and all of his faculties had returned. He no longer felt sick to his stomach. Now he sipped another tea that tasted like sweet berries.

Clark glanced around the shack, taking in his surroundings. A kerosene lamp burned in the corner. Bundles of herbs of different shapes and sizes hung from the rafters beneath a tin roof. A makeshift series of shelves constructed from warped boards covered one wall. Rows of glass jars with different-colored herbs and powders lined each one. A cot like the ones he'd seen at the AYUDO compound sat against another wall.

Outside, a rooster crowed. Clark looked out the open window behind the shadowy form of Mama Loa, who worked over a stove that had been fashioned out of a fifty-five-gallon drum. The first indigo tinge of dawn glowed on the horizon below a scattering of stars. Mama Loa turned from a pot she had been stirring and grabbed a small three-legged stool before coming to where Clark sat. After putting a cool hand to his head to check his temperature, she nodded to herself, apparently satisfied, then placed the stool beside him and sat down.

"Your sickness has passed," she said. "Soon you will be all the way back to your old self. I have never seen the zombie powder affect anyone the way it sickened you. Its magic weakens your magic, which tells me just how much you are aligned with the beings of the light who watch over us. It is no wonder my guides told me of you. I know why you are here."

"I can't thank you enough for saving me," Clark said, feeling that his words fell far short of the gratitude he felt toward this enigmatic woman whose power and charisma extended far beyond her appearance. "I would have died there."

Mama Loa waved dismissively. Clark sensed a bit of self-deprecation in her demeanor.

"You would have done the same and more," she said. "The white light of the magic that guides you is an extension of the purity of your heart."

Clark felt embarrassed. He said, "I'm here to find out how to cure someone who's become a zombie."

Mama Loa made the sign of the cross and her eyes took on a faraway look. "Zombies have always been a way of life here. For generation after generation they have come in the night like ravenous dogs, preying on those who are caught unprepared and defenseless. I have tried all my life to stop their creation, but I have no idea how to do that." She put her face in her hands. "And now they have taken my Baby Loa," she whispered.

"There has to be a way to stop them," Clark insisted.

"They grow bolder with each passing day, and, with the distilled potion that this American technology brings, their numbers have grown and the plague that they are has become worse—and now these soldiers."

Clark heard himself say, "Between your magic and my magic we have to end this."

Mama Loa sat up straight, her features set in firm resolution. "The girl, Marie-Claire. She escaped, yes?"

Clark nodded. "Yes. She's in my hometown right now. These guys have been after her. She took a sample with her, but they stole it." *I would have known right away that one of the components was meteor-rock if I'd had a chance to see it.*

"Among other things, she knows a lot of chemistry. She has a university education. She may be able to prepare the antidote. I can help her. Can you put me in touch with her?"

"I don't know . . ."

"You have the magic," Mama Loa said quickly. "It is within your power."

"I don't know how I can do that. If I went to her, she'd know I've been here to Haiti," he told her. "Back where I live my powers are secret. I have to keep it that way to protect my family and those I love."

"I know that, young warrior," she assured him. "I will never tell anyone about you. You have my silence."

"Thank you," he said, relieved.

"Your carry your gift with reluctance," she observed, cocking her head as she studied him. "You will never be like other men. There is no antidote for that which has touched you. The breath of the gods lives in your lungs. Your life will go more smoothly if you look upon your special attributes with more warmth."

"I'll try," he promised her.

"And so, to work," she said. "I may have already lost those that I love," Mama Loa said forlornly. "The zombie plague has an evolution to it. As time passes the zombies get worse and worse until they thrash and moan and gnash their teeth in fevered madness, then they die."

Clark flashed back to the sound they had made with their teeth . . .

Click clack click clack . . .

"What she needs is the fertilizer," Clark said. "That's what I came for."

She looked puzzled. "But you cannot carry it. It brings you sickness."

"If we shield it with lead, I'll be all right," he told her. "It stops the sickness. What about the AYUDO compound? They must have had lead of some type there."

Mama Loa brightened. "Yes. Maybe so."

She rose from the stool and grabbed a brightly colored shawl that hung from a nail on the wall. "Are you strong enough to walk?"

Clark pulled himself to his feet and took a few steps. "Good as new," he said.

She led him through a few cane fields, past a couple of farms, until they came to the remains of the AYUDO compound. Together they walked the ruins while Clark scanned the debris with his enhanced vision. Deep within the charred framework of the gutted infirmary he found the melted remnants of a lead blanket that had been used for medical X rays. Dragging it back to Mama Loa's shack, he stripped all the extraneous material from it.

Using his hands to work the remaining lead like clay, he molded it into a bowl and lid that fit tightly together, then he asked one of Mama Loa's helpers to fill it with the fertilizer, finishing it off by pressing the lid tightly into place over the top. Satisfied that it was safe, Clark pinched the edges with thumb and forefinger to complete the seal.

"The forces of light are with us," Mama Loa said, admiring the finished product.

"*You* are the forces of light," Clark said, turning from his work to hug her, then he picked up the sealed bowl. "Thank you, Mama Loa. If this works, I'll be back as soon as I can with enough antidote for everyone who's been changed."

She smiled, obviously embarrassed. "You are the light that came in answer to my prayers. One small flame that can push back the darkness of a whole room. Now go," she said, patting his cheek. "Get this vile poison to Marie-Claire so the flame can burn higher."

When Clark got the sample back to Smallville, he left it at the hotel desk for Marica. That was all, just the sample: no note, no explanation, and nothing to indicate that it was from him. He didn't even make sure the desk clerk took it; he simply left it at the reception area and moved away.

Maybe she'll think Lionel gave it to her secretly, he thought.

It was the best he could do . . . for now.

Then he went to the hospital to check on his mother.

CHAPTER TWENTY

Chloe had let the requisite twenty-four hours pass while she decided what to do about Rebecca's secret . . . and then another twenty-four.

She finally decided that the best thing to do was to let Rebecca know she knew, and promise her that she would never tell anyone about it.

A sharp undertow of anxiety flowed through her stomach as she strolled casually past the decorative acanthus columns of the Talon toward the bar. Rebecca and Lana were working together; Rebecca was smiling shyly, and Lana was laughing.

She reminded herself that it wasn't all about secrets. It was about motivations. She couldn't help but dig into the former, and the latter was the tiller that she needed to examine—to be sure her ship of truth stayed on course.

She didn't want a repeat of the Hacketts. But now she'd found out why Rebecca seemed so worried.

Duh. Burglaries in town and a convicted felon has just arrived in the neighborhood. It does look bad.

But she wasn't putting any of it in the *Torch*, no way.

Her motivation was to help here— and that was the key. The reason she felt so bad about Marshall was just that— motivation. It was, she'd decided, the difference between good and evil. The same actions, when taken from the standpoint of motivation could be either. Had she been trying to *help*—trying to bring a story to life that needed to be out— like if no one had *known* about the exchange and she'd been trying to help, it might have at least been a worthy action.

But it wasn't. She'd been airing out the dirty laundry after the fact, muckraking in high yellow-journalism style. Dragging it out to show how *clever* she was.

And while it was true that she'd seen that before she'd published the story—it had been too late for Marshall.

But not *this* time. This time it was just going to be a show of support, no *Torch,* no public broadcast.

Lana had just left the bar with a tray of coffee cups and pastries, giving Chloe a wave as she crossed to the other side of the room. That left Chloe and Rebecca alone, and Chloe felt even more nervous.

"So, here I am, intrepid reporter hat placed on the shelf for the remainder of the day." She smiled pleasantly. "Now, what was it you wanted to talk to me about?"

Rebecca looked back at her. Then she caught her breath. She turned pale and bit her lower lip; and Chloe knew that Rebecca had just guessed that her terrible secret was a secret no longer.

"You know about my dad," she said.

A beat, and then, "Yes. I do," Chloe said firmly. "And I just want you to know that I'm here for you." Chloe's voice trailed off.

Tears welled in Rebecca's eyes. Chloe hurried on. "It's okay. I'm not going to tell anyone. No one needs to know. Okay?"

Rebecca said slowly, "You *know*. And you still want to be my friend?"

"Well, yeah," Chloe replied, confused. She tilted her head and put her hand on her hip. "*You* didn't rob a jewelry store."

A tear slid down Rebecca's cheek. At first Chloe thought she was upset, but then she murmured, "Thank you, Chloe. You don't know what this means to me. I've hated keeping this all to myself. I feel like I'm about to burst."

"Do you want to talk about it?" Chloe asked.

"I . . . I don't know," Rebecca said. "There's talk about these zombies, but the burglaries . . . my dad . . ."

"Wow, you've had a lot to worry about," Chloe said.

Rebecca began to cry. "Yes. I have. And I am worried. Really worried." She gazed at Chloe. "I love my dad, Chloe. But it's hard. He was in prison, do you understand that?"

"Yes," Chloe said firmly. "He's a convicted felon."

"Oh, God." Rebecca swayed. "It's . . . I'm so scared. Every time someone finds out, they dump me. And he . . . he keeps going out, Chloe. I don't know where, and yes, okay, weird things happen around here, but the crime rate has soared since we showed up, right?"

"Um, well, 'soared.' That's a relative term," Chloe said.

Rebecca pinched the bridge of her nose, looking unutterably weary. "If I had to go to a foster family again . . ." She buried her face in her hands.

"Oh." Chloe put her arms around her and leaned her against her shoulder.

"Oh, God. Oh, my God," Rebecca murmured.

"What's going on?" Lana called out to the girls as she hurried over. "Rebecca, are you all right?"

There was a moment of silence. Then Rebecca said, "Thank you, Chloe. I'm going to tell Lana, too."

"You can trust her, same as you can me," Chloe told her.

Rebecca turned back around. Smoothing back her hair, she lifted her chin and took a deep breath.

"Lana, my father . . ."

"I know." Her face was soft and kind. "I've known for a while."

At Chloe's surprised look, she said, "A friend of Nell's was an alternate juror on your dad's trial. I was talking to Nell on the phone and it came up somehow."

"And you . . . you still want me to work here?" Rebecca asked uncertainly.

And you didn't tell me? Chloe thought archly, then realized there was still a bit of the muckraker lurking inside her . . . or was it the fact that she and Lana had agreed not to have any secrets, ever since that weird clone-guy had tried to date both of them at the same time?

Lana asked the obvious question. "Is there anything we can do?"

Rebecca shook her head. "Not unless you've got a crystal ball and can tell me where my dad goes at night." She looked at them with misery on her face. "You know what I'm thinking. You can see why I'm scared. These robberies . . . it might be . . ."

"We'll do what we can to help," Lana said. "Clark and Pete—"

"No. Please don't tell them," Rebecca pleaded. She swallowed hard. "Back home . . . back in Metropolis . . . once everyone knew . . ."

"It was hard, wasn't it," Lana said gently. "I so get that, Rebecca. I had my face on the cover of *Time* magazine when I was three years old, and some people still think of me that way. 'That poor girl on the cover of *Time*.' "

"I haven't been able to talk to people about my life." Rebecca's laugh was very sad. "When your father is a convicted felon . . ."

More tears streamed down her face as she searched Lana's face. "You can't know what it's like. He can't even vote. He can never vote again. He has a parole officer. We had to get permission to move."

"It's okay, Rebecca," Lana said warmly. "None of us would ever judge you because of your father."

"She's right," Chloe added. "Clark and Pete are good

guys. If something's going on with your dad, you should come to your friends for help. And we are your friends. All of us—Lana, Clark, Pete, and I. We want to help you."

Looping her dark hair around her ears, Rebecca firmly shook her head. "It's bad enough that you two know. I—I'd hate it if they knew, too."

"It'll be between us, then," Lana assured her. "Right, Chloe?"

"Absolutely." Chloe gave Rebecca a hug. "Don't worry. Our lips are sealed."

"So. Let's get back to work," Rebecca said, soldiering on.

Lana smiled. "We're about three mocha lattés and four espressos behind."

"At least business is good," Rebecca ventured, and Lana laughed.

"That's true." She gave Rebecca another quick hug.

Chloe hunkered down on her stool. "I'll sit here and do my work," she said. "I've got an issue of the *Torch* to proof. As usual."

"Thank you, both of you," Rebecca said. "This is . . . this is amazing. You're amazing."

"We're really not," Lana said.

She went off to make a slew of espresso drinks, while Rebecca set cups on trays and filled the orders for pastries. Then she picked up her tray and walked through the crowded coffeehouse.

All around her, people her age were laughing and gossiping. A guy from her math class was holding hands and leaning forward over the table, hanging on every word the cute blonde across from him was saying. It was such a different world from hers—more innocent, kinder.

She watched as a man slid into a booth at the back. He

was about her father's age, but not as handsome. He gave her the strangest look as he glanced at her name tag.

"Rebecca," he read. "Thank you, Rebecca."

"Sure." She didn't like him, didn't care for the vibes he was throwing off.

"Actually, I just glanced at my watch," he told her. "I didn't realize what time it is. I have to leave."

"Okay." She flashed him a smile. "Please come back sometime."

"I certainly will." He hesitated. "What time do you close tonight?"

"Eleven," she told him.

"Late for a school night," he observed.

"Well, not all our customers go to school," she replied, shifting her weight.

"I meant . . . for you."

"Yeah, well, as long as I keep up my studies," she said. Then she realized she didn't even want to be having this conversation, so she said, "Have a nice evening," and walked quickly away.

"Are you okay?" Lana asked, as the two met up en route to the bar.

"That guy," Rebecca murmured under her breath, as they stood beside Chloe, who was busily proofing her mock-up of the *Torch*. "There's something weird about him."

They both turned to see him making his way casually toward the Talon's doors.

Lana raised her brows, and said, "Well, if he comes back in, let me know, and I'll wait on him, okay? House rules: Any guy makes you nervous, someone else takes over his table."

"Thank you," Rebecca said in a rush.

Looking up from her mock-up of the *Torch*, Chloe

drawled, "He's probably had too much caffeine. Then her gaze trailed past them to the man, who had just turned his head to the left as he pushed open the door.

Her eyes widened. She whispered, "Oh, my God."

"What?" Lana asked.

Chloe blinked, dumbfounded.

"What?" Rebecca demanded.

"Rebecca. I think . . . I'm fairly certain that's Jason Littleton," Chloe blurted. "One of the men who was . . . involved with your father."

Rebecca's knees buckled.

"Oh, God, I knew it," she said miserably. "All the late nights. My dad . . . my dad and Jason Littleton are robbing stores." She pressed her hand against her mouth and began to cry.

Chloe got off her stool, took Rebecca by the shoulders, and marched her toward the staff lounge.

Lana announced, "I'll call the sheriff."

"No. No, please don't," Rebecca pleaded, whirling around. "That man and my father aren't supposed to make contact with each other. It's a condition of Daddy's parole. If the police find out, they'll throw my father back in jail with no questions asked. Even if it's . . . nothing."

Lana and Chloe regarded each other. Chloe's features hardened, and she said, "I'm going to do as Rebecca asks, Lana. Keeping my mouth shut. For now."

"I don't know," Lana said.

"Please, Lana, *please,*" Rebecca murmured.

"All right." Lana nodded. "But we have to find out what he's doing here, all right? Rebecca, I think you need to talk to your father about this."

Rebecca quavered inside. She and her father had never fully discussed the robbery. They had only skirted around it

But she sensed that doing so was a condition of Lana's not calling the police.

"All right," she said, sagging.

Lana put her arm around her and gave her a hug. "We're here for you," she reminded her.

Then Chloe walked her to the bathroom, and Rebecca broke down again and cried.

While they were gone, Lana paced behind the bar, trying to decide what to do. Finally, she picked up the phone and dialed the Kent farmhouse.

"Clark?" she asked breathlessly, but their answering machine clicked on. She had no idea where Clark was, and she realized that Jonathan Kent was probably at the hospital with Martha.

Then she remembered what Rebecca had said—that her father would be in violation of his parole if he was seen with Jason Littleton, and decided not to leave a message like that on the Kents' phone. It was too public.

She hung up.

A few minutes later, Chloe and Rebecca returned from the ladies' room. Rebecca had been crying so hard it looked as if her eyes were welded shut. Lana took one look at her, and said, "What can we do?"

"She wants to go home," Chloe informed Lana. "I'm going with her."

Lana's eyes widened. "You guys, that man is a criminal." Then she flushed as Rebecca jerked, and said, "I'm sorry, Rebecca, but . . ."

"I want to be with my dad," Rebecca insisted.

"Have you called him? Do you even know he's there?" Lana pressed. "And what if this guy comes looking for him? I really think we should call your father and ask him to pick you up here."

Rebecca hung her head. "This is awful," she croaked.

"It's going to be okay," Chloe assured her. "We'll let your dad know what's going on. He'll take care of it." She smiled at Rebecca, but her expression didn't reach her eyes. "Right?"

Holding back sobs, Rebecca nodded dejectedly. *I'm going to lose their friendship,* she thought. *Who would want to be my friend after this?*

Chloe pulled out her cell phone, and said, "Let's go outside so you can get decent reception."

"Be careful. He might still be around," Lana told them.

Rebecca felt a chill as she glanced toward the door; then Chloe said, "We'll go out the back way." She smiled at Rebecca. "Good?"

"Good," she murmured.

They turned to go, Rebecca in the lead. She headed for the exit, punching in her home number as she walked.

Then she heard Lana call Chloe in an urgent tone of voice. Chloe said, "Hold on, Rebecca. I'll see what she wants."

"Okay."

Rebecca loitered near the exit. Then the men's room door opened and someone came out.

Idly she looked up. She opened her mouth to scream just as Jason Littleton clamped his hand across it. Something hard jabbed into her ribs.

"It's a gun," he said calmly. "Let's go."

Tom Morhaim returned home from a late shift tired and eager for a beer and some TV. For a moment he was surprised that Rebecca wasn't home, but then he remembered her job at the coffeehouse.

Maybe I should take a walk to the cemetery.

He knew she'd been wondering where he went all the time. His excuse about needing to go on walks was wearing pretty thin.

If she only knew . . . but how am I going to tell her? I've got millions of dollars' worth of jewels buried in Michelle Madison's grave. They've been sitting there for over a decade, and I'm dying to dig them up. We'll be set for life.

But the more he thought about retrieving them, the more he wondered what Rebecca would think . . . and more importantly, how she would react. Back in prison, all those years that he had dreamed about his fortune, she had been little more than an abstraction. He had spun fantasies about how ecstatic she would be—no more scrimping, no more humiliation over wearing hand-me-downs. She was going to live like a princess.

The phone rang, and he expected it to be Rebecca. He hadn't made any friends yet, and he figured she was among friends down at the coffeehouse.

"Hey, Becs," he said pleasantly.

"Hey yourself, Tom."

His blood froze. It was Jason Littleton. Jason, from the robbery. Jason, who took the rap for shooting the security guard.

"Oh, God," Tom croaked.

"I've got your girl. Rebecca, say hi to your father."

"Daddy!" It was Rebecca's voice. "Daddy, help!"

"It's okay, honey," he said soothingly, but his voice was shaking.

Then Littleton was back on the line. "Guess what, Tom, old friend. You've heard about those burglaries? Me. And the weird white people? Me again. They're zombies, buddy. Just like the papers have been saying. And I have a little vial that turns sweet little girls into zombies. And I'm going to use it in, oh, about twenty minutes unless you get the jewels and bring them to me."

"I don't have them," Tom lied.

"Rebecca, open your mouth," Littleton said off the line.

"No! Don't!" Tom shouted. "All right! Just don't hurt her, okay? Don't hurt her."

Jason chuckled to himself. He was sorry that he hadn't realized the vial was leaking last night when he'd set it on the table at the Talon. It had soaked through the bag, and all he could figure was that the sugar packets in the basket on the table had absorbed the remainder of the liquid. It was all gone—although he knew any decent chemist could extract the molecules off the inside of the vial to re-create the formula for him. But that would take time. His imminent plan to change Tom Morhaim into a zombie would not come to fruition. It didn't matter too much; he'd planned to do so in order to get Tom to tell him where the jewels were. Threatening his little girl was proving to be just as effective.

"So you'll have them to me in twenty minutes, right?"

"No. I mean, they're buried. I have to dig them up." He hesitated, then sighed, sounding defeated. "They're in the graveyard."

"You're kidding." Littleton started laughing.

After he digs them up, I'll have the zombies kill him. No. I'll have them bury him alive. Turnabout's fair play. After all, he buried me alive, in prison.

So, we meet in the graveyard. Just like in the movies.

He'd handcuffed and gagged Rebecca and got her in his van. They drove to the cemetery through the fog, and Littleton parked off the road.

"This won't take long," he told her.

Dragging Rebecca along, Jason Littleton headed for the graveyard entrance.

You are gonna pay, Morhaim, he thought. He felt in his jacket for his Anschütz .22. *Pay and pay and pay. And then, you are gonna die, one way or another.*

He walked on, turning around occasionally to make sure no one was following them.

The fog gathered in layers, grayish white upon gray upon a milky, sickly sheen of moonbeams and mist. Streetlamps overhead became dull, clumpy orbs of watery light. A dog barked hysterically, as if protesting.

A bird cawed, and Littleton murmured, "*'Quoth the raven, nevermore.'*" That poem had been written by Edgar Allan Poe, about some guy's dead girlfriend. Poe was twisted and gifted.

Kind of like Shaky . . . speaking of whom . . . I wonder if he's just sitting in the crypt, waiting for orders from head-quarters. Maybe with the others. Maybe they ate him before he changed. Bet they're hungry . . .

Ahead, the arched wrought-iron sign rising above double towers of bricks announced that he had reached his destination. The Smallville cemetery lay dead ahead.

So to speak.

He pushed open the gate, which squealed on its hinges. It sent a delicious frisson up his spine. Reaching into his pocket with his free hand, he pulled out his flashlight and held it above his head, pointing it downward, the way police officers do.

The fog lapped at his kneecaps as he walked forward, moving solely on instinct. He and Rebecca walked into the thick soup; no matter how he tried to push it away, there was more, and yet more. It was like swimming in a pool of semi-frozen ice.

Then—

What the . . . ?

He fell forward, letting go of Rebecca as he tumbled, then landed on his hands and knees on something hard that collapsed beneath his weight.

As he flailed in the wreckage, he understood what had happened: *I fell into an open grave! I landed on a coffin!*

He swallowed. *Did I read any obituaries? Who died recently? More to the point, where's the body?*

Finding the flashlight courtesy of the dulled beam, he grabbed it and scrambled up and out. Rebecca was nowhere to be seen. He got to his feet and gingerly walked forward, feeling with his boot tip as he went, scanning the fog in search of her.

His foot hovered in midair, and he realized he had almost fallen into another open grave.

What is going on?

Perplexed, he scanned his flashlight in a half circle. The light simply bounced off the fog, diffused into a hazy glow. He moved on, feeling as he went.

He didn't encounter another hole as he made his way down rows of headstones, which he kept track of by placing his palm on the top of each one, trying to keep count. He figured he was getting near the crypt where he'd stashed Shaky.

"Rebecca? Honey?" he called out. "Come on, sweetie, make it easy on yourself. Come on out, now."

Then, reaching out with his hand to make a sweep, he made contact with the door of the crypt. It was wide open.

But I locked it.

He froze, listening. Heard nothing.

"Shaky?" he whispered. "Guys?"

Then all hell broke loose.

Skeletal fingers grabbed him; voices rose, howling and screaming and shrieking as several zombies converged on Jason Littleton. Some of their fingers broke off like breadsticks as he extricated himself, using karate moves he had learned in prison. He swept his leg forward, then executed a roundhouse kick, slamming his foot into ribs that detached, apparently, springing from a sternum and clattering to the stone floor.

The zombies screamed and grabbed for him.

Jason ran. Through the blinding fog and his blinding fear, he ran so fast that he overran, losing his balance and falling hard. His left hand made contact with a headstone, and his flashlight arced out of his grasp.

As he fought to get up, something burst from the ground beside his hand and grabbed him. He shook it off; feeling the sharp fingernails slicing into the topmost layers of his skin.

The dead are rising from their graves!

How . . . how?

It didn't matter how. What mattered was getting the hell out of there in one piece.

He brought his gun down on the searching hand. Bones cracked, and disjointed fingers flailed at him.

This is a nightmare. A living nightmare.

He fought down giddy fear as he flung himself away from the place where the hand had pushed through the earth, fully expecting a wrist to protrude next.

Then he lay as still as death on the ground, panting. He was in shock. Perspiration beaded from his forehead, stinging his eyes.

He tried to formulate a strategy for self-preservation. If there was one thing he was good at, it was saving his own skin.

It occurred to him then that if the fog was hiding the zombies from him, it was hiding him from the zombies. Unless they could somehow bring their other senses to bear—sound . . . smell.

Do they smell me?

He fought down his panic, trying to bring the layout of the cemetery to mind; there were gravestones in rows, then brass memorial squares set into the ground farther out, then trees and bushes. Just beyond the crypt—which was now behind him—there were plenty of trees.

Could hide me, could slow me down.

Shaky was missing; he had escaped from the crypt. No single zombie would have been strong enough to force the thick door open alone. It would have taken cooperation.

Or a lucky accident of combined brute strength.

He prayed it was the latter.

He sensed movement all around him in the fog. He heard wild shrieks.

Maybe if I get to the cemetery entrance . . . and shut the gate . . . maybe that will contain them.

It was his only plan; therefore, his only shot.

He rose, and began to run.

For a second, he heard only his own footsteps, and he smiled grimly. Wherever they were, they weren't around him.

And then the screams grew thicker and more concentrated; something swiped at the back of his head, and he gave a bellow of fear.

They were behind him, and they were running him to ground like a dog.

The cemetery gate was a lifetime away . . .

As soon as Chloe and Lana had realized that Rebecca was missing, they searched the Talon and the surrounding area;

then Lana told the head waitress to take over, and they raced out the door to Chloe's car. Leaping behind the wheel, Chloe nodded as Lana said, "Okay, I'm calling the sheriff."

"With you all the way," Chloe said.

Lana punched in the number, and said, "Hello? It's Lana Lang. A girl's been kidnapped." She gave all the details, including the identity of Jason Littleton. The deputy assured her they would check it out, and she disconnected.

"Let's go to her apartment," Lana suggested. "Maybe he'll take her there." Then she looked at Chloe. "Except I don't know where she lives."

"I don't either."

They looked at each other in frustration. "We'll have to start searching," Chloe said. "Just drive around until we see or hear something unusual."

"Like, um this?" Chloe asked, pointing through the windshield.

A man in a pair of jeans and windbreaker was racing toward them, his arms windmilling wildly. And behind him . . .

Chloe couldn't believe what she was seeing.

A dozen zombies, maybe more; some were half-decomposed and some looked pretty okay and some . . . some were rotting skeletons that straggled after the others.

"Oh my God," Lana gasped.

Chloe tried to drive up to Littleton, rolling down the window, and shouting, "Get in the car!"

He ignored her, or couldn't hear her, and then he was weaving into the brush at the side of the road.

The zombies howled after him.

Chloe gave chase.

Lana said, "I'm trying Clark again."

◆◆◆

Clark had just gotten home from the hospital. His mom was having a bad night, and his father was going to sleep at the hospital.

The phone rang, and he frowned; it was late.

It was Lana.

"Clark? Rebecca's been kidnapped by this man who knew her father. We're at the cemetery. It's . . . there are zombies!"

"Get out of there," he said. "I'll wait there for the sheriff."

"But Rebecca—"

"Get out of there!" he insisted.

He got in the truck and drove as fast as he could, realizing that he could make far better progress on foot. But as usual, there would be questions.

Then he saw a man—*must be Littleton*—and the man was not alone.

Five or six white-faced figures were converging on him in the fog.

Zombies.

Clark raced toward them, shouting, "Hey!" to the man.

In the clearing mist, Clark could see the man's face. He was terrified. Clark rushed toward him, remembering too late that the zombies had ingested something that included traces of meteor-rock.

Pain. Intense. Debilitating.

He fell to his knees. One of the zombies rushed up to him, snarling, and bent over him, trying to sink his teeth into Clark's face. Clark easily pushed him away, but another came to take his place. The zombies were on him, dogpiling him. The pain seeped into him, through skin, bones, and muscle; his head began to throb. The veins on the backs of his hands rose and burned.

The zombies were all over him, slashing at him, trying to

get a grip on an arm, a leg, seeking purchase anywhere so they could have a nice meal of raw human flesh. It was not their frenzied attack that debilitated him; it was the meteor fragments carried inside each of them, and the combined effect was sapping Clark quickly. Gasping and in intense pain, his ability to fend them off was evaporating.

He moaned, trying to at least roll away from the zombies, but they stuck with him, not giving him an inch as their teeth *clacked-clacked-clacked* in their heads.

A terrible stench rose from one of the zombies as Clark grabbed its arm, and the entire thing broke off in his grasp.

Then he heard footsteps, and Chloe saying, "Clark, it's us! Hang in there!"

Lana and Chloe ran toward him.

I told you to go away, he thought dully.

He heard punches and whacks; felt hands loosen their grip on him when the fog was split in two as he caught sight of his friends battling the zombies. He couldn't keep track of the action—he was fading fast—but he could tell that the girls were winning.

Then the pain and the poisonous effects took hold, and he was immobile, and nearly unconscious. Everything was a jumble of sound and sight, nothing clear. He heard breaking bones and growls and the occasional, "You guys okay?" as Chloe and Lana pushed back the zombie assault.

He had no idea how long they fought; then someone was grabbing his arms and someone else his ankles. They were hurrying him out of there, and he was grateful for that. Lana had her arm around him, and she was half-dragging him, half–being dragged by him.

CHAPTER TWENTY-ONE

The fog pressed in, feeling cold and clammy on Rebecca's cheeks and hands, muffling everything. She shivered, pulling her jacket tighter. She had gotten away from Jason Littleton, then had been surrounded by monsters. Running away, she had fallen, smacked her head on a gravestone, and passed out. Now, as she came to, she was eerily alone. The wind soughed through the shadowed branches of a huge elm that loomed over them, and the dim gray glow of the moon faded in and out from above.

Then she heard the distinctive sound of shoveling. She peered around the side of the gravestone.

It was her father, digging up a grave.

"Daddy?" she managed, but her voice came out a dry rasp.

Then a shot rang out. She screamed, and her father shouted, "Keep your head down, Becs!"

She started to lower her head, then saw Jason Littleton racing toward her father, who stopped shoveling and stared at him.

"Tom, long time," Littleton said. "Don't stop digging. Those kids slowed the zombies down, but you can bet they'll be back. We've got minutes at best."

He continued, "Thought you were slick, hiding *our* jewels here in someone's grave, making everybody think you're some poor slob, whining and sniveling over your poor dead wifey." His voice hardened. "If you had whacked that guard the right way in the first place, he wouldn't have lived to testify against us. You couldn't even do *that* right." He shook his head.

"Then you go and pop *me* for the deed," he added.

Rebecca gasped. Her *father* had shot the guard? Her *father*? Rebecca bit her lip to keep herself from screaming.

"Listen, Jason, I was hiding the stuff here for the both of us. As soon as I got things in line with my kid here in Smallville, I was going to come get them, fence 'em off, and send you your half of the green. Really."

Littleton motioned toward the gravestone with his head. "Michelle Madison know you were gonna take them jewels back from her after all these years?" He smiled. "Were you gonna stiff her, too?" He chuckled at his own sick joke.

"Real funny, Jason."

"Well, I'm going to let you prove to me that you were gonna do me right." Still training his gun on Rebecca's father, Littleton knelt down, picked up a spade, and tossed it to Tom. "Dig 'em up. And make damn sure the hole is deep and wide enough for a man."

Tom held the shovel without moving.

"Now!" Littleton said, stepping toward him. He cocked the gun and pressed it hard to Tom's forehead.

Tom did as he was told, shoving the spade into the soil and pressing down with his foot until he worked up a chunk of turf, then he shoveled again, digging deeper. "We can work this all out . . ."

Littleton kicked him in the side, making Tom double over.

"Shut up and dig it up quick so we can get this over with. I've waited too long for this." He looked over his shoulder. "If those damn freaks come back . . ."

Tom started digging again.

"Faster!" Littleton said, slapping Tom in the back of the head.

Only the sound of the spade biting into the ground followed by the thump of tossed dirt filled the fog-shrouded night.

Then Rebecca heard strange scratching noises and a faint *click-clacking* sound from somewhere behind them.

"Hey, shut up a minute," Littleton hissed, cocking his head.

Tom stopped digging.

Other noises came from behind and around them from all directions.

A chill tickled Rebecca's spine, and her mouth went dry.

Click clack click clack . . .

Then a loud *click* came from in front of them, from the shovel hitting something hard.

Tom dug and scraped more with the shovel. Then he ducked into the hole on his hands and knees, making more scraping and grunting noises until he pulled a plastic-wrapped metal briefcase free from the hole and tossed it up on the ground at the grave's edge.

Click clack click clack . . .

"Open it," Littleton said, with an edge to his voice.

Tom hoisted himself from the hole, crouched low, and looked around, eyes narrowed, listening. Both he and Littleton remained still for a long time, as if the whole scene had been frozen in video freeze-frame.

While they looked down, Rebecca saw the zombies—hulking, broken-down, half-human-looking shadows shuffled through the billowing mists. Arms stuck out at odd angles, fingers splayed stiffly. Rebecca heard low moans, wheezing, and the ever-present, wet-sounding *click clack click clack . . .*

Coming from in front *and* behind her.

"Daddy!" she cried.

Then she saw Clark, Chloe, and Lana, too, hurrying toward her. Clark was hurt!

Jason Littleton grabbed the half-rotted briefcase and turned to run. But the zombies formed a semicircle that extended behind Rebecca and Chloe, and around to where Clark and Lana stood. Clark looked terrible.

Littleton pointed the gun in the air and fired a shot that made Rebecca's heart jump into her throat. A row of vacant stares turned toward them and the zombies stopped their advance. Together they swayed as one, jagged teeth clicking, their drooling mouths gnashing, as if attending some ghoulish undead rock concert.

Rebecca got to her feet, shouting, "Daddy!"

"Honey!" Tom's voice was anguished. "Get the hell out of here!"

"Run!" Clark yelled.

Without a trace of fear, he turned to face the onslaught of zombies. But they scrambled all over Clark, pushing him down on his knees, as Lana hit and kicked at them.

Chloe shouted, "Clark!" and ran to join the battle.

"Daddy!" Rebecca cried. "Daddy, say you didn't shoot that guard!" If they were going to die tonight, she was going to die knowing the truth about her father.

"I didn't! I didn't!" he shouted back at her. "I didn't mean to!"

"You liar!" Littleton shrieked at him. Then he shot Tom Morhaim at point-blank range.

Rebecca screamed, collapsing to the ground. She crab-walked toward her father, shrieking, "Daddy! Daddy!" She smelled something disgusting behind her as a zombie lunged for her arm. She screamed again.

And then, without warning, Jason Littleton dropped to the ground, blood spurting from his chest.

"Stand back!" someone yelled—a male voice Rebecca had never heard before.

She paid no attention, intent only upon reaching her father.

A thick stream of diesel-smelling flame spewed out from between two monuments, spreading in a steady line across the zombies, who screeched inhuman shrieks that made Rebecca sick to her stomach.

As if connected by invisible cords, the zombies who had been clambering over Clark fell back and retreated into the chaos with all the others, as they ran helter-skelter in blind panic.

A man dressed all in black, wearing a hood, advanced with the flamethrower, methodically incinerating the zombies like some dark, postapocalyptic exterminator.

Rebecca ran to her father's side. He was lying on the ground, still gagging. His eyes had a faraway, glassy look. She looked back to see Lana, Chloe, and Clark, giving as good as they got, although Clark seemed half-dead himself.

The zombies burned.

They screamed.

Rebecca's father lay silent on the grass, blood gushing from the wound in his chest.

Then Pete Ross walked from behind the man who was dressed in black, saw Clark, said, "Hey," and collapsed.

Shortly after the mop-up operation was complete, T. T. Van De Ven was summoned to HQ in Metropolis. He stood at attention before the Project's board of directors—a committee made up of high-ranking military personnel and one civilian, Lionel Luthor, the industrialist who had made it all possible.

Luthor glared at him. "You imbecile. Who gave you orders to set my house on fire?"

"Before you go on, sir," General Montgomery said, "I'd like to point out that Field Operative Van De Ven successfully eliminated all evidence of the Project from Smallville and returned your son's friend to him fully restored to health."

"Then I would postulate that not all the evidence was eliminated," Lionel snapped.

The colonel looked confused. "We assumed that the return of this young man, this . . . Pete Ross . . . was imperative."

Lionel Luthor said nothing. But he turned and pointed at Van De Ven, and said, "I want that man court-martialed."

"Agreed," the general said.

Van De Ven's mouth dropped open.

"Sir," he began.

"Shut up," the general ordered him. Then he said, "Gentlemen, I move that we shelve the Project."

No one dissented.

Clark's mother leaned heavily on his arm as he and his father escorted her into the house. She was pale, but she looked better than she had in a long time.

Best of all, she was home.

Chloe, Lana, Pete, and Rebecca greeted the three Kents, jumping up and yelling "surprise!" as Jonathan opened the door, and Clark walked his mother over the threshold.

"We made you guys some lunch," Rebecca said. She smiled shyly at Chloe and Lana, who both smiled warmly back. "Sandwiches and fruit."

Tom Morhaim had survived, but barely. He had been taken back to jail in Metropolis in a prison ambulance, and was awaiting a new trial in the infirmary, as he had confessed that he, not Jason Littleton, had shot Lee Hinchberger.

Rebecca had no idea if she would ever be able to forgive him for that. His confession was much too little, much too late.

With the Kents' help, Rebecca was placed with a very loving older couple who had longed to become foster parents for a number of years. She would remain with them until she turned eighteen ... but Clark agreed with his mother's assessment that this new relationship was something that would last much longer than that: The Kendalls doted on Rebecca, and she on them.

The best thing was, no one had turned their backs on her in her time of need. Rather, they had rallied around her.

Rebecca Morhaim was finally among friends.

"What a nice thing to do. Thank you," Martha said warmly to the group.

"*Organic* fruit," Lana added. "No pesticides. We don't want you ending up back in the hospital!"

"Nothing to make you sick," Chloe elaborated. "Everything is yuck-factor free."

"Funny thing about that," Martha said, giving them all a look. "It wasn't anything on the fruit at Lex's house that landed me in the hospital. It was mold, growing on the peanuts we also ate that day. If there had been some kind of agent on the nuts to destroy the mold, I wouldn't have gotten sick.

"I got sick precisely because the peanuts were untreated."

"And I'm putting that in our report," Clark said to Pete, who smiled wryly at him.

"In a footnote," Pete shot back.

"A really big footnote," Clark said. "It's worth mentioning."

"Let's eat," Martha suggested. "I'm hungry. The only decent food I had in the hospital was the sandwich Jonathan smuggled in from the cafeteria."

Clark looked questioningly at his dad, who held up his hands, all innocence, and settled Martha in at the dining room table.

Soon the Kent family farmhouse was noisy with the laughter of a large family, celebrating life and health together, as families should.

Maria del Carmen Maldonaldo Lopez accepted a glass of champagne from the flight attendant and sipped it appreciatively. "Very nice," she told the woman.

"Thank you," the flight attendant replied. Then she turned the only other occupant of the private Learjet and asked,

"When would you like me to serve the filet mignon, Mr. Luthor?"

"You hungry?" Lex asked Marica.

"Not quite yet."

The jet waggled its wings as it crossed the fertile fields surrounding Smallville, each one a bright green or golden postage stamp as the aircraft gained altitude. Marica, wearing one of the many other outfits Lex had just happened to have in her size, leaned against the seat and sighed heavily.

"*Adios,* Kansas," she said softly. She glanced at Lex. "Do you still believe your father was involved with the creation of the zombies?"

"Oh, yes," Lex told her. "But he'll never admit it out loud. My father is all about discretion and subtlety." He shifted, facing her more fully while he sipped his champagne. "Maybe he couldn't give us the antidote. He wouldn't want me to know that. I think he was trying to make amends by leaving that sample for you at the reception desk."

She smiled to herself. With that sample, and Lex's lab she was fairly certain she had an antidote of her own Friends of hers were taking it to Haiti, and would be in forming her about its success.

"And in the bargain," he added, "the research you did o datura's effects on the brain have yielded some interestin; data on other neurological contaminants. It might even hel with MS. And, of course, LuthorCorp plans to be on the cu ting edge of that data curve."

"So your investors will be happy," she pointed out.

"Everybody wins," he concurred. Then he shifted, sippin his champagne. "Have you decided what you're going to c when you get home?"

She nodded. "Well, I do agree that it's no use trying to e: pose what went on back there. No one will believe me.

have to assume that the government realizes that, and will leave me alone. In return, I will work to improve a lot of developing nations as 'a lady,' as my parents would say."

She looked a little sad, as if the exciting part of her life had just ended.

"I have an education, and I have privilege. I'll set up a foundation and get all my parents' rich friends to contribute."

Smiling, Lex reached into the pocket of his Italian sports coat and brought out a leather checkbook. As he flipped it open, he retrieved a pen from his pocket as well.

"Will a million be a satisfactory first contribution?" he asked.

She momentarily looked dazed. Then she grinned at him and said, "Two million."

Without a moment's hesitation, Lex wrote the check.

After the party was over, and Martha Kent was resting, Clark took off, moving at a blur. He had a rendezvous to keep in Cap du Roi.

He was certain Mama Loa knew he was coming, and she would be waiting for him.

It was very late at Smallville Juvenile Hall. Most of the inmates were asleep.

But in a small office, in a soft, comfortable chair, a psychologist named Dr. Miranda Nierman sat, holding back.

Across from her, words spilled out of Marshall Hackett's mouth.

"I hate him! I miss him! How could he do this to us? How can I ever forgive him?" he demanded without taking a breath.

She listened, not speaking, aware that she was witnessing

the breaking of a heart. It was a wound that was necessary, if Marshall was ever going to heal.

"How am I ever going to stop hurting?" he shouted at her. "How do I make this stop?" He burst into heavy sobs, another horrible aftermath of his family's tragedy.

"It's not fair. I can't believe how unfair it all is," he told her. "I hate this. I hate it!"

You should, she thought. Her heart was breaking, too—for him. It was a struggle not to interrupt, to ease the tension she herself felt by giving him bromides—*It's always darkest before the dawn; time heals all wounds* . . .

It would be so easy for her to do that to him.

And so unfair.

Make me a witness, she thought, hearing an old song in her head.

And so Dr. Nierman kept vigil over Marshall's pain.

Kept silence.

Rebecca, Lana, and Chloe stayed up watching old movies and eating popcorn at the Sullivan home the night Martha Kent came home from the hospital. They sat in the living room, and didn't speak.

After a while, a tear slid down Rebecca's cheek. Lana gave her hand a pat. Rebecca leaned her head against Lana' shoulder and let the tears come.

No one spoke.

No one had to.

In Haiti, Clark learned that someone else had already prepared an antidote and administered it to all the victims in Cap du Roi. In addition, the secret government facility had been sealed up. Clark could see parts of it with his X-ray v sion; it looked as if it had been bombed underground. Huge piles of rubble filled the tunnel and the elevator shaft.

Lionel's doing? he wondered.

Mama Loa held a party to celebrate the liberation of her people and an end to the torment and fear. At her urging, Clark stayed for it, dining on roast chicken and mangoes, watching the dancers swirl in colorful clothes. The drumbeats sang in his blood.

She walked up beside him as he gazed up at the stars. He studied them, then turned to her, and asked sadly, "Why didn't they give me a message? Why didn't my parents tell me who I am, and why I'm here?"

The firelight crackled, casting her face in soft light. Beyond them, her son Baby Loa, who had fully recovered, strummed a guitar and began to sing.

"You know," Mama Loa said wisely. "You know who you are. And why you're here. Every day, your heart tells you, does it not?"

Clark gazed up longingly, silently, at the stars.

Listening to the sound of silence.

ABOUT THE AUTHOR

NANCY HOLDER has written over 50 novels and 200 short stories, essays, and articles, including many projects for *Buffy the Vampire Slayer, Angel,* and *Highlander: The TV Series.* Her books have appeared on the *Los Angeles Times* bestseller list, and she has received four Bram Stoker Awards for fiction from the Horror Writers Association. Her work has appeared on the lists of recommended works for the American Library Association, American Reading Association, *The New York Times* Library Association, and others. She lives in San Diego with her daughter, Belle, two cats, and a dog.

READ MORE

SMALLVILLE

NOVELS!

STRANGE VISITORS
(0-446-61213-8)
By Roger Stern

DRAGON
(0-446-61214-6)
By Alan Grant

HAUNTINGS
(0-446-61215-4)
By Nancy Holder

WHODUNNIT
(0-446-61216-2)
By Dean Wesley Smith

SHADOWS
(0-446-61360-6)
By Diana G. Gallagher

AVAILABLE AT BOOKSTORES EVERYWHERE FROM WARNER ASPECT

1212-E

VISIT WARNER ASPECT ON-LINE!

THE WARNER ASPECT HOMEPAGE
You'll find us at: www.twbookmark.com then by clicking on Science Fiction and Fantasy.

NEW AND UPCOMING TITLES
Each month we feature our new titles and reader favorites.

AUTHOR INFO
Author bios, bibliographies and links to personal Web sites.

CONTESTS AND OTHER FUN STUFF
Advance galley giveaways, autographed copies, and more.

THE ASPECT BUZZ
What's new, hot and upcoming from Warner Aspect: awards news, bestsellers, movie tie-in information . . .